ANTHOLOGY OF SHORT STORIES
BY
YOUNG AMERICANS®

2004 EDITION
VOLUME XLIV

Published by Anthology of Poetry, Inc.

Printed in the United States of America

To submit short stories
for consideration in the year 2005 edition of the
Anthology of Poetry by Young Americans®,
send to: poetry@asheboro.com or

> Anthology of Poetry, Inc.
> PO Box 698
> Asheboro, NC 27204-0698

Authors responsible
for originality of poems submitted.

The Anthology of Poetry, Inc.
307 East Salisbury • P.O. Box 698
Asheboro, NC   27204-0698

Paperback ISBN: 1-883931-48-7
Hardback ISBN: 1-883931-47-9

"We the people…"

From the moment those three words were penned in ink, on the most important document in the history of the world, the unique experience of what it means to be an American began. Those three words opened the door of hope to a world mired in oppression and tyranny, giving the opportunity of freedom to both domestic and foreign people. The remainder of the document that followed, has been defined by us, the people, as much as it has defined us.

Without question, the freedom of expression is the first of our freedoms that we employ. From an early age we begin to present ourselves to the world, to our families, to our young friends. The Constitution of the United States of America guarantees us the right to free speech via public speaking, artistic theatrical endeavors, the far-reaching and proven influential airwaves, and of course, the mighty written word.

In the pages that follow, stories are told, the freedom of expression unfolds itself before us in the form of the mighty written word. Our eyes will take it in, our brains and our imaginations will work in unison to assemble the written words into the inevitable pictures, and our ears will create voices and soundtracks necessary to move the stories along. And at last, each of the stories will culminate in a wave of rhythms and meaning, and the small warmth of satisfaction will sweep us in as we are woven together in story and we smile, quietly thank the author for sitting down and sharing with us the great freedom of expression.

"We the people…" dovetails our lives together. Though we are rugged individualists, we stand shoulder to shoulder as Americans. Together. Concertedly. Collectively. With our sights set on the future, and our minds and hearts wide open let us move forward in this unique experience that is known as the *Anthology of Short Stories by Young Americans*. Enjoy the stories as we have. These young Americans have impressed us once again in 2004.

The Editors

ONE MINUS ONE EQUALS FOUR

This story takes place in the poor part of a town in Missouri. Mya was a ten-year-old young girl, with long blonde hair. She always wanted a horse since she was five years old. Her parents told her that they couldn't afford a horse, because they didn't have a lot of money. She decided to save up money to be able to get a horse for herself. Then, she decided to put signs up all over town. She also went to peoples' houses to see if they needed stuff done like, walk their dogs, clean stalls, and rake leaves. On a beautiful Saturday, the Millers asked Mya to watch their animals for a week. Mr. and Mrs. Miller said that they would pay her two dollars a day.

When the Millers returned Mya was awarded fourteen dollars. Someone came to Mya's trailer. They said that they needed someone to walk their dog for a month. I will give you two dollars a day. It has been a month now. When the guy returned she was given sixty dollars. Now she had enough money to buy a horse. She could even buy a paper. When she got the paper, she saw if it had horses for sale.

She saw a horse that was only one hundred dollars. Then she thought and thought about the horse. The next morning she went to tell her parents about the horse. They asked how much money she had. She told them that she had five hundred dollars. Mya told her parents how she earned the money. They thought Mya was brilliant.

Then Mya went to a neighbor's house to ask to use their phone. They wanted to know why. Then she told them she had to call about a horse. After she told them why, they let her use the phone. The next day she ran to see the horse. Right when Mya saw the horse she handed the guy the money. She brought the horse home. She put Misses up in a stall. Then she found out why he sold her so cheap. That horse was frisky and mean. Mya trained the horse for a long time. That night it was stormy out. Mya went to put a blanket on Misses. When Mya got in the barn Misses was dead but beside her were four colts. Mya got some help. They took Misses away. They made sure the colts were healthy. After that Mya named the colts: Sir, Pie, Miss, and Velvet. They acted just like their mom. They lived happily ever after.

Carissa Schramke

Chapter One: Her First Race

Sofia Anne Lorenzo is a thirteen-year-old girl that was born and raised in a small town outside the state of Nebraska. When she was born, her parents never knew she had the love for running. Sophia was five when she first started having the love for running. Every day after school she'd run home and tell her mom how school went. When she got done talking to her mom she did her homework and then did her chores. After a while she went for a run around the block.

One day after school she dashed home to tell her mom and dad they were having a race at the school and she wanted to participate in it. Her parents knew how much she wanted to be in it so they said yes.

Saturday arrived and Sofia bounded out of bed. She got dressed and went downstairs to find her parents up early making breakfast. After breakfast, Sofia told her parents how much she wanted to win.

When they got to the track that afternoon Sofia jumped out of the car and ran to the starting point. Her parents sat in the middle of the stands to see Sofia better.

Then Sofia heard somebody say "On you mark! Get set! Go!" They were off! Sofia was on her last lap before anyone was on their second lap.

Sofia won first place that afternoon. She got a big shiny silver trophy that had first place engraved on the front of it.

When Sofia saw her parents, a big grin went across her face and theirs. She knew they were proud of her and what she had accomplished.

Chapter Two: Birthday Girl

"Yes, today is my birthday!" said Sofia to her best friend, Tammie. Tammie is a blonde and has green eyes with freckles and is as skinny as a pencil. She is the nicest and most caring person you could ever meet. Sofia loved Tammie like a sister.

"How old are you going to be?" asked Tammie as they were walking to school one day.

"Oh, I'll be twelve years old," replied Sofia.

"Are you going to have a birthday party?" asked Tammie.

"Yeah, I am. It's going to be at the Harmony Bricken trail, but I haven't gotten my invitations mailed yet," said Sofia.

"What do you want for your birthday this year?" asked Tammie with a big grin on her face.

"I don't know. Maybe a Walkman so I have music to listen to when I go out for a run."

"How can you love running so much?" asked Tammie.

"I don't know I just do," replied Sofia.

"Ok, class be quiet," said Mrs. Thornthread as they were walking into the classroom. Mrs. Thornthread was the sweetest teacher Sofia ever met. If you turned a paper in late, she acted like it was on time.

"Where in the world have you two been?" asked Mrs. Thornthread in a soft voice.

"Sorry we're late. We were talking about Sofia's birthday party," said Tammie as she was taking her seat next to Sofia.

"Yes, we're sorry," said Sofia.

"That's ok, but next time wait until lunch so you won't be late," replied Mrs. Thornthread with a smile.

Chapter Three: Surprise

It's my birthday party after one long week of planning. Sofia ran downstairs and saw no one was there making breakfast in the kitchen. There was no one there to take her to her party. There was no one home at all. Sofia checked the last room in the entire house. She opened the door and turned on the lights.

"Surprise!" everybody shouted. Sofia lit up like the sun after a rainy day.

"Did you do this for me?" asked Sofia with shock.

"Yes, we did," said her mother as she came out behind the table.

"Were you surprised?" asked her older brother.

"Yes, I was Kyle," replied Sofia. "Thanks for everything, Mom and Dad and everyone who could come. This is the greatest party surprise ever."

Chapter Four: A Year Later

"Wow! I can't believe I made the track team," said Sofia to Tammie.

"That's great," replied Tammie.

"Yes, it is. When I get older I want to be in the Olympics," said Sofia.

"Well, I don't," said Tammie as she was getting something out of her locker. "I want to be a school teacher or an acrobat."

"That's great," replied Sofia happily.

"Hey, do you want to come over?" asked Tammie.

"I'd love to, but I can't because I have practice after school," said Sofia. "I'm sorry," replied Sofia with a sadness across her face.

"That's ok, maybe some other time," said Tammie with disappointment.

"Class, settle down!" Mrs. Detention said as we were returning to our chairs.

Mrs. Detention wasn't at all like Mrs. Thornthread. Actually she was just the opposite. She was mean. If you turned a paper in late she ripped it up and threw it away. Her name fit her perfectly because she was always giving detentions out.

"Now class! Today we're having a quiz," Mrs. Detention said with a smile. As soon as she said, "quiz" everyone froze and started getting scared they wouldn't pass.

"Now I wasn't going to give you a quiz but it took you five minutes to get quiet, so it's your own fault," Mrs. Detention said as she was passing it out.

Sofia turned and leaned over to tell Tammie this wasn't fair. After she told Tammie this wasn't fair, Mrs. Detention said, "Now does everyone have a paper because if you do you can start."

After twenty minutes went by Mrs. Detention went around collecting papers. After a while they were graded and passed back.

"Wow, I got an A+," said Tammie.

"I didn't. I got a B-," responded Sofia. "I thought I knew division, but I guess I need to practice more," said Sofia with sadness.

"Well at least you passed," said Tammie with a smile.

"I guess you're right. I guess this isn't something to get upset over," replied Sofia.

Chapter Five: The Crash

"Tammie! Guess what?" yelled Sofia from across the room.

"What?" asked Tammie.

"I have been asked to go to the Jr. High team's race Sunday to be in it," said Sofia.

"Wow! That's great!" replied Tammie with a smile.

"Do you want to come?" Sofia asked happily.

"Sure!" replied Tammie.

"Ok, we will pick you up," said Sofia.

Sunday arrived and Sofia had to get ready for the race. That night when six o'clock came, Sofia was ready and so was her brother. Her mom and dad had to work late, so her brother, Kyle, had to take her.

They got in the car and fastened up. They got a mile down the road and, BOOM! A car came crashing into them.

One of the neighbors close to the crash called the ambulance. They arrived a half hour later after the crash happened.

Sofia was injured badly and had to be rushed to the hospital immediately. Her brother, Kyle, only had a broken arm and a few scratches but that was all. When Sofia got to the hospital she was treated immediately.

Sofia's parents arrived shortly after they got the call. Sofia's mom asked what was wrong with Sofia. The doctor told her she was in a coma and didn't know how long it was going to last. The doctor also told her she didn't know if she was going to live after the coma.

Chapter Six: Two Years Later

It's been two years after the accident and Sofia was still in the hospital and was still in a coma. On June 1, of 1999 Sofia Anne Lorenzo died.

Even though she died at the age of fifteen, her parents and her brother still wanted her dream to come true. They had a statue made of her running with a baton in her hand. On the stone she's on is a message saying:

Sofia Anne Lorenzo
Born-July 4, 1986
Died-June 1, 2000

If you dream hard enough and want it bad enough it will one day come true.

Monica Cooper
Age: 15

THE ADVENTURE

I am going to Mt. Vernon today with Grandpa to buy cows. We have the grain truck and the livestock trailer. We can fit twenty-eight in the front and eighteen in the back. The traffic is busy. I will be home by 10:00. But it is nice out here. There are a lot of semis. There are a lot of fields and ponds. It is not raining here. There are not very many houses but there are a lot of bridges. It is full of trees. It is a little muddy. You get to see farms a lot. It is colorful out here. I am getting shook up. It is 10:56 at lunch. I am hot, hot, hot and hot. People are fishing here. My whole family is farmers. I have lots of pigs. I already have cows. I ate at DQ. I had a hamburger for lunch. It was yummy to my tummy. There are not many pigs here but there are a lot of cows. I am still not there yet. It is quiet here. You can see horses. You can see old houses. I like it here. You can see farm stores. I am at the cow sale. There are a lot of trucks. We bought seventeen cows. They said you can ride a scary bull. You hang onto his large horns and the horns are big. There were a couple of wild cows. A cow broke through the fence. A bull jumped over the fence. It was a big bull. We bought a couple of bulls. We will castrate the bull. We bought calves. They sell goats. A cow rammed into the fence. It got a bloody nose. They picked the goats up by the horns. I petted our cows. I scared a cow with the whip. My grandpa used the zapper. The zapper is very long and very strong. I got home and went to sleep. I was cranky in the morning. I was not cranky at school.

Caleb Brown
Age: 8

5

AN UNPREDICTABLE ACCIDENT

About one and a half years ago, I was in a near-death situation. At about 1:45 p.m. we were arriving at a friend's house from a nearby creek. We were playing around with their dog Nikki, and that's when it happened. Taylor (the friend) threw the ball and the dog and I followed it, the dog and I raced so fast and so carelessly, I was unaware of the accident that was about to happen and that ball would be close to killing me. I just got to their laundry room and slipped on a rug that was placed on a slippery concrete floor and the top right corner of my head slid across a stepstool with a ninety-degree angle edge. I lay there on the floor unconscious bleeding badly. I guess five minutes after I fell Taylor immediately called my mother who arrived less than two minutes after the call. When she arrived she explained to me that I'd have to get stitches. After we arrived home before we got ready to go to the hospital I got dressed and my mom had to get the bleeding to stop which was pretty hard because I had a two-inch gash in my head. We went to the Carlinville Emergency Room.

The doctor said "The gash is too big and he needs a plastic surgeon and we do not have one here." So after that they gave us directions to St. John's Hospital in Springfield, IL. I waited patiently and then my mom called my dad's house and when they asked where she was calling from my mom said Springfield Hospital.

And my stepmom asked "Is Nick coming down this weekend" because they always call Thursday. My mom said I can't because I'm about to get stitches in my head and my stepmom gasped for air because she was stunned when my mom told her. So after they got done talking my mom gave me the phone. Before I even took a breath she asked me are you OK?

"Yes," I answered. Then my stepmom gave the phone to my dad who was freaking out and was actually crying over it. Then we talked for ten more minutes then I hung up. I sat down then the doctor called me in. When I got in the room she tested me for any major injuries and to check if I fractured my skull. Then she called the doctor over the intercom. He came in the room and said he would have to finish on his other patient and that would take an hour or two. My mom gasped in despair.

"That long?" she asked. The doctor left and sent another doctor in so in case I went into shock or whatever. The doctor, my mom, and I talked over the accident. The doctor was shocked. Then she left. My mom and I watched TV for a while then my stepdad, my sister and her boyfriend Jared, my little brother Justin, and my other sister Paula and her boyfriend Josh came in the room to see me. We all talked and joked then visiting hour was over. Finally, the doctor came in and uncovered the thing he put on me that he put on me an hour or so ago. My mom left to go to the restroom before surgery began. When she got back the doctor gave me twenty shots to numb my head. Five minutes after that surgery began. I was a little bit scared because if I moved my head in the slightest angle his hand could slip and puncture my artery that goes to my brain and I could bleed to death. But that did not happen. He just did stitch after stitch after stitch and he was done. Then my mom filled out the release papers and we left. We had difficulties getting home because going to the hospital we had three fourths of a tank plus the fact we drove to Carlinville to Hettick then we missed six turns then finding a parking space that was empty. Our gas gage was on E when we got more gas in the truck. When we got home after that horrible day it was 5:35 a.m. when we arrived. We were finally home at last! I was so thankful to God that I was not dead. Then my mom bandaged my head and I went to bed. In the morning I woke up and EVERYONE was at my bedside asking are you OK, were you passing out, and did the stitches hurt? I answered YES I was OK, NO I did NOT pass out, and NO the stitches did NOT hurt. My mom was hugging me and happy that I was not dead. And that was the unpredictable accident that almost led to my death at the age of nine.

Nichals Singleton
Age: 11

Hi, Mr. President! My name is Matt. Nice to meet you. I was just wondering if you could come to my school? And tell us what it feels like to be a president.

Matthew Rapisardo
Age: 7

Once upon a time, there was a dog. But, this dog was not the normal street walking dog, he could talk. His name was Charlie. He lived in a mansion with the Talman family. Charlie was a German shepherd. He did not like the Talmans because they abused him. Charlie had a small, dirty bowl and he lived in a cage too small for his own size. Charlie hated the dark, dirty room. All he ever wanted was to get away from the Talman's house and have puppies. One day, he had had enough. He got his old ball his mother gave him before he left home. All his things were taken by the Talmans but the ball. He slowly reached one paw out to the hook that the key to his cage was hanging on. After a couple more tries he got it! Then he put the key in his mouth and quietly opened the cage. Charlie grabbed his ball and lunged forward. Suddenly, he remembered that Mrs. Talman was having tea with her friends. It was going to be hard to get past them. He knew he had to, so he slinked down the stairs and into the living room. There, he saw Mrs. Talman and her friends. Charlie stuck his ball back in his mouth and slowly and quietly walked to the door. Then, he reached up and got the key and unlocked the big, tall door. The scent of victory rushed through him for seconds -- then it stopped! Suddenly, he felt hot breath on his neck and he looked up. There was a huge bulldog.

"Hello," said the bulldog in a sly, foxy voice. Charlie was frozen, rooted to the spot. The bulldog growled and before Charlie could say a word he and the bulldog were fighting! Charlie won against the huge dog. He walked on -- still a little shaken. There was a forest up ahead. He wondered if he could get directions to New York City in there. He was in Pennsylvania. Charlie had never been outside before. It was beautiful -- fields, grass, flowers, bugs, birds, trees, sunlight on the morning dew. It was wonderful to Charlie. When he reached the forest he saw a badger. Charlie asked him if he knew the way to New York City. The badger just shook his head no and walked away. Charlie saw a stream up ahead. He was very thirsty.

"Haven't had a big drink in a while eh, have ya?" said an old rabbit.

"No," said Charlie looking up at the old rabbit.

"How'd you like to come stay with me a while?" asked the old rabbit.

"Sure," said Charlie, "anybody but that bulldog or the Talmans."

"Very well, that is settled," said the old rabbit. "Come, come, let's not waste time."

"By the way, sir, what is your name?" asked Charlie.

"Ah yes," said the rabbit, "my name is Jingles."

"Oh," said Charlie. Then, something caught his eye, it was a small hole in the ground, just big enough for him to fit into. Much bigger than a rabbit hole. "Is this your home?" Charlie asked Jingles.

"Yes," said Jingles. "I sized it so you could fit in."

"You knew I was coming?" asked Charlie.

"Yes," said Jingles. "I can tell the future."

"Wow," said Charlie. Jingles and Charlie went into the rabbit hole. It was like flying down a long tube. When they reached the bottom, Charlie saw a small patch of dirt cleared for him.

"It's late," said Jingles, "better get to bed." He pointed to the cleared dirt patch. Charlie laid

8

down and fell asleep quickly. When he woke up in the morning, Jingles was already up. He had food for him and Charlie.

They ate breakfast and woke up a bit more, then Charlie said, :I think I should go now."

"Very well," said Jingles. He pulled out a small, glass bird. "Charlie," he said, "if it is time for you to go, you must go, but you must always remember me." He handed the glass bird to Charlie. "Go up," he whispered to the bird. Suddenly, the glass bird began to fly, pulling Charlie with it.

"Good-bye!" said Jingles. Charlie was amazed -- he couldn't believe his eyes. When he reached the top of the rabbit hole, he saw the most beautiful girl dog in the world. (The only girl dog he had ever seen in his life). She was brown with floppy ears. She had those perfect blue eyes. Charlie walked up to her. He smiled at her and she smiled back.

"Hello," she said.

"Hi," said Charlie.

"Would you like to come to the Firelit Forest Party?" asked the girl dog.

"Yes," said Charlie. "What's you name?" asked Charlie.

"Olivia," she said.

"Oh," said Charlie.

"Oh my," said Olivia, "if we want to get to the party, we better hurry. Follow me," she said. They bounded toward the stream. On the stream there was a log. "We have to cross the log," said Olivia. Charlie gulped. The log was very thin, but they made it. There was a bonfire, lanterns, hot dogs, corn dogs, hamburgers, and lots and lots of other animals dancing to music. "Come on, let's dance!" said Olivia. They danced and danced until the moon was about to go down behind the trees. Then Olivia said, "Come with me." Charlie followed her to an old fox den. "This is my home," Olivia said as they crawled inside the den. It was cozy. Olivia had a wonderful home, the floor was covered in dried leaves. She carefully made a place for Charlie to sleep. Then, she made herself a place to sleep. "Better get to bed," she said. Then she kissed Charlie's cheek. He blushed, then drifted off to sleep. The next morning when Charlie woke up, Olivia was still asleep. So, he went out to find food. He found plenty of food. When he got back Olivia was awake.

"Where were you?" she asked.

"Out finding food," Charlie said.

"Oh," said Olivia. "I was wondering if you would like to come to New York City with me?" asked Charlie.

"Oh yes, I'd love to." said Olivia.

"Right now?" asked Charlie.

"Yes," said Olivia.

"Let's go," said Charlie.

"How do you get there?" asked Olivia.

There was a silence, then a rumbling noise. Suddenly, a car drove up in front of them and a pretty girl clambered out of the car. The girl picked them up and Charlie said, "Hey!" so that the girl could understand him. The girl froze!

"What?" she gasped.

Charlie said, "I can talk to humans."

"You what?" said the girl.

"I can talk to humans," said Charlie.

"Wow," said the girl.

"Will you take us to New York?" asked Charlie.

After the girl came back to her senses she said, "Yes, as a matter of fact, I was just going there." She put them in her car, started the engine and drove away. Two years later, Charlie got his wish -- he got away from the Talmans and had puppies of his own. He and Olivia live in an apartment in New York City now, happily ever after.

Hayley Haskett
Age: 8

LIFE

Every Halloween night I act creepy! But every other day I'm funny!! On Christmas Eve I'm so crazy I can't wait for Santa Claus to come! Every single Saint Patrick's Day I act Irish pretty often. Every spring my sister, Samantha, and I play and do exercises until night. Before we go in, we wish on the first star that appears. Every sunny day in summer, we go swimming in our giant pool. On rainy days we play in the rain all day. Sometimes we go fishing with our brother who is twelve years old. Also on sunny days we trace each other on the driveway and make cartoons with the traced figures. When we're done we climb up the basketball pole to see them. Also on rainy days, we jump in puddles.

Amanda Helm
Age: 8

THE MAGICAL SPIDER

Once there was a magical spider. Then an eagle saw the magical spider and caught her. The magical spider used her powers to make the eagle disappear. It worked, but now she is falling. She used her powers to fly. It worked. Then she flew into the distance.

Kyle Baumgarten
Age: 8

THE DOG

Once upon a time a girl had a dog. The girl had soft hair and was nice. The dog had prickly hair but he was nice too. The girl's name was Tori. The dog's name was Pet. Tori couldn't pet the dog because it had prickles. Tori wanted to pet the dog really bad. One day she asked if the dog could get a haircut. They said, "yes!!!" So the dog got a haircut. Tori could pet the dog and she was so happy!

Sarah A. Kline
Age: 7

SPUD'S STORY

It was a gloomy Oklahoma day and Mariah Lane lay on her bed doing homework. "Mariah," she heard her mother call. "Go make sure the horses have food and your riding lesson is in an hour."

Mariah grabbed her coat and dashed outside to the barn. She ran over to her favorite horse, Spud and whispered to him. "Spud, today was the best day ever. We went on a field trip to a museum. They had a lot of really cool stuff. I wish you could have come."

Spud had really soft, white fur. He was the biggest of all her horses. She ran over to her other horses Cookie and Beauty to make sure they had food. She ran back inside and got her horse riding clothes on. Then she ran back outside to get Spud ready. Soon Kathy Culman, her horse-riding teacher was at her house for the riding lesson. Mariah always enjoyed her riding lessons. After two long hours Kathy told her about a horse riding competition in two weeks. She ran inside to ask her mother. Her mother said that it would be OK. Mariah never felt so excited in her life. She ran back outside and started practicing with her favorite horse Spud. It was the week before the competition and Spud had a slight limp but Mariah really needed to practice. Mariah didn't want to tell her mom that she had pushed Spud too far. She knew Spud was an old horse and that he couldn't take as much as her younger horses, but she really wanted to take Spud. She went to her mother and told her she wasn't feeling well so she didn't want to do her lesson. Mariah felt horrible that she lied to her mom but she didn't want her mom or Kathy to know that Spud was hurt. On Friday the day before the competition Spud couldn't even walk. Mariah went to her brother first, and her brother Cory said, "You better ride Cookie or Beauty". That didn't make her feel any better but she knew that that's what she should do. Mariah went back out to the barn to make sure Spud really did have a hurt leg. The next morning she threw on some clothes and ran out to the barn to see how Spud was doing. Spud's leg was worse than ever. Mariah sat on the bench in the barn and cried. After a while she slowly walked into her house and told her mom that she had pushed Spud too far. Her mother was disappointed. She decided that she would take Beauty. All the way there it was silent. She got seventh place. She was proud of herself for doing so well. On the way back home it started to rain harder and harder. Mariah turned on the radio. Within five minutes they heard that there was a tornado warning over their town. Mariah's mom admittedly pulled over to the nearest gas station and ran inside. Mariah thought about Spud but she was positive that Spud would be OK. When Mariah got home she ran straight out to the barn but the barn was no longer standing. She ran all the way to the barn without stopping and started searching the millions of shredded wood pieces. By the time her mother got over to the millions of wood pieces Mariah had found Spud who was dead. Mariah stayed out in the pouring rain all night. Finally at about midnight Mariah's mother came out and got her. She went inside and lay in her bed but couldn't go to sleep. After about three days Mariah started to think about other things and was not so sad about Spud dying. One week later was Mariah's birthday. Her mom took her over to the barn at her uncle's house and when they got there her mom told her to look in the barn. There was a little soft, white pony lying in the stall where she got Spud eight years ago. She ran over to the pony and gave it a big hug just like when she first got Spud. She named the pony Spud Jr. after her favorite horse of all time.

Mariah went and started racing with Spud Jr. and won the state championship three years in a row.

Emily Williams
Age: 10

THE RACCOON WHO WANTED TO BE A MOMMY

Once upon a time there was an old raccoon. She wanted a baby very much but she didn't know where to get one! So she went to her good, wise friend, Mr. Owl.

He said, "Eat lots of food!"

The raccoon said, "Why?"

But the owl didn't answer! The owl said softly, "When you are done eating, push hard!"

So the raccoon took his advice. She pushed so hard a baby came out! The raccoon is a mommy now!

Kali Bringolf
Age: 7

CAPTAIN CHRISTMAS AND COMMANDER COLLIE TAKING ACTION

"Captain Christmas and Commander Collie reporting for duty, sir!"

Oh, hi, I'm Captain Christmas, and this is my dog, ?Commander Collie. We're secret agents, and we work at a place called The Agency. See, what's cool about The Agency is not only people work there but dogs too. Not only can Commander Collie fetch, but she helps me fight crime. She's my best friend. Well, let's get back to the story.

"Captain Christmas and Commander Collie reporting for duty, sir!"

"Girls, take a look here," Boss pointed to the computer. "There have been six robberies at these museums. They all have one thing in common at each place. The burglars only took the diamonds. Six very special diamonds each worn by Queen Isabelle. She loved diamonds. All six were taken in 1800 but returned in 1805. Then each one of the diamonds was placed in a heavily guarded museum. They haven't been touched since, until yesterday. They were found missing."

"Right on it, sir!" I said. Commander Collie barked.

"Your plane is ready," Boss told me.

"Great!" I said. First I got all my gadgets and disguises, and we boarded the plane. I was acting like a blind girl and Commander Collie was my seeing-eye dog, so they had to let her on the plane. It was a quiet ride over to Ireland. That's where the diamonds were stolen.

We got off the plane. I put a wristwatch walkie-talkie on, and Boss made Commander Collie a walkie-talkie collar. I put on my sunglasses, which really, I can see through things. We headed to the first museum.

"May I speak to your manager?" I asked the man standing at the counter.

"Why, yes, little girl. Is there something wrong?"

"No, sir, there's nothing wrong except that you think I'm little. I'm thirteen."

"I'll go and get the manager."

"Thank you," I told him. A strong looking man came out of the back room.

"May I help you?" he asked me.

"No, but we're here to help you. Hi, I'm Captain Christmas, and this is my dog Commander collie. We're the agents here to crack your case." He started to laugh. "Is there something wrong?" I asked.

"Yes," he kept on laughing. "I asked the U.S. to send their best agents. They sent a kid and a dog."

I was getting mad. "Well, sir, we're agents and believe me, there's nothing we can't solve," I told him. "Now, tell me what happened."

"Well," he said, "we were closing down last night, and one of my guards heard something upstairs where we keep the diamonds. So he went to check it out. When he walked into the Diamond Room something hit him on the head. The burglar tied him up and stole the diamonds without even setting off the alarms."

"May I take a look around?"

"Sure," he said.

"Commander Collie put these on. They are sunglasses to see fingerprints and very small things on objects. You take this side of the room, and I'll take the other." I put some sunglasses on too. I found two sets of fingerprints but barely enough to tell on either one. Commander Collie also found two black hairs. I sent them to Boss at the lab where Cadet Smelly and Sergeant Salami could find out who they belonged to.

We left and went to the next museum. What was funny, we found the exact same things there. We were both puzzled. We stopped to get something to eat. We went to the next museum and the next. We couldn't believe it. The clues were all the same. By the end of the day Cadet Smelly called me on the walkie-talkie. They had found whom the fingerprints belonged to: Cleo Beacon. Commander Collie and I both looked at each other. We knew the name very well. She was a worldwide villain who liked any kind of jewelry. I should have known it was her. I stopped three of her crimes already. I called up Boss and told him my information. He seemed pleased.

We were on the case. I searched high and low for any more clues. None were found, so Commander Collie and I headed to find Beacon. There was another robbery over in China, so we headed over to Hong Kong. We thought that she might be there.

Commander Collie stopped me as we walked back to the hotel where we were staying. She heard a noise. I followed her as she led the way. She picked up a scent. We followed a couple of huge guys. They were dressed in all black. They led us to a small building, and there we saw her.

"Good work!" I told Commander Collie and gave her a treat. "Let's enter through the window. Be quiet!" She looked at me with her dark brown, puppy eyes. My heart melted. I got on my hands and knees. She jumped on me and up to the window. I put on my glasses. I could see the diamonds. Beacon was wearing some of them muttering to herself. I called for backup, but I knew it would take The Agency a while to get to China. I climbed up the drainpipe and got on the windowsill. There I took out my stinky smoke bombs and a chew toy or, at least, that's what it looks like. It was a net. It expands when it hits an object. I threw one of the stinky smoke bombs. The air filled up with gas. My sunglasses could see through the smoke. The men started coughing, and I could see Cleo Beacon grabbing the jewels and running.

Commander Collie was already on her case running as fast as she could. I threw Commander Collie the chew toy, and I took care of the scary men. They didn't even have a chance. I caught up with Commander Collie and Cleo. Commander Collie had her trapped.

"So, we meet again," she said to us with a sly smile.

"Well, hello, Cleo," I looked at her. Commander Collie barked and threw me the chew toy.

"I thought I had shut you down the last three times I caught you," I laughed.

"You and your stupid dog could never stop me." Commander Collie growled.

"What are you going to do?" she smiled.

"Send you back to jail," I told her.

"You may have stopped me before, but this time, girlie, I outsmarted you." Here came a helicopter. Beacon jumped out the window. The helicopter caught her. She was laughing all the way down.

I called Boss on the walkie-talkie. He sent a plane out, and he said that it would be there in a little bit. As soon as we stopped talking, here came the plane. Cadet Smelly and Sergeant Salami were on it. We caught up to Beacon. We boarded her helicopter. We took out some gadgets and kicked some butt. We took care of the huge scary guys, and Cadet Smelly took over the helicopter. It was just Beacon and me. Commander Collie grabbed the jewels. From behind I threw the net on her. She tried to get free, but we had her. Cadet Smelly steered the helicopter towards home.

We stopped her again. Boss was proud. When we landed, you could see it in his face.

"Great job!" I told the other agents. I looked over to Commander Collie. She came and gave me a big lick on the face.

"You were great!" I smiled.

"Captain Christmas, Commander Collie, good work, girls."

"Thanks, Boss," I told him.

"I can always count on you two."

"We're always there when you need us. Captain Christmas and Commander Collie signing off."

(Remember, you can always achieve your goals with friendship, imagination, and a whole lot of heart. You can do anything.)

Jacy Chapman
Age: 12

JINGLE GOES EXPLORING

There once was a hamster and his name was Jingle. He built a house and it looked like this. Pashmena thought it was a good house. One day he went out of his house. He looked for some flowers for his friend, Pashmena. She wore a pretty rainbow scarf. Don't you think it looks beautiful? I think it is. Jingle thinks it is, too.

Jingle found some beautiful flowers to match her rainbow scarf. He found red roses, orange poppies, yellow sunflowers, green leaves, blue pansies, and purple clovers. He gave her all of the flowers and she loved them very much.

Taylor Cooperider
Age: 8

A WINTER STORY

My family and I live in Missouri but it felt like the arctic here. Charleigh and I were playing in the snow in front of our house. We were waiting for Mom to come get us.

As soon as my mom came out, she said we were going to get our Christmas tree. So all of us tried to get in the Blazer. However, we could not get in because the Blazer doors were frozen. Therefore, my dad had to get the heater and soon we were in. On the way there, we went to the gas station to get some hot chocolate because I was freezing.

Soon we got to the tree farm. We saw the perfect tree but it had ice on it. No one cared about the ice or that there were snowflakes flying everywhere. Therefore, we cut it down with a handsaw. We strapped it to the top of the Blazer.

We were home in a short amount of time. By the time, we got the tree through the door I looked like a snowman. The snow on the roof and the tree just smothered me. As we got inside a blizzard or an ice storm blew all the decorations in the winter garden away. We were tired so we went to sleep.

Tyler Robichaud
Age: 9

A VERY SNOWY DAY

One school day I woke up and looked out my window. I saw snow up to my roof! I went downstairs, and saw icicles everywhere! Mom called my school to see if it was out. No one answered but the answering machine said it was closed.

I got dressed quickly and went out to play. I opened the door, fell in the snow, and rolled down the street inside a snowball! I was frozen. Then the snowball ran into Melissa. It was very chilly. Melissa said, "A snowstorm is coming let's get inside."

So we ran to my house but a Godzilla Snowman popped out from behind a tree before we got inside. It was enormous! Melissa had an idea. We took snowballs and threw it at him but it didn't work. Then we threw rocks but it didn't work either. Next we got hot chocolate and poured it on him, and he melted.

After that more snowflakes fell and it got really nippy. The snow glistened and sparkled. We ran inside and poured hot chocolate on everything. That night I had a hot chocolate bath and went to bed.

Missy Kohl
Age: 9

17

AGILITY

Hannah Carter walked her dog, Chipper towards the agility obstacle course that she and her dad had set up in the backyard. That year for 4-H Hannah was entering Chipper for agility. Chipper was a German shepherd that had a black ear with a brown speck on the tip. It looked like his ear was chipped. That's how he got his name. Even though Chipper hadn't been trained by a professional trainer, Hannah trained him very well. Chipper ran the obstacles like there was no competition! He ran so fast that Hannah couldn't keep up with him. When she fell behind, he kept going. He wasn't afraid of the obstacles either, and when the other dogs hesitated he acted like the seesaw was plain ground. It was like he shut everything else out of his mind. If a bomb went off, he'd probably pay the slightest bit of attention! That's what made him so good.

About a month later, Hannah took Chipper to 4-H. He was so excited with all the dogs running around that he went crazy when he almost sat on a tiny Jack Russell! There were tons of dogs! From the Papillion to the Great Dane -- there were dogs! It was practically raining dogs and the worst thing that could happen was to get a cat on the scene! Just as Hannah lined up to sign Chipper in, a girl taller than her came over, "A police dog!" she shouted. "Is he retired?"

Hannah raised an eyebrow. "Uh, no," she answered. "He's not a police dog. He's a German shepherd." The girl rolled her eyes.

"I already knew that! Not stop acting like I'm koo-koo and let's get down to business!"

Hannah squinted an eye. "What do you mean?"

The girl rolled her eyes again. "Do you know anything? I'm gong to borrow your dog for agility! That's what I mean! What's his name anyway?"

Hannah's eyes were about to bolt. She was so surprised she almost fainted. She finally told the girl what Chipper's name was.

"Well, thanks for answering a hundred years later!" shouted the girl. "What does Chipper mean anyway?" Hannah quickly explained Chipper's name.

Alex wrinkled her forehead. "Odd name. Mine's Alex. What's yours?"

Hannah was so shocked she thought she'd forgotten her name. When she did answer, it could barely be heard. When she could talk again she said, "Sorry, but Chipper's my dog and I'm running agility with him."

Alex crossed her arms and leaned towards Hannah. Then, she said, "And why do you think that, Hannah?!" She said it as if Hannah was a terrorist who had stolen Alex's dog.

"Because he's my dog," said Hannah. "Why'd you come here? To take peoples' dogs and do something that the dog and owner planned to do themselves? Huh?"

Alex didn't answer. Hannah knew she was right, because if she wasn't, Alex would have answered by now. She turned around and sniffed. "Fine. Chipper can be in agility with you. It's just that I've never had a dog and I wanted to know what it was like."

Hannah started to feel a little sorry for Alex, but she had made up her mind that she was to run agility obstacles with Chipper. This was a once in a lifetime chance and she wasn't going to let it pass because of some spoiled girl. Hannah sighed. "I guess you can come to my place and work him out before I take him to 4-H, and if you want to, you can feed him in the morning. Is it a deal?" Hannah held out her hand.

Alex's frown turned into the biggest smile Hannah had ever seen. She didn't know how somebody could be so happy about taking care of someone's dog, but who cared? Alex was happy and she was still running agility with Chipper. Hannah told Alex her address and got back in line to sign up. Alex got in line too. It was a long line, and when they finally got there Hannah felt almost thrilled. When the woman at the counter asked the owner's name, Hannah answered. When she asked Chipper's name, just as Hannah was about to say his name Alex told her first. "His name is Chipper. Hannah's his owner but she's letting me take care of him for a while. My name's Alex, but I'm not doing agility with Chipper." Alex beamed.

The woman looked at Hannah. She wanted to know if Chipper was his real name. Hannah nodded. "Yeah, it's Chipper," she said.

The next few days were exhausting for Hannah. She spent most of her time with Alex. They talked about each other's lives and what they were like. Alex's family was rich; she bragged about all the neat stuff she had. Hannah wondered why Alex was so rich, but didn't have a dog. She didn't ask, though. Alex talked for a long time without letting Hannah say anything. When she finally did get to talk, she wasn't sure she wanted to. She was afraid Alex would say things like "Why are you like that?" or "My life is so great compared to yours!" because Hannah's family didn't have much money. Hannah decided to tell Alex about how good Chipper was at agility. She guessed it was okay to brag a little after what Alex had said. Alex patted Chipper on the head. The two girls were sitting at the kitchen table eating brownies. Alex sighed. "I wish I could see Chipper do agility. Just to see how he'll react when I'm warming him up."

Hannah thought a minute. "You want to go outside to watch him?" Alex didn't answer. Instead, she jumped out of her seat, grabbed Chipper's leash, hooked it onto his collar, and ran outside with Chipper behind her before Hannah could move. When Hannah got outside Alex was trying to force Chipper to run the obstacles.

Hannah ran up to them and took the leash from Alex. "I thought you said he was really good at agility," she said.

"He is," said Hannah. "He just won't do it with strangers."

Alex wrinkled her nose. "I'm not a stranger you know that!"

Hannah crossed her arms. "He hasn't known you very long. That's what I meant when I said stranger."

Alex shrugged, and went to sit on the porch and watch. Hannah took one last look at Alex before letting go of Chipper's leash and running through the obstacle with him.

When the big day finally came, there were more dogs than there ever had been before. But there was one thing Hannah was curious of, Alex had vanished. Suddenly, two boys came over. "Have you seen our dogs?" one of them asked. "They were sitting over there just five minutes ago." He pointed at the fence that surrounded the obstacle course. The leashes had been taken with the dogs. The other boy started to describe them. They were both golden retrievers, bigger than Chipper. Hannah told the boys that she hadn't seen their dogs, but she had an idea of where they were, if only she could find Alex.

Then, Chipper started to pull on his leash, and before Hannah knew it, he was pulling her back behind the bleachers. There, with the golden retrievers, was Alex. She had seen Hannah and was running as fast as she could, away from the bleacher. Hannah knew she couldn't catch up with her. She looked at Chipper. He could run faster than any human she knew, and he understood that these weren't Alex's dogs. Hannah let go of his leash and he darted after Alex. "Get her, Chipper!" Hannah shouted.

Just as Alex was reaching the road he grabbed her jeans in his teeth and pulled her to the ground. Hannah ran up, and grabbed the leashes from Alex. She wouldn't let go, but when Chipper jumped onto her chest she did.

The two boys that were the golden retriever's real owners had followed. They came over and took the leashes from Hannah. "Thanks," said one of the boys. "We better get back to the obstacle course. The show is about to start." The other boy shook his head.

"We can't run an obstacle course and look after the thief at the same time."

Hannah grabbed Alex's arm and pulled her off the ground. "I'll give her to my parents so they can watch her." She tugged Alex back towards the bleachers. She had her sitting in them just as the show had started.

When it was their turn Hannah led Chipper out to the obstacles. He ran faster than he ever had before, and in the end it was announced that he won.

After the show, Alex came to Hannah and said, "I've learned my lesson, and I'll never do anything to hurt you again." After that, they were best friends and their favorite thing to do was to run dogs in agility.

Sammy Hendrix
Age: 9

A WOLF AND A DOG

A wolf and a dog were best friends. The wolf pups were black and white. They hunt for meat. The wolf caught a deer. The dog caught a rabbit. As they slept the wolf slept with the pups. They found a half wolf and half dog. They became best friends.

Cameron Ford
Age: 8

ALY'S FAVORITE BOOK

Chapter One: Aly's First Time Swimming

One day Aly was in her room reading her favorite book and hugging her favorite teddy bear. Ten minutes later Aly's dad called, "Aly, Aly, get your swimsuit on because we are going swimming!"

Aly's twin brother ran down the stairs he said, "Where are we going swimming?"

"To Queeny Park," said Dad.

Aly was pounding down the stairs, "I don't want to go swimming."

Mom said, "You have to go because everybody else is going. Now, go and get your swimming suit on."

Aly went upstairs and put her swimming suit on. She then went downstairs and ate her breakfast and went to the garage and got in the car and drove to the pool. Aly brought her book to read because she didn't really want to swim. Aly got in the car and began to read. The book was called Cinderella. Once they got there she got a chair and put a towel on it and sat down. She began to read Cinderella again. Then she got up and splash! Aly's twin brother Alan splashed water on her. Aly was mad and she went on chasing her twin brother.

Aly's mom and dad said, "It's time to go!"

Aly said, "Oh, can we go again?"

Aly's mom said, "Why not!" They went home and got in bed and went to sleep. The next morning the kids went downstairs and had breakfast peacefully and quietly.

Chapter Two: School RING!

The bell rang. Little Aly walked into her room with her twin brother Alan. Everybody sat down and the teacher Mrs. Coldens said, "Today we are going to learn about Dr. Martin Luther King, Jr."

Aly raised her hand, "Who is Dr. Martin Luther King, Jr.?" she asked.

Mrs. Coldens said "Here Aly, read this book and it will tell you all about him." Aly got the book from Mrs. Coldens and put it in her backpack. Mrs. Coldens passed out the Martin Luther King, Jr. books. Everybody loved it. Everybody started to read it. Then the class was over. Everybody packed up and went home. Little Aly was still reading it. When she got home she went upstairs and did her homework and began to read the Dr. Martin Luther King, Jr. book.

Fifteen minutes later her mom called, "Dinner is ready."

Aly said, "Just a minute!" She came down the stairs, ate her dinner and went back upstairs and began reading again.

Anjola Akande

THE LEGEND OF THE STRAWBERRY

Once, there was a man named Luerei Kbovn. He was from the city of Ositdnohna (pronounced /o SET njo na/) in the country of Grejnac on Plant Ephaa. In this land, there were many bad things like storms, famines and captivities. A neighboring country by the name of Aimbide had bumper crops, gold and prosperity. Here is the story that changed Grejnac, and in essence all of Ephaa, forever.

Luerei Kbovn went and got some of the scarce food of the Ositdnohna farms so he would have something to eat. He did not take much, however, for he was a wise and kind man who was caring for the needy. The needy, in turn, needed much more to sustain themselves than the well-to-do, and gave back to the wealthy small tithes which were accepted with great gratitude--something that was unique to that time period. They all worked hard and went through many famines, and their trust in each other persevered along with the whole thing. That was what kept them alive. Luerei was a kind and caring man.

It came about that there was a big wasp attack. They stung everything in their path and devoured everything in sight. They tore up wells. They devoured huts. They eroded houses. Shacks didn't stay very long. Tents were swept away by the plague. Entire cornfields were laid bare. Hay bales ruled the road. It was amazing what an army of little insects could do. Other things happened as well, and none of them were good. The ruler of the universe saw this and warned the Wasp King to end the battle or be brought to a bitter end. The wasp king did not reply. The wasps just kept on with the terrorism and the killing of innocent allergic victims. The ruler was tensified by this whole thing. He summoned the Wasp King and once again they negotiated the concept of ending the terror. Again, the Wasp King declined an end to his fun. So the Wasps continued with their work. In their work they got great exercise and nourishment so they were very happy and excited about any new attacks that they might be making. When their bodies got larger, their exoskeletons provided no room for excess growth, so when they got fat, something had to go -- in this case, their brains, which got smaller and smaller. The Wasp King was the only intelligent one among them after a few years, so it was not long until they could not understand him because the hearing and thinking parts of their brains had disappeared. Meanwhile, Luerei was in his house thinking when a mad-raven wasp army came and did him in. They stung him on his arms, legs and head. But, unfortunately for them, they forgot to remove their stingers, so they died all over the Kbovn Family Rug. Luerei was not doomed, however, because of his caring and faith. The needy pooled their sparse cash and had Luerei treated. All the bad blood vanished into the sandy ground of Ephaa. Soon, a green carpet crept up from the ground and blossomed into beautiful flowers. They became fruit. The ruler of the universe appeared in the air and said, "This planet is now called Earth." The sand became soil. "This nation will be named Greece." The citizens were filled with ambition, knowledge and intellect. "This fruit will be named the strawberry." Immediately, as if by magic, the whole world knew that this would be the name of the new fruit. They ate it because it reminded them of freedom, the ruler and Luerei Kbovn.

This tale tells how two things have happened: Strawberries come into existence, and wasps are dumb and scarce. Today the Kbovn family lives in joy, happiness and prosperity. To this day, they love and remember the strawberry as a reminder of their ancestry and their favorite fruit.

John Wiemer
Age: 14

WINTER FUN

Winter can be fun. Here are three things I like to do in winter. They are making snowmen, having a snowball fight, and building a snow fort.

The first thing I like about winter is making snowmen. Last year, we made a six-foot-tall snowman. It was taller than my dad! We had to roll a big ball of snow for the bottom and then we made a medium sized ball of snow for the body. Last, we rolled a tiny ball of snow for the head. We put eyes, a nose, a mouth, arms, a scarf, and a hat on him. When winter was over he melted. I enjoy making snowmen.

The second thing I like to do in winter is having snowball fights. My whole family usually plays. My dad always wins. Sometimes we make snow walls to protect ourselves from getting hit. We have to get a lot of snow! We hardly ever have enough snow to make four snow walls, so, sometimes we have teams. My dad and I play against my mom and sister. I love to have snowball fights.

The third thing that I like to do in winter is build a snow fort. There has to be a lot of snow to build a snow fort. When we build snow forts we usually get my neighbor, Alex Hunt, to help. It is very hard to make. My sister and I brought over some containers to use as molds. Once we got one row around the bottom, I got in and made sure that they wouldn't break. Then we started to build some more. When we were finished we realized there was no door. We had to take some blocks of snow off so there would be a door. Suddenly, David, Alex's brother, came with a wagon full of snowballs. We were very glad we made the snow fort, because he couldn't get us. Once he ran out of snowballs, we got out and started getting snowballs and throwing them at him. He finally gave up. We were glad that we won. It is fun to build snow forts.

As you can see, I like playing in winter. It is very fun. I enjoy making snowmen, having snowball fights, and building snow forts. I love winter!

Tim Barnett
Age: 9

"Are you really going to go through with it?" Chelsea asked. "I mean, it's a lot of hard work to be in something like this."

I brought my bike to a halt and stared in disbelief at the girl. "Don't give me that again. You know how much being in 'The Nutcracker' means to me."

Ever since my dance teacher, Miss Johnson, had mentioned the auditions for the ballet, I'd immediately signed up. I'd always loved doing shows, but I never seemed to get in them when I had to audition for a part. This time, despite past events, I had gotten in.

"But every time you get involved in a show, you always end up throwing something," she complained. "Remember last year? It cost you big time."

I shuddered at the thought. Maggie Daniels wouldn't be talking to me any time soon.

I began pedaling as hard as I could. "I don't know what you're talking about." I shot a glance at her.

She let out a quick laugh, running a hand through her long, silky brown hair, and added, "no one could forget something like that. I know you. I know how you worry about things."

I tightened my grip on the bike handle. "Why don't you try out for a show?"

"Lily, you know I can't dance to save my life." Chelsea removed her hand from her hair to emphasize her anti-dancer's body.

"I bet you could pedal!" With that, I took off and tore down the sidewalk, my legs almost getting tangled in the process. Chelsea wasn't too far behind, as expected. She was perfect for helping me train and build up my leg muscles. The sun's rays beat on the back of my neck, but the cool March air helped me glide through the neighborhood, as I watched every tree I passed by.

"Legs worked up yet?" Chelsea shouted from behind.

"No way!" I exclaimed, and pedaled even faster, if that was possible.

"Maybe you should stop," my friend's voice seemed to have changed from excited to worried.

"What's wrong?" I turned my head to see that her eyes were wide with fear.

"No!" she screamed.

That's the last thing I remember, before my whole world went black.

***

"Hang on, I think she's coming about."

I opened my eyes, to see a blurry man dressed in all blue hovering over me.

"Who are you?" My voice came out hoarse, as if I hadn't used it in days.

"Lily," my dad appeared next to the gray-haired man. "This is Dr. Fields. You're in the hospital."

"Joy," I muttered sarcastically.

I tried to sit up, but the second I made the slightest move it felt as if I'd been injected with pain.

"Hold still," I heard my mom's voice, and she appeared on the other side of me.

I decided to ask what people in movies would ask in a situation like this, "What happened?"

"You crashed into a tree," Dr. Fields said, nervously rubbing the back of his neck. "You were badly hurt, but luckily your helmet saved you from any further injury."

"How bad?" I demanded.

"Lily, maybe we should get you something to eat," Mom interrupted. "After all, going three days without proper nourishment, you must to be ravenous."

"Three days?" I yelled, as instant pain came to my head. "I was out for three days?"

She nodded sadly. "We thought you were in a coma, but you seem to be doing better."

If only she knew how badly I was feeling then. Especially when it hit me.

"What about 'The Nutcracker'?"

"Honey, it's next Monday," she told me, and I think I saw a tear fall from her eye. "I don't think you can make it."

"But it's a week away! I can get better by then!" I felt tears welling up in my own eyes.

They made it seem like my mom's red hair was shining. I don't know why I noticed it. The shining hair just made her seem important in a way, as if she knew what was best.

Despite that, what she was saying wasn't fair. The one time I auditioned for a part in a show and actually got it, I had to go and crash into a tree. Then I remembered Chelsea.

"It's a week away," Mom repeated. "Only a week away. I want you to rest. I don't know what you did to that head of yours, but I certainly don't want you in a show."

I ignored this comment. "Where's Chelsea?" I asked.

"Oh, your friend Chelsea may have saved your life." Dr. Fields smiled. "When she saw you go down she immediately knocked on the door of the closest neighbor's house."

I smiled. "Where is she?"

"She went home a couple days ago," Dad informed me.

As Mom and Dad continued running through the events of that past three days, I couldn't keep my mind off of "The Nutcracker." What was I supposed to tell Miss Johnson? After five months of rehearsals, they were all going to waste -- every single one of them. Now the understudy, Martha Sandberg, was going to be the Snow Princess.

"Perfect." I closed my eyes, half expecting to be lying in my bedroom when I opened them.

I was disappointed, though. The hospital seemed to be holding me hostage, because even as I tried to move, the bed was holding me back. For the first time, I surveyed the room. The walls were bright blue, decorated with butterflies and rainbows.

"Humph, must be the children's hospital," I whispered.

I looked for Mom and Dad but was surprised to see that they weren't there. I must have fallen asleep when I closed my eyes.

"Please, no... please, no," I repeated under my breath. "This can't be happening."

I wanted to be in that show so badly, that my head started spinning with the slightest thought of it. I began to think that my injury was hurting more emotionally than physically.

I wanted to see Miss Johnson, to tell her I couldn't make it. I wanted her to know that I cared. I reached up to feel my head. It felt as if it was covered in a thick bandage, which it probably was.

25

I wanted to fall asleep forever, at least at that moment I did. I closed my eyes again and waited, for what seemed like an hour, until I finally drifted off.

***

When I woke up my eyes were fixed on a young woman who was rummaging around the dresser next to my bed. She said her name was Nurse Kate.

"It's time for you to go home," she explained, "but you'll need to rest a lot. Get in at least three days of relaxation."

"What day is it?" I asked her.

"Thursday," she replied.

My heart sank. There were so many rehearsals at the end of this week, followed by the performance on Monday. Martha Sandberg hadn't hit her head on a tree. Martha Sandberg hadn't let the whole cast down. She was going to dance her heart out, her blonde hair dazzling and shiny teeth sparkling.

When I got home, Mom helped me into the house. As I set foot into the kitchen, I devised a plan. For two hours straight I rested my head on a pillow in the living room, taking in deep breaths. Then I sat up slowly and swung my legs over the side of the couch. I stood up as carefully as I could and walked into the center of the room. Then I began dancing, lazily at first, but I started getting sharper. I did all of this with my eyes closed, imagining myself in front of the audience.

I repeated the exercise on Friday and Saturday. On Sunday, I asked Mom to drive me down to the dancing school for the rehearsal. She seemed reluctant at first, but then agreed.

When I saw the school, all the pain disappeared. I marched into the auditorium. The cast was busy practicing on the stage.

"Miss Johnson," I said to my teacher. "I can do my part. I'm going to perform tomorrow."

She seemed surprised. "But your head -- I thought it was injured."

"I feel fine," I stated.

That's how it went down. On Monday, I removed that bandage and went onto the stage. The pain was gone the entire time. I danced my heart out, just like I had imagined I would. I stared out into the audience to see Chelsea seated in the front row. She winked at me and gave me a thumbs-up. I had proven to her that I could get past an injury and do what I love to do, but even more, I had shown myself.

Jamie Schlansky
Age: 13

THE ACCIDENT

Sarah lay in bed that night, wondering why this had happened to her, even more, to her best friend. When she lifted her head from the tear-stained pillowcase, she thought maybe it wasn't true. Maybe the terrifying phone call wasn't real. Could it all have just been a bad dream? Why did it have to be Nicole to die in the accident? Why did she have to get in the car with Mike, who she had known had had too much to drink? All these questions ran through Sarah's head. Nicole had always been a great kid. She was in the drama club, on student council, always did her work, volunteered in her community. So why did someone decide to knock her off this earth knowing she would be missed and that she was of value to everyone around her?

A day ago, everything had been normal in fifteen-year-old Sarah Daniel's life. She walked down the hall with her best friend since sixth grade, Nicole Swanson. They chatted about many things, one including the party that would be held at Mike Jenison's mansion-like home.

When Sarah got home, she told her mom about the party she wanted to go to so badly. As she told her mother the news, she noticed the calendar behind her. The calendar noted that the party was on the same day as her aunt's wedding. She knew there was no way out of the wedding, so she did not argue with her mother and went to her room. When she got there, she called Nicole right away and told her she couldn't go, but that Nicole still should. Nicole was upset, but went to the party knowing it would be a shame for Sarah to miss all of the fun.

At the party, Nicole realized it was midnight and decided it was time to go home. She walked outside and breathed in the cool night air. Too cold to walk home. She thought to herself, so she asked Mike for a ride. She could see that his eyes were a little foggy, but she needed a ride and got in the car.

A week passed after Nicole's death, Sarah was still devastated. One night, she lay in bed thinking and fell asleep with one thought in her head. That Nicole was probably in a better place and would want Sarah to move on with her life.

The next day, Sarah was not as unhappy and as the days passed, she got better. The one thing that did stick, though, was that she knew it all could have been avoided if Mike and Nicole both had made a better decision.

Haley Luke
Age: 13

WHY DID IT HAVE TO HAPPEN?

Waving good-bye to my older sister, I thought about what she had said to me before she left. She said that the government was failing, condemned to subjugation. I do not know what she meant, but I believed her. The very last thing she told me was to be careful. There was something about the way she said it though. It wasn't the average 'take care of yourself' or 'be a good girl' there was a fierce tenseness in her voice that I didn't understand.

Usually I walk home from school with my older brother, Elijah. Today will be the first time I am allowed to walk alone. As I walk around a corner that leads to one of the main streets in town, I see many odd-looking men I have never seen before. The men were dreadfully tall; the very sight of them scared me. They looked like giants. Feeling very small, I tried to slink past them without their terrible, cold, eyes catching me. I was about to turn the final corner when I felt a cold, hard, hand weighing itself down upon my shoulder. Slowly, I turned my head around. The giant wasn't looking at me. He was looking at my dark hair, my dark eyes. I ran home as fast as I could.

As soon as I was home I ran to Mother and told her all about the soldier. Later that night I could hear Mother and Father discussing my encounter with them. "Bina, you knew we would have to leave someday. If one of the Nazis followed Dela home they could come for us within the next few days, perhaps even tomorrow. Even if they didn't follow her they have their way of finding out who is disabled, who is Jude, and who is not one of them!"

"I know we have to leave it's just that, we raised our family here, I was born here." Mother said, I could feel the pain in her voice.

"It will be hard leaving here, but it we leave now we might have a chance, our fate may not be in a concentration camp." Father said this in his comforting voice that I had often heard him use. What were they talking about? Tovi must have heard them too, for just then he opened the door and quietly crawled into my bed.

"Odelia, why are Momma and Vati yelling at each other?" Tovi said in his sweet little voice.

"They're not yelling at each other they're just," I didn't know what to say, were they yelling at each other? How could I comfort Tovi when I knew just as much as he did? "I don't know Tovi, I really don't know."

"Is something bad going to happen?" he said

"I don't know that either, but I promise that whatever does happen, I will never let anybody hurt you."

The next day Mother didn't let Elijah or me go to school. "Is school closed today Momma?" I asked.

"No, we're just, going on a vacation. Now, go on and pack away a few of your outfits." A few hours later violent knockings were set upon our door.

"Erschlieben Sie! Open up!" Mother had a terrified look upon her face I had never seen an adult use before.

"Go to your rooms, do not come out" she said in a hushed yet demanding voice. All three of us huddled in the same room.

"Search the house, leave nothing valuable!" Just yesterday I had heard those harsh voices for the first time. Now they were everywhere. When there were no more sounds we crept out of the room. What we saw was a sobbing woman crouched on the floor that couldn't possibly be our mother. "They took everything! Nothing is left!" We looked around the room realizing the horrible truth. Almost everything was gone.

"Momma." I didn't know what to say. All of us crowded around this woman that had to be our momma.

Tovi knelt down, looked her in the eyes and said "But Momma, they didn't take us."

When Vati returned from work he and Mother talked for a long time in hushed voices. I only heard a little bit, but what I did hear swam through my mind in a mass of jumbled confusion. Finally Vati told us that there were people after us, the giants. He said that we had to hide from them or they would send us away. A few hours later Momma, Tovi, and I dressed up in dark cloaks. We said good-bye to Vati and Elijah. The three of us left the house and proceeded to walk down dark alleys until we reached the outer part of the city.

When we finally stopped we were at a run-down cottage. Momma knocked on the door. A tall man with gray hair and a mustache opened it. He led us to the back of the cottage to a barn. Once we were there he led us to a wagon. At the bottom of the wagon where hay usually is, the man opened a small door. On the other side of this door was a little opening about six-feet long, five-feet wide, and one-foot deep. The man motioned for us to crawl inside. There was a violent jolt and the wagon was moving. I do not know how long we were in that wagon, but it felt like a lifetime.

Finally we stopped. "I will be back for you tomorrow. Do not leave this area, if someone comes, hide." The man had left us in the middle of a forest with nothing but the clothes we had brought, a loaf of bread, and a promise that he would be back for us. When we could no longer hear the rolling sound of the wagon wheels, I turned to Mother.

"Is that man really going to come back for us?" I was terrified, how could he have just left us here? Were the giants going to find us? Would they really take us away? Where would they take us? I felt so confused, what was going to happen to me? Why were we in this cold, dark, woods in the first place? Why wasn't I at home right now?

"He will come back for us."

That night it was hard for me to fall asleep. When I finally did I was awoken many times by frightful nightmares and mysterious noises. The next day slowly dragged on, when the sun started to disappear, we heard a faint noise in the distance. "Follow me. Be as quiet as you can." Mother led us to a fallen tree that had been hollowed out from decay. She motioned for us to crawl inside. The noise was growing closer, I was shaking with fear. Peeking out the various cracks I nearly squealed with joy. The same wagon we arrived in was passing into a clearing close by. Momma must have seen it too, because she grabbed Tovi by the hand and raced towards the wagon. When the man saw Momma he stopped abruptly. Momma and the man unloaded the hay. When it was all gone the little trap door was the only thing left. Out of the door crawled a tired-looking Elijah and Vati.

We started walking through the forest. A few hours later the trees started to thin out. We were walking to the edge of a city. This city looked exactly like my home. Yet it was oddly different. Vati said we couldn't walk down the main streets, so once again we were forced to walk down dark alleys. After we had walked for a long time we came to the back of a big building.

"Odelia, if the Nazis catch us, even see us, they might take us all away to a horrible place." Vati's comforting voice soothed me. "You have to understand that Momma and I will be going away for a little while. One day we will come back for you though, and everything will be better." Going away? Where were they going? How long would they be gone? Were they leaving Elijah and Tovi too?

"Momma, where are you and Vati going?" How could they leave us?

"Odelia, you have to understand!"

"Momma! I don't want you to go!" Tovi was grabbing onto Mother's skirt. "Please don't leave us!"

My momma and Vati had sent us to a Catholic orphanage, they did not return for a few years. When they did return they came with visas. After being taken out of the orphanage and smuggled to the nearest port, we managed to get on a ship to America. I wonder what would have happened to me if the Nazi hadn't stopped me, if Vati wouldn't have hid us. Would I have died with the other twelve million people? Why didn't the Nazis realize that nobody is perfect, that nobody ever will be? Why did the Holocaust have to happen?

Haley Sinea Conner
Age: 13

MY SISTER'S THE COOLEST

Up until last year I thought my sister Jessica was the coolest. It's no lie that I wanted to be like her, who wouldn't? Ever since I can remember she has been popular, athletic, good-looking and smart! Everybody always liked Jessica and she seemed to know everyone. She played on the school soccer and softball teams, made pretty good grades and even ran for election to the student government. When she turned sixteen she got a really cool job at a movie theater! She would sometimes get me into movies for free! Because Jessica is six years older than me, she didn't spend a whole lot of time playing with me. Especially when her friends came over, then she would usually tell me that I was too little and to get lost.

About a year ago, during her senior year of high school, Jessica's grades started to get bad. She was spending all of her spare time at work, hanging out with her friends and even started skipping school. My mom and dad were upset a lot about the friends she was skipping school with and tried to ground her. Jessica would just sneak out. She got her navel and tongue pierced and started dying her hair a different color every week! My parents were really worried about her grades and what she was doing at night. They tried talking, grounding, yelling and crying. Nothing seemed to matter to Jessica anymore but hanging out with her friends and partying. This was not cool!

Three months before my sister was supposed to graduate, she dropped out of high school and moved in with the friends she had been spending so much time with. My mom and dad were real upset and tried to get her to take the GED if she wasn't going to go back to school. Jessica said that she didn't need to because she had a great job at the theater. I missed Jessica, she didn't come over very often.

It's been almost a year since she dropped out of school and a couple of weeks ago she came and talked to my mom and dad. Jessica said that it was hard living on her own because she was always broke after paying the bills. She told my mom and dad that she had tried to get jobs that paid more money but couldn't because she didn't have any skills or education. She asked if she could come back home to live, take her GED and go to college. My parents were really happy because that's what they wanted her to do this whole time! I'm really glad she's home too!

I love my sister but I don't look to her for advice. I learned from my sister that the one thing you need more than anything is a college education. Back when I was younger I wanted to be cool like my sister, now I just think it's cooler to be me.

Chelsea Engelhard

31

THE LONELY GIRL

Once upon a time there was a little girl named Princess. She was very lonely. At home her brothers and sisters did not play with her and her mom and dad ignored her.

At school no one would play with her or talk to her, but when they wanted to insult her. But what she didn't know was that a girl wanted to be her friend and a boy had a crush on her.

One day she went to school and did her work. It was time for recess. They went outside for recess. Princess was just sitting there as stiff as a rock all alone. Then the girl that wanted to be her friend decided to tell Princess that she wanted to be her friend.

But first she had to sneak away from the popular club. You see the girl named Flower, the one that wanted to be Princess' friend, was in the popular club.

So she kind of backed off and ran over to Princess. Flower said, "I've been wanting to be your friend for a long time."

Princess said, "But you're in the popular club."

"I know, but I really don't like it."

"Does Star the leader of the club know about this?"

"No, said Flower, "but she soon will because here she comes."

"Are you over here making fun of Princess like we always do?" asked Star.

"No, I am not and you better not either, because Princess is my best friend and I won't let you."

"How dare you go to the non-popular girl and leave me?"

"I can if I want."

"No, you can't," said Star.

"Yes, I can." said Flower, "Because you are not my boss."

"Yak", said the rest of the popular club.

Then the most popular boy in the school came over and said, "I, I, I, I have a, a, a crush on you, Princess."

Princess started to smile and blush. His name was Doney.

Star said, "Yuh! Why don't you have a crush on me?"

Doney said, "Because you're mean and bossy, plus I like Princess, not you."

Doney said, "Get away from Princess, Flower."

Princess said, "She is my best friend and she is not in the popular club anymore because she doesn't want to be in the club."

"OK, I am sorry, Flower, I didn't know that," said Doney.

"That's ok, Doney," said Flower.

"Let's go play," said Princess.

"Do you want to play on the bars?" said Doney.

"Sure", said Princess and Flower.

They played on the bars and they flipped and twirled. Recess was over and everyone went inside.

The teacher, Mr. Harley Davison, was the only teacher that really had paid attention to Princess' actions and expressions. Princess found it out that he did.

That day Doney walked Princess home and Princess said, "Did you really have to come all this way to walk me home?"

"No," said Doney, "I just live across the street."

"Oh, then I will see you later, OK?"

Then everyone paid more attention to Princess. Later on in life, Princess and Doney got married and lived happily ever after.

Elizabeth Mae Fraley
Age: 10

FLYING FROGS

One day deep in the woods lived a girl and her grandma Jane. The girl's name was Molly Jean. Molly Jean believed that frogs could fly. So one day Molly Jean went into the woods to find a flying frog. Finally she got to the creek. She saw a frog hop. She caught it. Then she took out a jar and put the frog in it. She took the frog home and watched it. But it won't fly. Her grandma was calling her, it was time for supper. That night she had a dream if she let the frog go, it would fly. So the next morning she let the frog go and it flew. My dream came true. It was so popular it was on the news. But everyone was bugging the frogs. Molly Jean felt bad, so she went to tell the frogs to only fly at night. They had a deal. Everyone came to take a picture, but the frogs wouldn't fly. Everyone stopped believing in them, but Molly Jean believed. If you look out your window at night, you might see a flying frog. If you believe...

Jasmine Stults
Age: 11

LOCKER SIX TWENTY SIX

Locker six twenty six is the best locker ever.
No it's not locker number two sixty two is best
Julie and Rachel stop fighting over lockers.
No said Julie!
Please said Ali.
Fine said Julie and Rachel.
I'm sorry said Rachel.
Me too said Julie.
That's better, said Ali.
Thank you said Julie and Rachel.
Yeah yeah said Ali let's go see how clean our locker is said Ali.
I bet my locker is cleaner than yours said Rachel.
Whatever said Ali.
It is said Rachel.
I'm not arguing any more said Ali.
Fine said Rachel.
Fine said Jule.
Our locker is the cleanest said Blake and Addie.
STOP fighting! said Kaylyn.
No our locker is cleaner said Will and I.
Will you please stop fighting.
I guess.
Thank you.
Now children. It is time for recess.
Come on let's go play football said Quade.
Dyllan and I have to stay in and clean our locker.
Ali and I have the same locker this year, said Julie.
Me and Blake are cleaning our lockers too, said Will.
Even though they don't need it, said Blake.
Hey Blake can we take your football out?
Whatever.
No Blake go outside, said Alex.
No said Blake. It's fun in here.
Yeah I know.
Mrs. McGehee said to come inside, said Addie.
Tell her I don't feel good.

I'm not gonna lie to her.

Addie Mrs. McGehee want to know what's taking so long, and she said if you're not cleaning out your locker to come outside.

Ha ha I am cleaning out my locker.

If it doesn't need it come outside so Addie and I don't have to spend our recess inside.

Blake and I are going to a Mighty Ducks game tomorrow at noon. Don't tell Mrs. McGehee she thinks we're going to the doctor.

Blake you can't.

Why?

Cause you have to clean your side of the locker.

Will you clean it?

Fine but you have to clean my side of the locker for a month.

Your side never gets messy. OK

You have to clean your side for a month. If you do I'll give you my Red Sox tickets.

All Right.

OK.

Jaclyn Pearce

This is how I make my breakfast. I use flour, milk and eggs and vanilla to make pancakes. This is how I make pancakes. That is my favorite breakfast.

Pauly Sparks
Age: 7

THE MYSTERY OF THE MISSING TEACHER

Hey Alexander race you to the playground. Blake said. Ready set go! I'm going to beat you.
No you're not.
Yes I am.
Yes I win! Alexander said.
Hey guys what are you doing asked Will.
Oh nothing just having a little race.
Yeah and Alexander won.
You guys want to play some football?
Sure why not. All right another score! RRRRING!!!
Yes we win!
Come on guys time to line up. Everybody lined up and went inside.
Mrs. McGehee said time to put your journals up and get your writing folders out. Start writing.
I think I know what I'm going to write about.
What said Blake?
Dirt bikes! Ok fine with me.
I know what I'm going to write said Lyndsay.
What is it.
It is going to be a poem about fall.
Oh very nice said Blake.
Writing's over.
And I was almost done with my story said Will.
Time for recess. You might want to take a jacket.
Hey guys what game you want to do said Jaclyn. You want to play shark?
Sure why not!
Not it!
Not it!
Not it!
Jaclyn's it!
I'm going to get you!
You are it!
Blake's it!
Hey I'm not playing. Never mind. I don't want to play this anymore said Jaclyn. I'm going to go play four square.
Hey guys can I play?
Sure said Lyndsay. Let's get the server out, that's Lyndsay.
I'll get you out before you get me out.

Come on guys Mrs. McGehee blew the whistle. Get your math books out. You're going to have a math paper for homework tonight.

Yes, I love math papers.

Do you love them so much you could marry them said Blake.

No said Jaclyn! I don't love it so much I would marry it.

Yes you do.

No I don't.

Okay whatever.

Turn to page 114. Do odds only.

Odds only, why said Blake?

Because I said so.

Okay said Blake.

Don't forget to do daily math.

Yes I'm done. Now I can do daily math.

Done that was easy.

Done said Jaclyn. Now I can do daily math too. This is way too easy. You can do this in a second.

Then Mrs. McGehee gave us something to work on. Then it was time to go to lunch. I was having fun like always sitting, eating, and talking. We were first in line. Mrs. Taylor dismissed us and we went outside. Then we came back in after recess. We couldn't find Mrs. McGehee anywhere. We waited for a long time. Mrs. McGehee never came in.

Then Alexander said... Mrs. McGehee is a missing teacher!

Blake yelled PARTY!!!!

Jaclyn said no Blake a teacher will hear you.

Sure enough, a teacher heard him. She came in and asked what we were doing.

What do you think we were doing?

We're having a party Blake shouted!

Mrs. McGehee came in the room. Everybody saw her they sat down and were as quiet as a mouse. Then Julie stood up and said Alexander said you were a missing teacher.

We have been here for an hour.

It has only been five minutes.

Oh, sorry.

After that it was just a normal day. The next day at school it was the same as always. Then at lunch the same thing happened only Mrs. McGehee didn't come back. Then everybody started to get up and Blake's little bratty brother Bucky yelled party! No teacher heard him. So everybody started a party. Bucky stood outside the door looking for teachers. Mrs. McGehee came out of the lounge. Bucky ran in and said TEACHER!! Everything was a mess so everybody started cleaning up. By the time Mrs. McGehee got in the classroom... everybody had sat down and it was like nothing had happened. Sorry class she said I lost track of time. Everybody screamed why can't there by a REAL MISSING TEACHER!

Addison M. Shreve
Age: 9

THE MITTEN IN THE KITTEN -- A DR. SEUSS STORY

There once was a kitten who swallowed a mitten. The mitten was in the kitten's tummy. The kitten thought it was very yummy. The kitten had to see the vet but he was not better yet! The vet opened his belly and it was full of jelly. Where oh where was the mitten? Of course it's in the kitten!

Devin Barnett
Age: 7

THE ELEPHANT PUMPKIN

On a cool fall day, Pete the pumpkin was enjoying the nice weather with his friends. They were all talking about Halloween, and about how they would soon be transformed into scary jack-o-lanterns. Halloween was the most thrilling night for all of the pumpkins. As they were discussing their plans, they heard the farmer tell his helpers that his pumpkins would be going to the local bakery to be made into sweet pies. The pumpkins were very shocked when they heard this... especially Pete. Pete was horrified because he did not want to be made into a sweet pie! He wanted to be made into a big, scary jack-o-lantern.

Pete was so mad he came up with a plan to leave the patch. He knew that the Reed School kindergarten would be coming to their pumpkin patch tomorrow. This was his way to pumpkin freedom. The next morning he saw the bus arrive. When Pete discovered that the kindergartners had left their backpacks right next to him, he knew it was time for action. He climbed into one! Once he got into the backpack, he knew he needed to come up with a disguise so that he would not be taken to the bakery. After he thought for a while, he noticed he was sitting on something. When he looked down, he saw a book. Because he did not know how to read, he only looked at the pictures. When he opened up the book, he noticed pictures of animals he had never seen before on his farm. While he was looking through the book, he saw an animal that looked similar to his shape. This could be the perfect disguise for him. Unlike other pumpkins, Pete's stem did not grow from the top of his pumpkin. His stem grew from where his nose should be. He could easily look like this animal!

All of a sudden he heard footsteps coming towards him, and then he felt himself being picked up. After a long bus ride, Pete finally arrived at Reed School. When the kindergartner opened up her backpack, Pete rolled out and ended up under Mrs. Galloway's desk. There he found a bunch of cool art supplies to use to disguise himself. When he was finished, he looked like the strange animal from the book. Pete sat there so happy to have avoided being made into a pie that he fell asleep.

The next day, Mrs. Fitz's fifth grade class visited their kinderbuddies. Pete looked so funny dressed up like an elephant that Alli took him back to her classroom to decorate her desk. The next day she was going to take Pete home. She couldn't wait to give him to her dad... the town's baker!

Allison Perry
Age: 10

THE CHAIN LETTER

Audra had only heard the news just a few minutes ago, and already it was setting in like concrete. She didn't know what to think, yet thoughts were swarming through her head like a fly swarming above a sandwich left out in a summer picnic. She didn't know what to feel, yet all her feelings and emotions were sprawled out in front of her. The shards of broken glass of what she and Mike had were shattered into a million pieces, and if you looked down deep into each broken piece, you could see a little bit of what they had, a little bit of their love.

Love. Had they been in love? No, no. They were only in high school. But as she thought about it more and more, they had been in love. Deeply in love. If there was one word to describe what they had, it was love. But that was over now. Mike was dead and there wasn't anything she could do about it.

Mike wasn't just dead, though. He had killed himself. He had ended it all for himself. And for her. She was still rather unsure why. He didn't seem unhappy. But he had written her a letter and that might explain some of it. She didn't think a letter would do justice, though. She needed him. She needed to feel the warmth of his body and the magic touch of his kiss. She needed his love.

She opened the letter that Mike's mother, Patricia, had given her. She felt tears coming on as she pulled the letter out. It read:

Audra,

I'm sorry. I'm really sorry. I just don't want this anymore. I can't handle it. All I feel now is hate and it sickens me! Sickens me to the point where I can hardly function! Oh! Anger and hatred swim through me and I don't think I can take it much anymore. It's not you. Believe me. I've thought about this for a long time and it's not you. I really don't know what it is. I just... never mind.

Well, there is no easy way for me to say this, but good-bye. I'll miss and I'll always love you. I do have one thing to say before I leave, though. Live on. Live on for yourself and live on for the sake of living. Don't do it for me or for anyone else. Do it for you. I hope you understand.

Good-bye.

I love you,

Mike

She read the letter over again, slowly and carefully. The tears she had felt coming on were now pouring out like a waterfall. She still didn't understand. Why, Mike? Why, oh why, oh why, oh why? The letter hadn't done it justice. She needed more. She needed him.

***

As she was walking home, the end of Mike's letter was stuck in her head. "Live on. Live on for yourself and live on for the sake of living. Don't do it for me or for anyone else. Do it for you. I hope you understand." But she didn't understand. She didn't understand anything. She was slowly falling apart. Everything she had once loved and cared about didn't seem to matter. She was slowly losing her will to live.

When she got to her house, no one was home. She walked in and said, "Hello. Anybody here?" No answer. That was okay. She wanted to take a nice warm bath, anyways.

She walked to the bathroom, hardwood floor creaking lightly under her feet. When she reached the bathroom, she started to draw the water and suddenly burst into tears. She couldn't hold it in anymore. She needed to cry.

After she had gained control of herself, she undressed and slipped one leg into the water. A warm, dreamlike sensation zoomed through her body. She stuck her other leg in and the sensation doubled. The rest of her slipped into the water and she was now hidden by a wispy cloud of bubbles. She smiled for the first time in a long time, and slid down deep, deep into the water, letting its warmth caress and embrace her.

***

Two hours later, Audra's mother came home. She walked into the silent house and called out Audra's name, and when there was no answer, she got a little worried.

She walked into the living room and called out Audra's name again. No answer. She walked into Audra's room. No sign of Audra there, either.

As she was heading into the kitchen, she passed the bathroom. The door was closed and a heavy white light was flooding through the crack at the bottom. She hesitated a moment, feeling a little scared, but then opened the door. What she saw almost gave her a heart attack. There was an array of blood splattered all over the floor and walls. The entire room had been painted red with Audra's blood. And Audra...

Audra's body lay in the red water of the bathtub, lifeless, dead. One arm hung out of the tub, wrist slit and blood slowly dripping onto the floor. Mike's letter lay beside the small puddle of blood, little red drops splattered across the white envelope. Another letter lay next to Mike's and Audra's mother picked it up with trembling hands. Her bottom lip quivered as her shaking fingers opened it.

She read the first line of the letter and her watery eyes burst into tears. She let it slip out of her hands and fall onto the bloody floor. She slowly walked into the kitchen and sat down at the table. She pulled out a pad and pen and began to write.

After a few minutes, she finished the letter to her husband and placed it underneath a vase on the table along with Mike's letter to Audra and Audra's letter to her. She got up and stood there silently for a moment. After a minute, she walked towards a drawer and opened it, revealing various utensils that they had collected over the years. She pulled out a long butcher knife and held it firmly against her throat. She hesitated for a moment, making sure she was really going to do this...

Joshua Murray
Age: 13

BASEBALL LAND

On the afternoon of April 1st, Sean was cleaning the attic for his mom. "Sean are you done sweeping the attic yet?" asked his mom.

"No Mom." he said.

"Well keep working at it, I want this all done by 3:30" his mom told him. It was already 2:30 and Sean hadn't even started. All he had done the past two hours was play baseball in the attic. Baseball was Sean's favorite sport and all Sean wished was that he would be called up to play on a farm team. At age seventeen Sean knew he was good enough and also knew that if he went to play baseball he wouldn't have to listen to his pesky mother any more. Sean looked at the attic again. It looked horrible. All the bags were out of line, all the toys untidy, and worst of all the floor was covered in dust. Sean couldn't think how he was going to clean all this by 3:30. Then at the end of all the rubble Sean saw a little box, with a little envelope taped to it. The letter said, "Open this immediately!" At first Sean saw nothing and then as he looked closer he noticed a little dot at the bottom of the letter. He kept looking at the dot and noticed that the dot was becoming gradually bigger, then the dot became too big for the page and turned into a humongous whirlwind sucking Sean in with it. Then suddenly Sean heard a "CLUNNCK." Everything was blurry to Sean. Then when things became clearer Sean saw that he wasn't in his attic anymore he was in Baseball Land! There were stadiums, training centers, baseballs, bats, everything he had ever dreamed of. As he kept looking around he bumped into a strange figure. He wore an MLB logo on his shirt and pants and if Sean didn't know better he'd say he looked like a scout.

"Name please." asked the scout.

"Sean Hoffman." Sean replied.

"We've been expecting you." said the scout, "You're assigned to the Cubs, right around Ruth Park."

"And where would I find that?" Sean asked not knowing a thing about this strange world.

"It's right around the corner of Legends, which is two blocks across from the Devil Rays' training center. Sean asked the scout how long he would be in Baseball Land. The scout told him "You'll be kept in Baseball Land until you prove yourself good enough to head you to the minors."

"What are the minors?" asked Sean.

"You know the minors in America in the real world." said the scout, this overjoyed Sean. This is my chance Sean thought, I'll be going to the majors in no time.

Suddenly a thought occurred to Sean, what if he wasn't good enough to go to the minors, he could be in Baseball Land forever! That wasn't even half of it for Sean. Even though he might be in Baseball Land forever what would his mom think happened to him. Maybe this wasn't Sean's dreamland after all.

Now Sean had to get out of Baseball Land. As Sean neared the Cub's clubhouse, thoughts of home surrounded him. Once Sean got to the door he found that the door wouldn't budge.

"Sorry kid only team members are allowed here." said the doorman,

"Hi I'm Sean Hoffman. A man said for me to come here." answered Sean, looking confused.

"Well why didn't you say so, come right in." said the doorman.

"Ah you must be the new guy, we've been waiting for you." continued the doorman after opening the door for Sean. "Your room is 129. By the way you can find your possessions in your room." Sean was baffled he didn't think he had brought any belongings with him to Baseball Land. Sean fell back on his bed and thought of the day's events. Everything was going too fast he thought. The one thing that scared him the most was if he was ever going to go back to the real world. Once he looked around he saw a telephone with listed numbers. Maybe the scout will know how to get out of Baseball Land thought Sean. Well there was nothing to lose he thought, so he called him up.

"Hello," said the scout.

"Hi I'm Sean Hoffman, you know the one you told how to get to the Cub's clubhouse?" said Sean.

"Yeah, what's your problem kid?" asked the scout.

"We'll I was thinking, well how do you get out of Baseball Land?" Sean asked.

"Okay kid, here's my way. Every week some kid from every team is sent up to the minors in the real world. These kids are the best on their teams." said the scout.

"But I don't have a week!" said Sean.

"Well there are other ways. But they're not mine, if you want it just ask any ump or manager. Okay?" answered the scout.

"Okay, bye" said Sean. Then Sean just fell asleep with fruststration.

"Get up kid!" Sean heard. "I said get up! Sean heard again.

"Ahhhh." answered Sean.

"Do you want to miss the game or what?" asked the voice. Sean raced downstairs to the lobby, grabbed a piece of toast and just narrowly caught the bus.

As Sean finished up his toast he asked the guy beside him, "Hey where are we going?"

"We're going to Legend's Field to play against the Astros." he answered. Once they got there Sean hopped off the bus and traveled into the stadium. As he wandered around he saw an umpire. Remembering what the scout had said he went up to the ump.

"Hey, a scout told me that you knew a way to get out of Baseball Land." said Sean.

"You're right I do!" said the ump. "Well here's my way. Every year there's a World Series right, well the team that wins it all gets sent up to the minors in the real world." said the ump.

"Okay so how are the Cubs doing?" asked Sean.

"Your team is in last and doesn't have a chance to make it to the playoffs." said the ump.

"Oh OK." said Sean.

"Good luck kid." said the ump

"Thanks." said Sean.

The Cubs beat the Astros 10 to 1 that game. Sean was the star of the game. He belted two homers, batted in seven runs and put the ball in play five out of five times. As Sean was about to board the bus the ump stopped him. "You played a great game kid, and if you keep at it you could make it to the majors." complimented the ump.

"Thanks, by the way do you know any other ways to get out of Baseball Land?" asked Sean.

"I don't but if you ask Babe Ruth I'm sure he'll tell you." said the ump.

"Thanks a lot." said Sean. As he got on the bus all he could think of was if he would ever make it back to the real world.

Once Sean got back, he asked his manager where to find the Babe. His coach told him exactly where and Sean raced off to meet the Babe. At the corner of Heroes Avenue Sean found the greatest baseball player ever to live.

There Sean asked him "Mr. Babe sir, I was wondering do you know how to get out of Baseball Land sir."

"I sure do kid and I'm glad you asked. See you know Cy Young? Well kid if you hit a homer off him you're home free."

"Thanks Mr. Ruth." said Sean.

"Hey kid." said the Babe.

"Yeah Mr. Ruth," answered Sean.

"Who are you playing tomorrow?" asked the Babe.

"My team's playing the Boston Red Sox Sir." said Sean.

"That's his team." said the Babe.

"Thanks." said Sean as he ran back to his clubhouse. That night all Sean could think of was the advice the Babe gave him. When they got to the stadium the next morning Sean was tense and nervous. When the time came Sean walked out to the batter's box and swung his bat around a couple of times. The ump waved Sean to the plate. He dug his foot in the dirt a couple times and put in a practice swing. Cy Young checked the sign and nodded. He came in the windup and the game was underway.

"STRIKKKKE!" yelled the ump. Sean had thought too fast. As Young pitched the ball again Sean, off-balance and unready swung at the air for strike two. Young threw the next one home for ball one. Then another came "BALLLL!" yelled the ump, the count was two and two. The next pitch was a mile high so Sean didn't swing. "BALLLL!" called the ump, it was a full count, three balls, two strikes. The next pitch was right down the middle and Sean connected with it. The ball was going to be a home run! Sean did a little hop and rounded the bases. The minute Sean crossed home a whirlwind came down for Sean. As he went up in it he could hear cheers coming from all of Baseball Land. He exalted and waited. It seemed like a year for Sean but finally Sean heard the same CLUNNCK! Sean was back in his attic. It was all clean, he looked at his watch and it was 3:30.

"Sean are you done yet?" his mom asked.

"Yes!" Sean answered in relief.

"You can come downstairs now!" said his mom.

"One second!" Sean yelled back. He looked over at the letter, that letter was like a staircase to Heaven for him, but he knew for someone else it would be as bad as losing all your candy on Halloween. So Sean ran over to the letter, took a final glance at it, and tore it up.

"Sean someone is on the phone for you, something about playing for the Atlanta Braves." his mom said, Sean looked back again and smiled. He didn't know who sent the letter but he did know that high school ball was over. Welcome to the majors!

Drew Padgett
Age: 11

PLAYING FOOTBALL AND BASEBALL

Football is very fun for me. I like to catch interceptions and run it for a touchdown. In case you didn't know that's when you catch a pass from the other team's quarterback and run it to your end zone. I also like catching long passes and going far on the field and I also like to watch my friends play and I also like to watch professional football on channel two. Football is one of my favorite sports.

Another one of my favorite sports is baseball. I like to get big hits like grand slams, and home runs out of the park. The bases are loaded, and I hit the ball way hard and far so everyone gets home or, if I just get a big hit and I get home too. I also like to watch baseball with my friends or, by myself. I like when a game is on, and I invite a lot of my friends over and we watch the game.

Samuel R. Smith
Age: 11

MYSTERY SQUIRREL

It was Halloween night in Squirrelville. Here in the village there was a sacred acorn. This acorn was the biggest in the world. It was in the middle of the museum, which was a fairly large oak tree on the west side of town.

It was on this night when one sneaky squirrel stole the acorn. "It was so large that he and his partner in squirrel crime could barely carry it back to their secret hideout from what I could see." Said Squirrel Guard the next day at Squirrel headquarters. "It looked to me like a flying squirrel and a gray squirrel."

"Well." Replied Squatson, I think that we have a mystery on our claws. What do you think my trusty squirrelkick?

"I think this looks like a job for the Squirrel Agency." Answered Squirrellock Holmes. "We will get on the case as soon as possible."

Squatson muttered to himself, "When do we start?"

Overhearing his small mutter, Squirrel Guard blurted out quite anxiously, "They were heading toward the east side of town near High Canopy Road.

After hearing this Squatson and Squirrellock went looking for clues and suspects. They decided to go check on Homeless Squirrel who lived in that part of town. Squatson then asked him for his alibi. He answered, "What makes you think it was me?"

They both challenged quickly, "You are always looking for ways to get money."

They then figured out that he was visiting the mayor at the time of the crime because he was trying to get some money from him. They then decided they would go ask Richie Squirrel, the richest squirrel in town.

Squatson asked, "Where were you on Halloween night?"

Richie Squirrel questioned, "Who wants to kno..."

Squirrellock Holmes interrupted, "We do!"

"Fine," he exploded. "We were all here at my Halloween party."

"Really?" rambled Squirrellock.

"I didn't invite you guys because I don't like you two and neither does anyone else. We all think you guys are nerds." Laughed Richie Squirrel.

After hitting him in his little wet nose they went back to the Squirrel Agency to try and figure this out. Then Squirrellock Holmes said, "If the guard saw this happen why didn't he go after them?"

"That is a clever thing to say Squirrellock, if only we had thought of this earlier." Mentioned Squatson.

They then went back to the agency and talked to the mayor and Squirrel Guard. He denied doing it, but they got a search warrant and found the acorn in his basement.

In the end Squirrel Guard went to Squirrel Prison and Squatson along with his Squirrelkick got a huge reward. With the money they opened up a real Squirrel detective center.

Michael W. Belford
Age: 14

SLIDING ON THE ICE

One winter day last year, my friend Cathy, my sister Lauren, and I saw a spot on the road that was covered in ice. The ice was freezing cold. It was hard enough to slide on. All of us decided to do some sliding. We did knee, belly, and back slides. It was a lot of fun.

After a while we went inside to warm up, and get some food. We had some hot cocoa and snacks. Some of the snacks we had were smores, peanut butter and jelly sandwiches. It was really sweet.

After a while we went out in the cold again. We started to have a snowball fight. After a few balls were thrown a big snowstorm hit and we went back inside. As we watched it falling, the flakes looked like tiny crystals.

Jason Konersmann
Age: 10

THE DIARY

It was Halloween in this new little town. Peter and his family had bought a rusty shack in the outskirts of town.

"This town is very mysterious," said Peter's father.

"Yes it sure is!" his mother answered. They had just driven into the town and turned onto the street where their new home would be. As they turned into the driveway and parked the car, Peter got out and looked around.

"Where are all the children that should be playing in the yards?" said Peter looking at his mother. There were no kids playing baseball in the streets or playing tag in the yard like his mother had told him there would be.

"I do not know, Peter," his mother said looking very confused.

They all went inside and the moving truck came to drop off all their things. While his parents were unloading the boxes, Peter went to the cab of the moving van to look for the man driving the truck.

"What do you want Squirt?" the man in the moving van said rudely.

"I was just wondering if there were any children that could be my friends in this neighborhood"

"Ha!" shouted the man in the truck. "There ain't no people even livin' in this whole town!"

"What?" questioned Peter, "No people anywhere?" Before he could hear him the moving man drove off down the street and Peter watched him until he couldn't see the truck any longer.

Peter carried all his boxes into the house and picked out his favorite room of the shack's two bedrooms. In the room he had picked there was a box. It was fairly small and thin. Peter opened the small box and there was a book. It was old and had a leather cover that was ragged. He opened it being very curious. The book screamed! It was a horrifying screech of a scream.

"Ah!" Peter yelled "Oh my!" he said as he shut the old book as quick as he could. For the next couple of minutes Peter studied the book's front and back covers. It was nothing except the brown torn leather.

He went into his parents room and found his parents unloading their things in the other bedroom.

"Hey Mom!" Peter yelled at his mother. "What kind of book do you think this is?"

"Hummmmm," Peter's mother said as she studied the book's front and back. "Looks like some kind of old diary."

"Oh cool!" Peter answered grabbing the book and running back to his room.

When he got to his room he thought about the strange diary. So he tried to open it one more time. He slowly opened it with his eyes shut tight. But to his amazement it didn't screech like the first time. On the first page it said:

Diary of Andrea J. Sweden
1803

"Oh my," said Peter, this diary is two hundred years old!" He turned the page and it said January 13th 1803, and Annie Sweden told about her birthday and how her father had bought her a new diary. She went on and on through two months of entries to her diary. Peter was so interested in it. It was almost like someone was forcing him to keep reading.

When he got to about the month of April she started to talk about practicing witchcraft. Peter became scared. He shut the diary and looked into the box again and there was an old newspaper dated back to the 1800's when Annie Sweden was alive. The front-page headline was "Witch hung on Halloween Night!" Peter gasped. Then he grabbed the diary again then opened it and all of a sudden words started to appear on the page. They read:

"I am Annie Sweden and I died for practicing witchcraft on Halloween night
in 1803, ever since I died in this town every child who may be born shall die!
There shall not be any souls alive in this town after Halloween night!"

Peter was so astonished. He shut the book and put everything back in the box and burnt it all.

The next morning Peter and his family had died. They all were hung from the ceiling as Andrea J. Sweden was two hundred years ago.

Liz Placek
Age: 12

Rainbows came from God. God sent rainbows because it was a thank you note to everyone to say I will not send a flood again. He did not do it again.

Mariah Davis
Age: 7

THE JACKSON FIVE

One day, the Jackson family woke up and smelled some pancakes and bacon. They knew that it was going to be a good day. So, they got out of the bed and went downstairs to eat. In the household, there are seven people: Mom, Dad, and the kids who are Tommy, James, Monica, Jasmine, and Mildred. Tommy is fifteen years old. James is thirteen years old. Monica is eight. Jasmine and Mildred are both ten years old because they are twins. After breakfast, the kids went to their rooms to get dressed for school. When they were all dressed, they got their lunchboxes off the table and walked to the bus stop. Their bus route was 3014, and their bus driver was white and didn't like them. But today, they had a substitute bus driver, and she was black. Tommy, James, Monica, Jasmine, and Mildred felt comfortable talking to her, so they told her how the other bus driver would call them names. The substitute bus driver asked them if they had told their parents how the bus driver would treat them. They told her yes, but every time they told their parents, their parents would call the bus company, but the bus company couldn't prove that the driver was saying these things to them because the other kids that rode the bus were white and didn't ever tell on the bus driver.

When the Jacksons got to school, they just did their work and prayed that the rest of the day would go well. When school was out, they went home and told their mom and dad about the nice bus driver that they had today. As soon as they finished talking to Mom and Dad, they went upstairs to their rooms and got on their knees and prayed that they would have the same driver for the rest of the school year. That night, they ate some roast beef and mashed potatoes. After dinner, the kids took a bath and got ready for bed.

At 6:15 a.m. the next morning, the kids ate pancakes and sausage links for breakfast. When they finished eating, they got their clothes on for school. When they got to the bus stop, they saw bus route 3014 coming. When the bus got closer they saw that their regular bus driver was back. The rest of the day at school didn't go so well because kids were hitting them and talking about them. When school was over, the Jacksons went home, took a bath, and went to bed without dinner because they had such a long day.

At 4:00 a.m., the kids woke up and got ready and made themselves some breakfast. They decided that they were going to walk ten long miles all the way to school just because of the way that the bus driver treated them. The Jacksons got to school forty-two minutes early. Since they were so early, they went to their homeroom and told their teacher why they didn't ride the bus and why they were so early getting to school. The teacher gave Tommy a tape recorder to record exactly what that bus driver was saying to them. The rest of the day went well. When the Jackson five got home they told their mom and dad that Tommy's teacher gave him a tape recorder, so that he could record what the bus driver and the kids were saying to them on the bus.

So when the Jackson five woke up the next morning, they got ready, ate breakfast, and they walked up to the bus stop. Tommy put the tape recorder in his pocket so the bus driver wouldn't see it and take it away from him. When they got on the bus, Tommy pressed record.

Then the bus driver said, "Get in the back, you black Negroes."

As the Jackson five were walking, the kids were shouting out at them, "You better hurry up black boy" and "You better hurry up black girl before we hurt you." So, when the Jackson five got to school, Tommy pushed stop on the tape recorder and went to homeroom. After school, they got back on the bus, and Tommy pushed record on the tape recorder again. But, this time, the bus driver didn't say anything to them because he had found out that they had been recording him. That night the Jackson five told their mom and dad that the bus driver had found out that they had been recording him from someone.

At 11:17 p.m. the oldest child, Tommy, woke up because he smelled smoke. Tommy went downstairs, and he saw that their living room was on fire, and their window had been busted. Tommy ran back upstairs and woke up his younger brother and sisters so that they could go outside to the other side of the street. When Tommy was going back to get his mom and dad, the doorway was completely on fire. So he couldn't get back in the house. Tommy ran back over to his brother and sisters and told them that he couldn't get their mom and dad out of the house and that he was going to the neighbor's house to call the fire department. Tommy ran over to the neighbor's house and told them that his house was on fire, and he couldn't get his mom and dad out of the house because the doorway was on fire, and he couldn't get in any other way. The neighbors let Tommy call the fire department.

When the firefighters put the fire out, they asked Tommy what were his parents' names, ages, and where they worked. Tommy said his parents' names were Lola and David. His dad was thirty-one years old, and his mom was twenty-nine years old. His mom was a lawyer, and his dad worked at the barbershop. When the firefighter finished asking Tommy questions, they inspected the house. While the firefighters inspected the rest of the house, the Jackson five walked up to the bus stop, which was only two blocks, and they just stood there and prayed that their mom and dad were all right and made it out of the house safely. When they walked back to the house, the firefighters said that their mom and dad were all right and were on their way to the hospital because they had inhaled too much smoke. Tommy went down the street to a good friend's house and asked his friend's mom if she would take Tommy and his younger brother and sisters to North County Hospital to see their mom and dad because they had been trapped in a fire at their house. He told them that his mom and dad had inhaled a lot of smoke. So Tommy's friend's mom said that she would be happy to take them to the hospital.

When they got to the hospital, Tommy, his brother, and his sisters went to the information desk to ask which room Lola Jackson and David Jackson were in. The lady at the information desk said that Lola Jackson was on the third floor in room 321, and that David Jackson was on the third floor in room 332. Tommy thanked the woman and he and his brothers and sisters ran to find an elevator. They got on the elevator, pressed three and got off on the third floor. Tommy stopped at the information desk on the third floor and asked the women which way would room 321 and room 332 be. The lady instructed them down the hall on the left and to the right. When they turned right, they saw room 321. So, they quietly opened the door and went inside. They saw their mom on the bed. She was resting so the kids tried not to wake her up. But, the youngest child, Monica, hated to see her mom in the hospital bed, lying helplessly. So, Monica jumped on the bed and hugged her mom and cried all over her. After a while, Mom woke up and said that she was all right. When Monica stopped crying and hugging on her, the rest of the kids gave her a hug and a kiss. Then Tommy told his mom that they were going to see their dad in room 332.

When they got there, they saw their dad's feet hanging off the hospital bed and went over there to see him. But Dad wasn't asleep; he was wide-awake watching the news. When they went over to talk to Dad, he was very happy to see them. When they finished talking to Dad, they went back to room 321 to tell Mom that they were going to leave. But when they went back, she was gone. She had a heart attack and died. The kids couldn't take it so they just left.

One year after their mom died, their dad died of a broken heart. To make a living, the Jackson five sold the property where their house once was for one thousand dollars, and they went to stay with Tommy's friend. Each of the children got two hundred dollars a piece out of the one thousand dollars they got from their property.

As for the mean bus driver, he had to go to racial management classes for a couple of months, so he could learn how to talk to kids of different races.

Tommy let all his younger siblings stay with him. He got a job as a football player at the age of twenty-four. From then on, the younger kids had successful futures.

The futures of the other kids were: Monica grew up to be a beautician, Jasmine and Mildred both were doctors, and James grew up to be a barber, just as his dad was.

Mariah Kareé Ellis
Age: 12

A WINTER STORY

In 2002 on a cold wintry day there was a big snowstorm. It was blistery and frosty. I was freezing. My dad was brutally cold. The roads were covered in ice. The snow was dazzling, and my pool was all ice. It was like a blizzard outside.

For over a week we had some crazy weather. It started to hail and the school was closed. It was closed for one week. We had fun playing in the snow. We restarted school after a week. While we were in school it started to sleet. The sleet stopped one hour later as we were getting out of school.

That was the end of our snow days. We went back to school. I started to think about summer vacation.

Nicholas James Helferstay
Age: 10

SELENA'S BIRTHDAY

It was April 4, 2004, five days until my sister's birthday and she hadn't said anything about it. When I asked her she said...

"Julia I don't want a birthday party."

"Why?" I asked

"Cause I'm going to turn five and no party means no turning five."

"What in the world are you talking about, Selena?"

"When you blow out your candles it happens."

"What happens?" I asked

"And you're supposed to be in the sixth grade, and I'm not even in school yet, and I know what happens. When you blow out your candles you turn five. Well I am anyway. But you get the point. Which means I won't be able to do the same things I do now 'cause I'm going to get taller which means I won't be able to go in the Chuckie Cheese tunnels." said Selena

"That's the fun part about it. You get to do new things with us big kids."

"Like what, Julia?"

"Well, like going to school and riding your bike without training wheels."

"Julia, I don't have training wheels on my bike."

"You don't?"

"No."

"Well you get the point."

"I get it."

"So you want to have a party?"

"I guess so. But I'm going to have the same boring party like I do every year."

"What do you mean?" I asked

"Pin the tail on the donkey, musical chairs and sitting there doing nothing."

"It won't be boring. Trust me."

"OK, Julia whatever you say."

So, once I got Selena talking about her birthday, I wished I hadn't, 'cause she wouldn't stop talking about it. I started talking to Mom about party decorations and the cake, and she had it all planned out. It was going to be a Mickey Mouse theme.

When it was Selena's birthday, I asked my mom to take Selena to the park and she did. All of her friends came with lots of gifts, and she had a great time. As a present, we rode our bikes together all up and down the street.

"Thanks, Julia for throwing me the best party in the world," said Selena."

"No problem. I am glad that you had a good time. That's what I wanted this party to be."

Ieshia Reneé Ray
Age: 11

53

JUST WORDS

Words can hurt more than anything in the world. Why? Because when you say them you can never take them back. That can scar us for life; hurt us as well as the person. We could say something to them and then lose them, forever.

It started like a normal day. Fifteen-year-old Crystal woke up and got dressed. She walked downstairs and saw her mother talking to her five-year-old brother Joey and making breakfast.

"Morning Mom," said Crystal as she sat down at the table, her mother looked over at her and gasped.

"Crystal Don Aries, do you think I'm going to let you out of this house like that?" asked her mother as she pointed to her outfit. Crystal was wearing a black spaghetti strap shirt over a black fishnet shirt with black baggy jeans.

"What's wrong with it?" asked Crystal. Before her mother could start to explain she stood up from her chair and started to yell. "What is it to you? It's my body I'll dress it the way I want to."

Her mother looked at her then yelled back. "It may be your body, but I made it, this is my house and my rules!"

Crystal rolls her eyes and starts to walk away. "You know why I hate you so much I... oh!!!" with that she walked out of the house grabbing her backpack and house keys.

"Uh-oh," said Joey as he watched his sister stomp out the door.

Crystal walked out of the front door. She saw her mother's "friend" pull up to the house as he walked by her he smelled strongly of beer. She ignored this fact and continued to walk. Her school was only three blocks away. She reached the school and realized that she was an hour and a half early. She took a seat on one of the benches they had on the playground. "Great," she said sarcastically.

Dave walked in the front door right into the kitchen and looked over at Amy (mother), "You..." he walked up to her and swung at her, knocking her against the wall. He walked to her once more and started to beat her. Joey started to cry and ran up to Dave. He started hitting his legs.

"Stop hurting my mommy!" he yelled.

"Dumb kid," with that he kicked him away, but Joey got back up and ran up to him and started to hit him again.

"Joey run!" yelled Amy.

"But Mommy..." started Joey.

"GO!" Joey ran and hid in a closet. Whimpering, crying, praying for help. Dave continued to beat her. Blood spilled from her nose and mouth, her eyes were bruised. "Dave what's... wrong?" she asked as he pinned her against the wall by her throat. "Yo-you're drunk ar-aren't you?" asked Amy. He didn't answer her just pushed down harder on her throat.

"MOMMY!" yelled Joey as he ran out of the closet, kicking and hitting Dave.

Crystal waited for school to start, looking at her watch. She sighed when she saw she still had an hour left. She started to look through her backpack and noticed she was missing her math book. 'I must have left so quickly I forgot it.' She slowly stood up and looked in the direction of her house. "Guess I got to go back." She started to walk to her house. She kept thinking of how her mother was going to yell more at her and tell how she took care of her as a baby and stuff. "She may have given me life but she sure has ruined it." She rolled her eyes as she walked past Dave's car. She never got along with Dave; she thought he drank too much. She balled her fist, trying to suppress her anger. She walked up to the car and kicked the tire three times. "I hate you too!" She stomped away from the car to the front door. It was slightly open. "That's a little strange." She walked in and closed the door all the way.

"Mom? Joey?" she yelled. She walked to the kitchen. She gasped at the sight she saw, Dave pinning her mother against the wall by the throat. She watched Joey run up to Dave and hit and kick him. She reached and grabbed a frying pan. "Get off her!" she yelled as she started to beat him on the head until he let go of her mother and was unconscious. Her mother fell on the floor. She rushed over to Amy's side; she kneeled down by her side and held her close. "Mom..." started Crystal, but her mother stopped her.

"Crystal,... Joey... I love you two so much, do you remember... the song I sang to you... when you were little?" asked Amy in a weak voice. They both nodded. Amy began to sing, "Hush my child it's all right, I'll wipe the tears from under your eyes, listen to my song as it dances through your ears." She began to cough. "I'll hold you close and fight away your fears, I'll hold you tight all through the night, 'til the sun comes out and shines bright, I --" she began to cough again. "I know you'll grow up someday, but you're always going to be my little ba --." With that the breath escaped her body and she stopped moving.

"No..." whispered Crystal.

"No Mom come back I love you, I didn't mean it when I said I hated you, I need you. Joey needs you. Please Mom?" pleaded Crystal. Tears began to roll down her cheeks.

"Crystal... what's wrong?" asked Joey as he walked up to her and put his hand on her shoulder. "What's wrong with Mommy?" he asked as he pointed to his mother's body. She gently put her mother's body on the floor and put her hand on both of his shoulders. "Is she sleeping?" Joey just kept asking questions about his mother. Crystal tried to think of the words to explain this to him. But how do you explain death to a five year old?

"Joey, do you remember when Dad got sick and wasn't around anymore?" she asked. Joey nodded his head. "Grandma and Grandpa too?" she asked him, he nodded once more. Her eyes welled up with tears. "Well umm... the same thing happened to Mommy," she explained.

"But she can't I need Mommy," he said as he began to cry.

"Oh Joey I know I know," she hugged him close to try and calm him down.

"I want Mommy back!" Joey cried. She started to cry as well.

"I know Joey I want her back too." They both stayed like that and cried. Soon Crystal called the police to take her mother away.

"Don't worry it's going to be okay kids," explained the officer.

Crystal regretted those few words. They hurt her for life. So always tell those you love that you love them. It may be the last time you get to say it to them.

Samantha Hornbeck

PRAYERS BEING ANSWERED

Hi. I'm Chaya and I live in Jerusalem, Israel. I'm ten years old and I'm a girl. I have a sister named Dinci Merach who's fourteen, and a brother named Micha Melech, who's seventeen. My family and I have been very depressed lately because my father, Uhashoah, died in a bombing by the Palestinians. My friend, Ben, has been trying to make me feel better by saying, "You have beautiful brown hair and pretty blue eyes. And you're so tall and thin and just plain PRETTY!" But it hasn't helped. My dad and I were very close. He had blue eyes; I have blue eyes. I am the youngest, he was the youngest, and I just can't get over the fact that he is gone, forever.

I'm in fifth grade and this is my last year in school because my mom can't afford it. My brother and sister went to ninth grade and eleventh grade, and they have to stop, too. I love school and I don't want to leave; I want my dad. I don't have a pet and no one to really talk to. Today my friend, Ben, took me to the Western Wall to pray to my dad and run around. The Western Wall is a wall in Israel and it is famous for praying, too. I haven't been out since my dad died, and I'm kind of scared, but I couldn't tell Ben that.

Then, Ben and I left. I was still pretty scared, but I still didn't utter a word. Usually when Ben and I are scared, we twirl. Ben and I always twirl and spin each other around and around. It calms us. While we were twirling, I noticed there was not a sound in the whole city. I thought for a minute something was wrong. I told Ben that I thought we should pray to my dad and then go home. I prayed to my dad and this is what I said, "Dad, I miss you so much I want you to come back. Everything is wrong. You're gone and we have to drop out of school because Mom can't afford it, and Mom can barely get food on the table. I think I am going to get a job so that we can have food for everyone. Dad, let Israel be peaceful. I'm so scared I'm going to lose Ben, Dinci Merah, Micha Melch, Mom, or anyone because of these awful bombings. I already lost you; I don't want to lose anyone else. Please, please keep me company and tell G-d that I love Him or Her and to keep the rest of Israel alive and safe. Thank you Dad, and I love you. Pray soon, Chaya."

Ben and I finished our prayers and then we ran back to my house. I ran in and asked my mom what in the world was going on and why was it so quiet. She scolded me for asking too many questions. I apologized and she told me. My mom, Ava, had been offered a job in North America, and we would be able to go to school. We would move to a place called St. Louis. Ben was standing right next to me with his mouth opened like an "O." I was astonished. But then I realized it had nothing to do with the silence outside. But my mom was not finished. She told me the bombing had slowed down and that was why it was quiet, but she still hadn't finished. She said Ben's mom got the same offer my mom did, so Ben and I could move together!!!

When my mom said that I jumped for joy!! I was going to be able to to go school with Ben, without being so cautious. I was thrilled! When I finally calmed down, my mom said that Ben's family and mine were leaving in three days. I was ecstatic! During my last three days in Israel, I was packing all my belongings to get ready to go to Missouri. At first, I was so excited, but then I realized that I was leaving home, I was leaving my friends, and I was leaving the Western Wall. I thought how could I be so excited about such a rotten thing like that. After a while, I realized what I was excited about. I was excited to be safe again and go to school. I thought about all the good things and did not even think about the bad. I was going to miss Israel so much. Right before we left, I went to the Western Wall with Ben. We twirled and prayed. But this time, these were my prayers, "Dear Dad, you've responded to my prayers wonderfully. I get to go to school with Ben in St. Louis, Missouri and get to be safe. I could not ask for anything more. Keep Israel safe for me and please keep responding to my prayers. Tell G-d thank you and I love you and G-d SO much. Love you Chaya."

Those were my last prayers at the Western Wall. We left Israel on a plane to Missouri.

We arrived there a day later. Mom says she didn't want my classmates to call me Chaya, because it would be too hard, so she gave me another name and it was "Carly." I like it, kind of. I went to school the next day at a school called, "Old Bonhomme Elementary School." My mom works and my sister and brother are "Zach" and "Kayla." Mom is "Eve" and she is a teacher with Ben's mom "Margie." They teach at "Ladue Early Childhood Center." I prayed to my dad tonight in my new room. This is what I said, "Dad, Missouri is great, but I miss Israel terribly. Mom says we will go back to Israel after the bombs are over. I am so excited to be here but I do miss Israel. I met some nice people today and my teacher's name is Ms. Barrier; she's very sweet. Don't forget I will never stop praying ever nor will I ever stop twirling. I will pray soon, I love you SO much! Love, Chaya, or Carly."

Carly Rudolph
Age: 11

A POT OF GOLD AT EVERY END OF A RAINBOW

There was a boy whose name was Henry. He was always bored when it rained. He always says, "Mom what can I do, I'm so bored."

His mom said, "Use your imagination."

He said, "No, I don't want to. Fine I will be bored for the rest of my life." So then he sat by the window. Then it stopped raining. He looked outside and there was a rainbow.

So then he said, "Mom, I'm going outside."

She said, "O.K."

So he went outside and he followed the rainbow. There it was, a big pot of gold at the end of the rainbow. He was so happy! He could buy a big house for him and his mom. But when he looked back it was gone. He was so disappointed. But he knew that what they have is enough! They were happy just the way they were.

Samantha Pitts
Age: 10

A STEP MAMA AIN'T THAT BAD!

Everyone knows the story of Cinderella, and it really is the story of Cinderella. Well, she told it anyways, but that ain't the real truth, honey. She just told a bunch of baloney lies about my two daughters and me. You see we're not bad, she was just mad at us because she wasn't the center of her father's attention anymore. So let me tell you the real truth child.

It was one of those once upon a time times, and Cinderella's father and I had just gotten married. It was a real fancy wedding, too. No sooner after a few months the poor man died. The poor soul, it just broke my little, old heart into pieces. Now, of course, he left all his money, treasures, and house to me. You would think Cinderella would be glad I had all the burden of responsibility on my back instead of hers, but no she went ahead and got all mad. She gave my daughters and me all kinds of trouble with that little blonde head of hers. How dare she accuse me of marrying her father for his money. The nerve! I loved her father very much (even though he wasn't all that), and he loved me, too. Well, for the next few weeks that little girl has been nothing but trouble. If it was up to me, her tush would be so red she wouldn't be able to sit in that chair and pout anymore. Why don't I just tell you what happened.

You see Cinderella always believed in tidiness, unlike my other daughters and me. Whenever we messed up one little thing, she would always come fussing after us like we started the next Fairy Tale War.

"Don't you ever clean up after yourselves?" she asked us every day.

"Cinderella, leave it 'til later," we always replied.

Until one day, the royal messenger came to our door. He announced the prince was having a ball to find his next wife. How grand! Of course we were all excited. We couldn't help but make a big mess while we were getting ready. This was big news, so me and the girls went out shopping for new dresses immediately. Imagine our shock when on the day of the ball, Cinderella came into the parlor dressed in her usual rags.

"Cinderella, why aren't you dressed?" I asked the poor girl.

"I'm not going," she answered, as if it was the most obvious thing in the world.

"But why?" we asked her. We were all dressed and ready to go, so why wouldn't Cinderella come.

"I don't have anything to wear," Cinderella answered us.

"That's ridiculous!" I answered, such intolerance. "I bought you a wonderful gown yesterday, and if you don't like it you could borrow one of ours. I'm sure there is something you like in there."

"I don't think so," she said, as if she was too good to wear anything of ours.

So, regretfully, we left for the ball on the diamond-starred night. And as soon as we entered the ballroom, I regretted leaving the child back home. The castle was gorgeous, and we had a splendid time. We danced, and laughed, but what truly got everyone's attention was that late-coming beautiful girl. She looked just like a princess, wearing a stunning blue gown, and charming glass slippers. She danced with the prince, surrounded by ooohs and ahhhs. And, to our surprise, the princess had fled the building as the clock struck midnight. She ran out of the ballroom, with the prince right behind her.

"I must go," she yelled over her shoulder, and ran out into the darkness. We heard a last neigh of a horse, and the sound of carriage wheels, before the air was filled with silence.

"But what is your name?" the prince asked the cool air, weakly.

That night, as we came home, we bombarded Cinderella with wonderful details from the party. But she had not seemed excited or interested. We had offered her to come with us the next night.

Her reply, though, was a simple, "No, thank you."

So, same as the night before, we dressed and hurried out the door, begging Cinderella to come. She still refused. And again as the night before, the beautiful princess returned. And again, she fled as the clock struck twelve, but this time the prince had returned with a glass slipper in his hand.

The next day, the prince came into the village. He announced that whichever maiden in the village can fit the shoe, then he shall have her hand in marriage. Of course, my daughters and I rushed out to try on the shoe. Sadly, we failed. We had started back to the house, when we were greeted by Cinderella."

"I would like to try on the shoe too, if you don't mind," she said coldly.

"But you weren't at the ball," I said.

"And?" was Cinderella's last reply, as she turned and headed straight to the prince. Her tone was so cold, a volcano couldn't melt away the bitterness.

She insisted on trying on the shoe, so we stayed out of her way. And wouldn't you believe it! Her little tiny, pale foot slipped right into the shoe. We just stood stunned and shocked, as the prince announced that he and Cinderella would be married the next week, and everyone was invited.

We never figured out how Cinderella fit the shoe, but she did. And while she went cruising with the prince, we went bruising with the rumors that we were trying to ruin her life. For Pete's sake, she was practically my daughter! I was happy for her, and so it would be my pleasure to announce that not all stepmammas are bad!

Sumeja Seferovic
Age: 13

59

WATCH OUT FOR GIRLS IN POINTY HATS

A few weeks ago I was at the bus stop near my house. A tall, thin, elderly gentleman was waiting for the same bus. The downtown bus pulled up and we stepped onto the bus. The old man and I exchanged greetings and upon learning of my plans to get off at the Saint Louis Gateway Arch, he said mysteriously, "I've heard a story about the Arch. Do you want to hear it?"

I said that I would like to hear it, and he shared this story.

Jason, a local teenager from the Italian area of Saint Louis known as the Hill, took some friends from out of town to the Arch. Bill, Mark, and Kim were two brothers and a sister who used to live on Jason's street, but had moved away and wanted to see the famous Arch again. Jason's mom asked him to do this while she was at work. He drove the family car and parked in the Arch garage along the Mississippi riverfront. They climbed the stairs out of the garage and saw the wide lawn under the towering metal structure, glistening in the sunlight.

When they reached the entrance, the heavy glass door swung easily under the tug Jason gave. The polished floor was angled steeply downward which helped their speedy entrance. They were now fifty feet underground.

Jason's group joined a long line for the tram tickets. After twenty minutes of inching along, Jason remembered locking their wallets in the trunk earlier in the day.

"Rats!" he exclaimed, "I will run fetch our wallets from the car. If I am fast, I'll beat the pace that the line is moving." Jason ran to the car. He was almost out of the parking garage with the wallets when a strange looking girl called to him from the stairway behind him.

"Will you marry me?"

Jason turned and stared at a pretty girl about his age wearing a light blue robe and a black pointed hat.

"Are you joking? No way. I don't even know you."

The odd girl looked unhappy. She yelled back, "Then I will turn you into a rat!" She waved her hand and disappeared.

Jason was stunned. He walked the rest of the way back to his friends wondering if he was just dreaming or did that strange, weirdly-dressed teenaged girl really say that she would turn him into a rat?

He found his group at the ticket line. He told them all about his unusual experience. They all laughed and bought their tickets. A few minutes later they were getting into an egg-shaped compartment with five seats. The tram started moving, but halfway up, Bill said, "You are getting hair all over your face!"

Kim looked and said, "Your fingernails are getting pointier and longer!"

Jason was shocked. Was that girl a witch?

Then Mark exclaimed, "You look like a RAT!" Jason was growing a tail. Jason was turning into a rat! By the time the tram reached the top of the Arch, Jason had shrunk and his voice was squeaky. His friends were worried and only took a short look out the small window to see the long drop down to the ground. It was so wonderful but they knew they had to get Jason the rat home.

They drove the car back to the Hill as quickly as they could. It was hard for the friends to concentrate on driving because their guide was now a rat with a very squeaky voice.

When they got home, Kim ran into the house and told Jason's dad what had happened. His dad did not believe her until Bill and Mark came in carrying the scrambling rat. The rat told his father the freaky story. Jason's dad was astonished. He did not believe in magic... until now.

Jason's younger sister Emily overheard the conversation. She ran to the bus stop and took the bus downtown to the Arch. She was almost to the entrance of the Arch when she saw the odd girl just like Jason had described. She stopped the girl in the pointed hat by tapping her on the shoulder. Emily asked the girl how to get her brother transformed back to a human.

The girl said, "If you go to the Mississippi River right across the street, you will find a small piece of red slate on the bank, get it and smash the rat with it. Your brother will turn back into himself." With that, the witch disappeared.

Emily followed the girl's instructions. She walked to the mighty Mississippi and instantly saw a rat-sized piece of red slate. She ran back to the bus stop holding the slate carefully. When she arrived home, everyone was in the living room frantically talking about what to do with Jason the rat. Jason was scurrying around the floor. As he ran behind the couch, she quickly smashed him with the piece of red slate. He instantly turned back into himself. When the family saw Jason, they jumped for joy, and everyone hugged each other. With a relieved look on his face, Jason said, "Watch out for girls in pointy hats!"

Right then, the bus pulled up at the Arch grounds. The old gentleman gave me a mysterious smile and stayed on the bus as I said good-bye and got off. I walked to the Arch making sure I didn't go near any girls in pointy hats.

Rachel A. Boehm
Age: 10

HOW RAINBOWS CAME TO BE...

God sent one as a thank you to Noah! After a rainstorm a rainbow came. It went across the sky, and I looked at the rainbow. My heart was excited.

Anna Miller
Age: 6

A GIRL'S WORST NIGHTMARE

It was two years ago that the worst thing that can happen to a thirteen-year-old girl happened to me. I was at Camp Wilber and as I was unpacking I saw this black limo pull up and I immediately thought, what drama queen is being forced to come to camp this year, then as I continued to watch that's when I saw the horrible part, my cousin Malana got out!

I know that to most girls their cousin coming to camp would NOT be their thought of the worst thing in the world but, when your cousin is Malana you find that it really is the worst thing in the world. The reason is because I live on a farm and am not afraid to get down and dirty, Malana on the other hand doesn't even like the outdoors mostly because she is a snobby thirteen-year-old with friends just like her. How do I know all of this you ask because one year I had to actually spend the summer with her!

I was not about to let my summer at camp be ruined so we established some boundaries and one was that after this year we would never ever see each other again. Little did we know that two years later she was going to be spending Christmas at our farm!

That camp experience was two years ago and this Christmas was the one she was going to be spending with us and I wasn't exactly excited even though my mom was. My mom always asked "Why aren't you and Malana friends, Shanna?"

And I would always tell her "because she is a stuck up, hates the outdoors and we are complete opposites!"

I was looking out my window when I saw that same limo pull into my driveway. I rushed downstairs to see my Aunt Krista and Uncle Leonardo. That's when I heard the doorbell ring. I answered the door and to my surprise I saw my cousin standing there along with sixteen suitcases.

My mom made a great dinner and then the worst part of the entire week came. My mom said "Shanna why don't you take Malana to your room to get unpacked." At that moment my stomach sank because I knew she would have some remark about how it was too small or that my horse posters were stupid or that she couldn't believe I owned no makeup.

That night I helped Malana unpack and then we both went to sleep. In the morning my dad woke us up at 5:00 am and of course Malana complained that seven hours was not enough beauty sleep. I finally got her out of bed but then she started putting on her good clothes and putting on makeup. I convinced her that she didn't need to look great to do a few chores.

We went outside to start my chores. I figured it would be best to start with the easiest chore first, cleaning and riding the horses. You should have seen her try to ride that horse. She had so much trouble getting on that I had to help her, then when she rode she looked like she was in a rodeo the way she was throwing herself all around with every step the horse took. When we got down to cleaning the horses Malana refused to even touch an animal that filthy.

Then it was time to milk the cows and I was in for the time of my life. I got out two buckets and did the math to figure out that each of us would have to milk eight cows to get done. I started and told Malana to watch. She saw me do it real easy and figured she could do it easily too, but when it was her turn it didn't come as easy. Every time she pulled the milk either sprayed onto the floor or onto her. By the time she had gotten sprayed in the face twice she was done and I ended up milking a lot more than eight cows.

The last chore to finish was to shovel the old hay out of the cows' barn and put fresh hay in. The minute Malana found out why we had to do, she headed inside. When I had finished I went inside to relax with a warm cup of Mom's hot apple cider. As Mom was fixing my cider I heard Malana coming down the steps and you should have seen what she was wearing, a leather halter top and a mini skirt in the middle of December. The next thing I know she is in the kitchen asking my mom if she could go to the mall with a few friends, and that she would be back by ten, and my mom said yes!

That was the last straw for me I ran into the kitchen before Malana could leave and told my mom "Mom why does Malana get to go to the mall all by herself and wearing something that I know you don't approve of and she doesn't even deserve it because she didn't do any of the chores because it was too gross for her! And why does her curfew get to be 10:00 on a Wednesday when my curfew is 8:30 on weeknights?" My mom could tell I was mad and she sent me to my room and told Malana to go ahead to the mall. I ran to my room and slammed the door.

At ten Malana came into my room and started changing into her pajamas. "I am sorry for not helping out and getting things you don't and being stuck up." said Malana. I told her that I knew she was a city girl and didn't like the country and wasn't used to it and that it didn't matter.

The next day Mom took me and Malana to the mall to shop for Christmas presents for everyone since tomorrow would be Christmas. We all split up and started looking for gifts. I got my mom a antique doll for her collection and I got my dad a new blue toolbox, I even got Malana something but I am not telling anyone.

That night I wrapped my presents and put them under the Christmas tree and went to bed. The next morning I woke up to the sound of Malana's voice telling me it's Christmas. We went downstairs and saw that our parents were already up. We started opening presents and every now and then I would glance at Malana and even thought she said thank you I knew she really hated the clothes my parents gave her. Then Malana left to go get something and came back with a small box for me. I ran upstairs and got her present. She opened her present first and saw that I had given her a bracelet that said Best on it. I then pulled up my sleeve to show her I had one that said Friends on it. She just smiled. I opened mine next and saw that she had gotten me a blanket that she had sewn and it said YOU'RE MY FAVORITE COUSIN ANYTIME AND ALL THE TIME!

I helped Malana pack and then we said our good-byes. It seems to me that as much as I hate Malana I will still miss her, but I know that she has that bracelet and I have still got her blanket.

Sara Whitman
Age: 12

THE MAGICAL TRUNK

Sean and his mom were cleaning out the attic in their house at 8:00 in the morning when they found an envelope on top of a dusty trunk.

The letter read:

> HELP ME! I am stuck in this trunk. I need your help to get out! You see, I was looking through this trunk and I fell in. The only thing that made it out was this letter.
> P.S. Be Prepared!
> Jason T.

Sean wanted to help him, but he didn't know what to do so he went to his mom for help. She turned him down. She said that he was hallucinating and sent him to bed. He got as mad as a snake when someone picked it up by its tail. Then he tried to forget about Jason, but he soon felt guilty and decided to go to the attic to save him. He packed only the essentials; food for two days, water, a blanket, a flashlight, and a rope. He left a note on the refrigerator that said,

> Dear Mom,
> If you are looking for me, I am in the trunk in the attic. I am OK.
> Sean

He climbed up the attic stairs and went in the trunk. He fell down a portal and landed on a man's lap. After the man stood up, Sean asked the man what his name was and the man said, "Jason Tapper."

It was 3:00 and they were very hungry. Sean took out the food and they feasted on a good lunch. While they were eating, Sean asked Jason how he survived. Jason explained that this place was another world. It was kind of like Florida, and he had been eating the mangoes off of the trees by the beach to survive. Jason was in a rush to leave this place because he missed his family dearly and he would lose his house in twenty-four hours if he didn't get back. His house was a very old mansion with grand ballrooms, gigantic libraries and huge fireplaces. It would be sold to a museum if he did not get back soon.

Sean said he was tired from his fall and needed to rest before he could save Jason. He pulled out his blanket and soon fell asleep.

The next morning he woke up to a loud THUMP. It was his mom! He looked up at the sky and the portal was open. His mother came to see if Sean was okay because she read the note and she was frightened. Sean went to his mother and embraced her. She said, "I missed you and I wondered if you were okay." He gave her the biggest hug he had ever given her. Then the man woke up and Sean's mom asked who he was.

He politely said, "Jason Tapper." She asked him for his name again. He said, "Jason Tapper." Sean's mom ran up to the man and gave him a hug. Sean was confused and asked his mom what was going on. His mom said that this was his great-great-grandfather and that he had been lost.

Sean took the rope out of his backpack and lassoed the lever that opened the portal. Then they made a human pyramid and climbed out using the rope.

After they were back, they ran down the attic stairs and got into the car. They drove to the museum to claim Jason's house. They made it five minutes before the twenty-four hour deadline was up.

After that, Jason invited Sean and his mother over for dinner. They had the best family dinner ever!

Sarah Rothberg
Age: 10

Before I go to school I eat breakfast. Then I change my clothes and I brush my teeth. Then I comb my hair and then I pack my backpack. I pack my folder and my mom packs my lunch box and a snack inside my backpack. My mom brings me and my brother to school. It is a short trip.

Jared Pudlowski
Age: 6

WHAT A SURPRISE

"Stop that you two!" Mom hollered.

"Sorry, we're just so anxious!" Jimmy said.

"About what?" Mom asked.

"Going to Disney World." Sara said.

"How did you find out about our surprise?" Dad asked.

"It's a very long story." Said Jimmy.

"Go wash up for dinner." Mom said.

That night at dinner, it was so quiet, hardly a sound. There was only the occasional sound of soft chewing and the slurp of drinking. The silence was broken by the sound of a dropped fork hitting the kitchen floor. It was Sara, she was playing with her food.

Later when Jimmy and Sara were in bed, they couldn't sleep. They both kept thinking of what they were going to do at Disney World. They hadn't been to Disney World so what all they were thinking about was what they had seen on a commercial on the big screen plasma television in their living room.

Jimmy was imagining a lot of roller coasters like The Tower of Terror, Space Mountain, and The Rockin' Roll Roller Coaster. Sara was imagining all the rows and rows of gift shops. She like Jimmy couldn't stop thinking about all the thrilling roller coasters at Disney World.

Those next two weeks until they left for Disney World went by very slowly. Jimmy and Sara both could not sleep. They had the same dream over and over again about them going to Disney World.

Finally, the day that they were to pack came. When Jimmy got home on the yellow bus from his last day of school at Howard Bentley School, his mom had all the suitcases lined up in neat nice rows down the first floor hallway. Jimmy and Sara had learned that messy rooms are not tolerated by their mom in the Smith house.

"My mom is one big neat freak." Jimmy has always said.

When Jimmy's dad came home from work, the table was set for dinner and Jimmy and Sara were upstairs packing for the big trip to Disney World tomorrow.

"Wash up for dinner you two." Mom yelled from the bottom of the steps.

Jimmy and Sara answered their mother and were downstairs in about two minutes. All four of the family members sat down at the table and said grace. They were having chicken and dumplings with mashed potatoes and gravy. Mom wanted to cook one good home-cooked meal before they left for Disney World. After dinner, Sara and Jimmy took showers and went to bed right away because they had to get up so early the next morning.

Jimmy that night dreamed about Goofy, Mickey, Mini, and Donald. He dreamed of getting their autograph and a picture with them under the Magic Kingdom Castle in the middle of the park. The next morning Jimmy and Sara were so excited. Today they leave for Disney World.

Jimmy's mom asked him to take the house key over across the street to Mrs. Whitefeld's house so she can get the mail and watch the house for them. Jimmy really did not want to go over there but Jimmy knew he had better do it or else his mom would make him go get a stick from the yard and give it to her. Jimmy would turn around and his mom would switch him on his hind parts. No, no, no, I am just kidding Jimmy would just get a look then he would go over across the street.

When Jimmy walked up to the house, he saw Mrs. Whitefeld's dog in the window. Jimmy politely rang the doorbell and stepped back from the door and waited. Mrs. Whitefeld opened the door and said "How nice it is to see you, Jimmy. What brings you here?"

Jimmy answered, "Our family is going on vacation to Disney World and we need someone to watch our house for us while we are gone."

Mrs. Whitefeld said "that would be fine with me, Jimmy."

Jimmy handed the key to her and headed back home. When Jimmy got home, he got ran over by his family running to go to the car. Jimmy grabbed his stuff and headed for the family's suburban parked in front of their house. Jimmy got to have the whole back seat to himself. It seemed like an eternity just to get on the highway. When Jimmy and Sara had not been in the car for ten whole minutes, they had already begun to get on each other's nerves.

Jimmy fell asleep about a half an hour later and was out the rest of the way. When they were entering the hotel parking lot, they woke up Jimmy. The next day they decided to go to M.G.M. Studios and ride all the rides.

Jimmy and his dad went on the world's fastest roller coaster, Rockin' Roll Roller Coaster first. While Sara and Mom went on a shopping spree for a gift for Sara's grandpa. Then they all went on the Tower of Terror ride together. Jimmy and his family spent the rest of the day riding rides and watching some theme shows like "A Bug's Life" and "Star Wars."

They all stayed until the park closed. The next two days, we went to Magic Kingdom to meet all their favorite Disney characters. The next day went horribly wrong. All the rides our family went on, we got stuck in. Somebody spilt a root beer soda on me. Obviously, it was Sara's fault. Then my dad got tripped by Mickey and started a big huge brawl with every Disney character at the park that day. It lasted only about five minutes or so because my dad had got beaten up by Goofy, Donald, and the rest of the Disney gang. We had to take my dad to the first aid office at the front entrance of the park. My dad looked back at Mickey and he still had a smile on his face.

"Doesn't that guy have a clue that he can't move his face?" my dad said.

"Yes he does, dear. It is just a mask." My mom answered.

"Ohhhh!" he exclaimed.

After we got out of the first aid office, we had to go back home to Montana because my dad had gotten our whole family banished from the park forever. On the way home it was really loud in the car. All of us were ganging up on my dad for making us go home. We forgave him and spent the rest of the summer outside in the backyard pretending that we did not remember, but how could we ever forget!

Tyler Martchink
Age: 12

THE AMERICAN DIAMOND

This is the American Diamond. Of course she hasn't always been the American Diamond. She used to be just a normal girl. This is her story.

Once upon a time, there was a girl named Jennifer. She was a normal girl. She was beautiful, smart, talented, silly and fun. There was one problem. Her teeth were crooked. Her worst day ever was picture day. She hated it because she had to smile for her picture.

Most of the time she tried to hide her teeth. One day, after school, her mother Mary noticed Jennifer's teeth. Mary took Jennifer to the orthodontist. The orthodontist said that Jennifer needed braces. Jennifer got to pick out the color she wanted her braces to be. She picked silver.

The next day at school, people were being nice to her. When she went home she felt very good. So she started to clean her room. Then she started to clean the rest of the house.

When she was finished the whole house sparkled. Her mother noticed how much work that Jennifer had done. Mary was pleased and gave Jennifer an advance on her allowance. She got fifty dollars from her mother.

Jennifer had been saving her money and she had already saved fifty dollars. Now she had one hundred dollars saved up. Jennifer went where most teenagers with money go, the mall. When she got home she had bought new makeup, shoes, clothes, and accessories. She felt happy. She had not felt this good in a long time.

The next day at school everyone in the school noticed Jennifer's new look. She felt beautiful and popular. Guess what else? Eric Shocker asked Jennifer to go to the prom.

One girl at school, named Brittany, was jealous of Jennifer's new look. Brittany used to be the most popular girl at school. Brittany told Jennifer "You will never take my place in this school!"

Then Jennifer said," Sorry Brittany, I already have." Then Brittany turned her head and walked away.

At the prom Jennifer and Eric were together. Then in walked Brittany and Adam. The two couples started talking and dancing. Eric was making fun of other people, calling them names. This made Jennifer mad when he called other people names. Because she remembered what it was like to be made fun of and called names. Jennifer broke up with Eric and began to have a crush on Adam.

At the same time Brittany decided she did not like Adam. They decided to break up. Brittany had a crush on Eric. Jennifer began talking with Adam and then he asked her to dance. The same thing happened with Brittany and Eric. All four of the teenagers began to like each other a lot and enjoyed dancing with each other. That night Eric asked Brittany to be his girlfriend. Then Adam asked Jennifer to be his girlfriend. They both said "yes."

The next day at school, Brittany came by Jennifer's locker. She told Jennifer that she was sorry. "Do you want to hang out after school and do our homework together?" asked Brittany.

"I would like that a lot," said Jennifer cheerfully.

Brittany said, "I think you need a nickname Jennifer." Jennifer stated that she thought that was a cool idea. "Your nickname will be... the American Diamond because your teeth sparkle like diamonds," said Brittany. Brittany told Jennifer that her nickname was "School Jewel."

Just then both Eric and Adam walked around the corner. They stopped at Jennifer's locker to talk. They all seemed happy and satisfied with their day and went home smiling, because they all knew it is better to be friends than enemies.

Erin Taylor
Age: 9

ALIEN SPACESHIP

Once there was an alien spaceship that had different colored lights and had water spraying out of holes in its sides. Soon the aliens saw a red ball. As it got closer, the aliens saw land. So the aliens landed on a gigantic island named 0, or to them, The Canyon. When the people saw it they panicked and fled, all except for one brave boy who went aboard the spaceship.

What he saw was amazing! There were billions of computers and bunches of aliens that you could hold in your hand. There was a big column in the middle of it all and there were hundreds of the aliens seated around it. The boy hoped they wouldn't see him and it's a good thing they didn't. He decided to explore, so he went to the next room. The next second he heard the door closing which meant he was all alone on the spaceship. So he just had to get to the control room so he could take off. So he turned around but the door refused to budge. "Oh, no!" cried the boy. "There must be another way to get out." But the room didn't have a visible door or window. Then he saw a glass cone with two hundred and fifty-nine tubes coming out.

First he went to one of the seats and saw where he would go if he pressed a button. He pressed "observatory" and walked into the cone and felt a sucking and started through a tube. Then he found himself looking out at a totally different room. This too, had a column in the middle, but there were hundreds of computers and monitors showing where the aliens were. He noticed some coming towards the ship. So he pressed "control room," and when he looked out he saw a small room with just one chair. He sat down in it and saw the button for "launch" and looked out the window. There they were in the distance, the aliens. He pressed "launch" and the spaceship shot up in the air! But then it fell. The smell of burnt sulfur laid thick in the air. Probably the engine was broken. Just then, an alien appeared in the glass cone. "A human!" The boy yelled and ran out of the spaceship. And the aliens went back to the planet Earth.

Andrew Creighton
Age: 9

69

FAR FROM HOME

Chapter One: Away

Chains are making my wrists bleed. I can't feel my legs and it's starting to get dark. My bare black feet are cold and numb. The only thing running through my mind is the way Mama looked when the master took me and the other slaves away. The last thing she said was to try to find the underground railroad. Papa said, "Keep walking unless they say not to."

The only noises I heard were whips cracking followed by cries. If anyone turned to see who was the unlucky person, they would get chained by the feet and wrists. I saw a fast running river. Everyone stopped, I saw sharp rocks sticking out from the water.

I heard the master yell, "Well, go on!"

Then a man said, "You can't do this to us -- it's torture!" The master took him off his chains and though he was being freed, he was chained to a tree and left to die. Everyone started to cry. I felt extremely bad.

Then I heard the master scream, "They'll be many more deaths along the way so pull it together or next it will be you."

I felt the chains go forward so I began to walk into the muddy river. My feet felt the water and it was a wonderful feeling but then the current became way too strong. I began to slip like the others. I fell on a rock and couldn't get up. The older lady behind me helped me up right before the master saw me. The lady's name was Nancy and she held my back so I wouldn't fall again. I saw land then I felt Nancy's cold hand on my shoulder.

She whispered, "Sweety, it's quicksand." My heart jumped. I knew that if I fell into the strong river I would get stuck in the quicksand. I felt a hard yank on the chain – everyone walked -- some people got stuck and were left behind. When it was my turn, I got stuck. Nancy picked me up and put me on the safe grass. I watched Nancy fall, but quickly she clutched the grass and pulled herself to safety. I helped her. She was as light as a bird.

The master said, "We'll rest here for tonight." He pulled me aside and said, "You will make the meals and serve them." He gave me a push. I fell on the ground and crawled away like an animal. I knew we were treated worse than animals, we were treated like scum!

Chapter Two: Where's The Sunshine?

Master quickly locked me in the cook room. The recipes looked like this:

Slave Meal	Master Meal
1 piece bread	1 glass of wine
1 cup oats	2 pieces of hot turkey
1 cup flour	2 cups warm potatoes
1 cup pond water in cup to drink	10 crackers with cheese

I made his food first and did exactly what it said. I walked over to give Master his meal. He grabbed it and said, "Get back to work!" I quickly walked to the meal hut and made the slave meals. I showed Master and he told me to serve them. I did and ate some myself. The master called Nancy. I saw her frail body jump out of worry as she walked over to him. He pulled her to him and said, "We need your chains." He pushed her on the ground and asked his helper to hand him a whip.

I said, "My friend!" and ran as fast as I could to her. It felt like as I got closer she got whipped harder. Her back was hunched over. Then her body was flat on the ground. I was standing right next to her.

Master said, "Too late." I burst into tears and master whipped me about seven times. He left me with her weak bony body. For the night I laid my head on the ground next to her.

Chapter Three: All Alone

I woke next to her body and began to cry. Master came walking towards me. He grabbed me by the wrists and he whipped me four times on the back. I didn't cry until I noticed I was bloody. He chained me up like the rest of the slaves. We began walking -- I was almost falling when I took my first steps. We were heading towards the forest.

The man behind me stopped and told the master he had ringworm on his foot. The master yelled for us to all sit on the ground. He pulled the thick and rusty chain back towards him. He unchained a woman in the front and told her to make a fire from scratch. I saw her swallow -- then she began. After about an hour of sitting on the muddy sand the fire started. Master told that poor woman to get the stick that had a hook edge. She limped slowly to it, picked it up and handed it to Master. He quickly chained the poor woman. Master lit the stick on fire and told the man with the ringworm to stick out his foot. Master put the fire on the man's foot. The man screamed and Master pulled out two ringworms. Then the man fainted. Master tied an old muddy blanket to the end of the chain. He picked up the young man and set him on the blanket. Master announced, "We will all have to walk an hour extra because of that break." I know it will be harder because of that man.

Chapter Four: Wolf Call

We start into the deep, cold forest. Master shouted in a terrified voice, "We are entering the deep forest. Wolves roam all around the land and they attack those with blood on their bodies. Many will become food for the wolves so we will be making a lot of noise so I won't have to spend more money buying slaves. Carry on!" he shouted. I started to cry -- that was a lot of noise -- then I started to slap my arms. There were mosquitoes and everyone started to slap themselves. Master said, "There must be a swamp nearby. Keep your eyes out for alligators or worse. Leaches! Leaches! Leaches!" I felt mud slush in between my toes. It felt smooth and soft. I saw a man with a lantern.

He spoke with a Texas accent, "Whatch ya'll doin' on my property?"

"It's me, Ivy Green," said the master.

"Oh yeah, you're here to sell me those slaves."

Master said, "Yes sir." The man limped over to master and handed him twenty dollars. Our new master clutched the chain and we all jerked forward. I knew I had to escape!

Chapter Five: The Big Escape

My escape will be at night when we are unchained but locked in a tent. I will dig in the wet mud deep enough to slide through. I shall look for the North Star and that will lead me to freedom. I'm sure I will run like the dickens!

This is the night the new master is just now locking our tent. I can see through a crack the master in his warm hut. I cupped my hands and began to dig. It was going awesome. When the hole was big enough I crawled through. I put my foot in the hole and screamed the loudest scream ever. A big fat leach bit my foot. Master slammed out of the door and was stomping so loud that you could hear it in the thick mud. He shouted, "What happened here?"

I said in a weak, whimpering voice that I fell out of the tent and a leach got me. "I'm real sorry Master," I said but he just grabbed my arm and said,

"That'll cost ya," and whipped me seven times on the legs. I felt like a rag doll the way he flung me around and shoved me inside the packed tent. I fell on a man who pushed me on the lap of a young and sweet lady. She held me like my mama. For a minute I thought she was my mother.

The young lady said, "My name is Bella and I'd love to help you escape to freedom so let's make a plan." My voice hurt whenever I spoke but I told her that we should run away at night. "I'll make the plans and you do the physical part," she told me. The plan was for Bella to scream and while master pays attention to her, I will make a run for it. I'm ready -- Bella screamed just as planned and I made a run for it. Master didn't even know that I was gone!

As I was running I tripped over a black woman so I knew it was safe. She whispered, "I'm Harriet. Harriet Tubman." She picked up my frail body and walked me through the underground railroad. At the end I saw my mother. I was sure my smile reached my eyes. Then I fell asleep in my mother's warm arms. I knew I was safe.

Harper Smith
Age: 9

WHY PIGS HAVE CURLY TAILS

Pigs have curly tails because it goes with their body. Pigs have curly tails because it makes the pig look cool. Pigs have curly tails so the mud drips off. Pigs have curly tails because God made tails like that.

Nathan Andrews
Age: 6

MY DOG

One morning my dad heard barking so he woke up my mom. She heard it too. So when I got up she told me. When Abby got up I told her. It went on and on. Last night my dog was lost. We looked all over. I found my dog Brandy. She had one little bite and one big bite. I was very sad, but Abby wasn't sad. I cried a lot. My dad picked Brandy up. My mom got some meat that had medicine in it. We let her in the garage. I cried and cried. Then I stopped and went to bed. She got better in nine weeks. I was so so so happy.

Alaina Thoele
Age: 6

SUPER KITTY

Once upon a time there was a little kitten that always wanted to be a superhero. The next day the kitten's owner said, "I've got the purrrrfect name for you, it's Sabrina." Then she took a red cloth out of her bag and tied it around her neck and mumbled, "It's beautiful," and went upstairs. Sabrina ran around the house with her cape and tried to fly but she couldn't. So she took a nap instead. Her dream was about saving people and taking bad guys to jail. Sabrina woke up and thought to herself, "I'm going to be a great superhero."

The next morning Sabrina's owner had everything in boxes. Sabrina was confused, even she was in a box. Then her owner said, "Well it's time we moved," as a tear fell from her eye. Sabrina started to meow because she didn't like to be in this hard blue box with bars on the door. Sabrina was scared. Then her owner put Sabrina in her car and followed the big truck in front of them. When they got to a stop there was a beautiful three-floored house. When her owner got out of the car, Sabrina again was confused because her owner was talking to her stomach and saying, "I'll be seeing you in one month."

Sabrina was taken into the house and all the boxes were unloaded in about three hours. Finally Sabrina took a long nap. Sabrina was awakened by a loud ring. It was Sabrina's owner's husband. He said he was on his way home. After that Sabrina fell asleep again. That's when it all began, (Sabrina's dream)

Sabrina woke up to greet her owner, but she wasn't there. That only meant one thing, kidnapping, her owner was kidnapped. Sabrina flew to the door at full speed and crashed badly. Even though bleeding, she got up, this time opened the door and then went full speed. She flew through the clouds and after ten minutes, spotted her owner in the arms of a bad guy. Sabrina did a nosedive straight into the bad guy, got out her handcuffs, put them on the bad guy, and put him in jail. When she was done with that, her owner again was missing. She flew around the whole town and then spotted her owner. She was dropping into a pool of sharks! Sabrina took out her pocket knife and just in time, got her owner. (Sabrina woke up)

Sabrina stretched out her legs and tried to fly once again, but this time she flew and when Sabrina's owner saw this, Sabrina's owner's husband walked in. They both fainted.

(After one month) The owners of Sabrina were now used to their cat flying. While the happy family was eating breakfast, it was time. Sabrina's owner screamed, "Oh dear, it's time!" Sabrina flew over and picked up her owner and her husband and flew to the hospital right away. As they all came to a stop, Sabrina burst into the door and grabbed a wheelchair and put her owner in it and her husband took her to the first room. Sabrina didn't know what was happening to her owner. She was scared again. She began to weep of sorrow. After about two hours Sabrina saw her owner and she had a strange figure in her arms. Sabrina heard crying and a lullaby being sung. Sabrina trotted to the door which was closed right that second. She was upset because her tail was stuck in the door. She meowed as loud as she could and nothing happened. So finally Sabrina got out her jet pack and blew up the door. Everyone was scared but Sabrina's owners were just fine, but now the baby was wailing. They were furious with Sabrina. So they locked Sabrina up in her cage. But that wasn't good enough for Sabrina who had melted the door with her laser beam which had always come in handy. Now they put Sabrina on her leash, but again Sabrina had a way to get loose. She bit it with her razor sharp teeth. Finally they all gave up. Sabrina's owners put their baby on the ground, and let Sabrina play with her. When they saw how great both of them got along, Sabrina's owners said "we'll call her Sabrina Jr." And everyone laughed.

(Three days later)
Sabrina's family came home including Sabrina Jr. And they all had a super power life. Pow!

Kathleen Foley
Age: 9

MY DOG

It wasn't even the evening time it was Friday at 3:00 she had an invisible fence and she didn't care that she got shocked. In my backyard woods she got hurt by a coyote, maybe two or three. We were calling her name over and over and she couldn't hear. I was really worried something big was going to happen. Finally, when she came she was bleeding all over, but mostly near her neck. We were really sad because we love her so much and we thought she might die. We could hardly believe she would go into the woods and get attacked by a coyote. She came inside and lay on her bed. My mom picked the bed up and, took her to the vet. My mom asked the vet to help carry her out of the car so, she couldn't get hurt more. And when she was there they said she might have surgery. But she had to sleep over that night. The car ride was probably terrible but, I wasn't there to know because I was too afraid to go. My mom was afraid every time she went over a bump because, she was so opened that more blood could come out. But the bad thing is on Saturday my mom got a call from the vet that she would die in pain or we could put her to sleep. I didn't know yet so I was wondering why they were crying. My mom and dad picked to put her to sleep because they didn't want her to die in pain. (I think they picked a good choice.) When, my sister, my brother, and I got home from school my mom told us the horrible news. She tried to keep it a secret as long as she could. I really didn't want to know the news but I would figure it out anyways. I'm always going to remember and have all the memories with her. I will always remember when she wagged her tail every time we came home from school. I liked when she greeted us every time we came off the bus. She was my first dog and only three. I wish she could come back but I know she can't.

Rachel Mormol
Age: 10

THE HITCHHIKER

It was said to only be an urban legend, about hitchhike killers, but on the night of April 7th, 1991 in a small town of St. Louis it became reality. There was an old man about the age of fifty, wandering on a busy highway. The Highway 270 was covered with rain and full of speeding cars. The man had on a black raincoat with a hood over his face. He walked on the side of the highway with a gray suitcase. He wore black pants, which looked like they were bloody from being in a butcher shop. He also wore a golden goatee that glowed in the darkness of the night. He was walking and walking, waiting and waiting for someone to pick him up. "I like the way you move, Bump! Bump!" Mark McKalister and his son Marcus McKalister were on their way home listening to their favorite artist, Maroco. Mark had spotted the old man walking on the side of the road. I wonder if this man needs any assistance wondered Mark. He drove off the side of the highway, pulling up right next to the man.

"Excuse me sir, do you need any help?" asked Mark. At first, it seemed like the man ignored him, but a few seconds later the man opened the back door and entered the car. "So where were you headed, sir?" asked Mark. The man then coughed and spit out blood right on the seats of Mark's Jaguar. "Wait a minute, are you all right?" exclaimed Mark. Mark was very frightened then.

The man whispered, "H.I.T.C.H.H.I.K.E.R."

Marcus turned around and asked curiously "What are you spelling?"

The man whispered back "Hitchhiker!" The man then opened his gray suitcase and pulled out a razor. For Mark the rest was history. The car swerved out of control, driving off the road. The car twisted, turned and finally landed upside down. Mark was dead and Marcus beat up from the car crash. Marcus opened the car door and escaped the car. He ran and ran, not looking back until he came upon a small corner store, Reflection Food. He ran into the store and explained to the clerk what had happened. The clerk called the police and came to the scene. Marcus called his mother and she picked him up at the corner store. The police explained to the mother what had happened and with much grief Marcus' mother Judith and Marcus drove back home. Marcus was devastated to see his father killed by this mysterious hitchhiker. The tragic day was over.

The next day Marcus and Judith went their separate ways, to work and to school. At school Marcus had been teased and ridiculed about what had happened to his father. After school Marcus was picked up by his grandfather. He went over to their house and waited for his mother to pick him up after she got off work. Judith was working for the mayor of St. Louis, Mayor Adams and she had to work overtime. She got over to her parents' house around 7:30 p.m. She picked him up and they drove home. As they were driving home they came to a stoplight. Attached to the stoplight was the street name, Howard Blvd. The light turned green and she sped away. Blinded by the heavy rain she ran into a man, who hit the windshield and rolled off. He wore a yellow coat and a golden goatee that glowed in the darkness of the night. She picked up the man and put him in the car. Marcus was in the backseat dozing off. She sat the man in the front seat and started to drive him to the hospital.

He suddenly coughed really hard and started to whisper some words "H.I.T.C.H." the man then coughed again really hard, interrupting his sentence.

Judith appeared frightened. "What are you trying to say?"

The man yelled "Hitchhiker!" The man pulled out a razor blade and Marcus' eyes suddenly widened. Judith hit the brakes really hard and the man's razor blade flew out of his hand. Just as the old man was assaulting Judith, Marcus grabbed the man's hand. The man opened the car door and snatched Marcus and disappeared into the night. He or Marcus was never to be heard from again.

"Now, you're asking yourself, who am I? I'm the person who followed Marcus and Judith and Mark the whole time. I'm the person who's responsible for Mark's death. I'm the person who kidnapped Marcus. I am the H.I.T.C.H.H.I.K.E.R!"

Marcus P. Howard
Age: 13

SHEN'S FIRST BATTLE

One day a boy named Shen and his henchmen were walking in a deserted canyon. After five hours of walking there was a giant blast that scared them. They wondered what had happened so they went to check it out and what they saw was an old man. He looked about fifty-three and he said his name was Tom.

He said, "I have been looking for a good fight and so far I can't find a good enough opponent. Can you satisfy my need to fight?" Tom answered, with a grin on his face.

"OK." Tom told Shen to follow him. Shen did not trust the old bat, but he followed him anyway. After five minutes of walking Tom led Shen to a dark cave. Tom went in first. Then Shen came in after him. Once Shen got in the cave Tom was nowhere to be found. Shen was looking around trying to see if he could smell Tom's scent. But he could not smell him anywhere. So he spread his hands and started to spin real fast. While he was spinning, a tornado started to form. The wind was so strong it pushed Tom out of his hiding place.

Then Shen said, "I will make you a promise to only hit you once, OK?"

Tom smiled and started swinging first. His fists moved, LEFT, RIGHT, LEFT, RIGHT. After thirty-six punches, Tom realized that if he lets Shen hit him once, Shen can't hit him anymore. So... Tom stood there waiting for Shen to hit him. Shen ran towards Tom and hit him in his stomach. Tom's eyes got real big, he fell to the ground and went to sleep. Then Shen vanished...

...To Be Continued.

Xavier Brown
Age: 13

THE BATTLE OF LORENZA

An ice arrow whizzed over Milo's head and froze a rack of weapons. The year was 1315. Milo and fellow fairies were locked into a battle against cyclopes.

The cyclopes had one eye, were six feet tall, and loved to fight. The cyclopes were wearing crude leather armor and wielded silver bladed swords.

"I need another ice breaker spell over here!" Milo shouted to a wizard. The wizard Blightzar hobbled over to Milo and performed an ice breaking charm on the frozen weapon rack.

Blightzar was a tenth-year wizard from the world of Marconi. He cast a spell that transferred himself from his world to Zork, Milo's world, called teleportation. Blightzar was a valuable weapon against the cyclopes because of his magic, and one of the reasons that Lorenza had not been overrun.

Blightzar finished casting his charm and asked Milo how the battle was going.

Milo was the Commanding Officer of the Lorenzan Fairy Army, and unlike other commanders Milo loved to be on the front line of battle. Milo looked like a brown-haired human except for his pointy ears, and his wings. Milo was an excellent archer and swordsman. He was the best soldier in the kingdom of Lorenza.

He turned to Blightzar and said, "Unless we get some help from the Titans on top of Mt. Typhoon, it is likely that by tomorrow morning Lorenza will be overrun.

Milo turned his attention back to the battle and fired an arrow through his spy hole. He heard a cry of pain and grinned to himself.

Blightzar teleported from Lorenza to Mt. Typhoon about a half hour after he talked with Milo. He found eighty Titans suiting up for battle. "Great!" thought Blightzar the battle would come to an end soon.

Blightzar teleported back to the outer sanctum just as the door collapsed. They cyclopes had broken through the front gates and frozen the first line of troops.

A great wave of fury swept over Blightzar. One of the troops frozen was his best friend, Mycroft. He struck the cyclopes with a lightning bolt from his staff, and defrosted the troops.

Milo's voice rang loud and clear through the bloodstained air, "Fall back to the inner sanctum, I repeat, fall back." Milo shot one more arrow at the cyclopes and fled.

The other troops followed their commander and fled to safety. Blightzar found Milo and reported his news about the Titans. "If we can just hold the cyclopes for ten minutes, the Titans will arrive," Blightzar said.

Milo sprang into action and barked out orders to his troops. "All troops that do not have bows, help fortify that door if the cyclopes break through the battle will be over in minutes. All troops that have bows fall back with me if the cyclopes breach that door we will have to take them out," Milo exclaimed.

The Titans appeared just as the great stone doors collapsed. The Titans were nine and a half feet tall and wore titanium armor, which was rumored to be gift from the gods. The Titan's commander, Blueshiek, gave Milo a reassuring smile, and used his ancient magic to summon a glacial spike and shot it at the cyclopes.

The Titans followed their commander's lead, summoned their own ice spikes and fired them at the cyclopes. The leather armor that the cyclopes were wearing might as well not have been on their bodies. The spikes found their targets and impaled some of the cyclopes.

The cyclop general, Spero, was taken completely by surprise at the arrival of the Titans. It took him several minutes to devise a new plan.

"Everyone summon rock shields," Spero yelled. A couple seconds later every cyclop was safe from the Titan's glacial spikes.

The Titans were caught off guard by this brain blast and switched to their diamond bladed swords. "Have your men open fire on the cyclopes as soon as we have broken through their shields," Bluesheik whispered to Milo. Milo then turned and spread the word to his men.

The diamond bladed sword cut through the rock shield like a hot knife through butter. Arrows zipped through the air and struck the cyclopes in the chest.

The cyclop general was faced with no other option, but to retreat. Before going he vowed to one day return and kill the king of Lorenza.

When the cyclopes retreated back into the hills the troops found the wounded and gave them care. They found the dead and buried them. A silent alliance was made that day between fairies and Titans.

The Titans returned home that day after a marvelous victory feast. The feast consisted of roasted duck, croissants, malt beer, and other gourmet foods.

Milo and Blightzar met with each other soon after the departure of the Titans. Milo thanked the Marconi wizards repeatedly for their help. He also promised that if the wizards ever needed assistance in the future they could count on the Lorenzan fairies to be there for them.

The remains of Lorenza can still be seen today on a far out island in the middle of the worlds Marconi and Zork. If you look very closely at the walls of Lorenza you can see the face of the great fairy commander Milo.

Michael Wankum
Age: 13

ELEMENTS OF THE UNREAL
A Not So Epic Tale Of Epic Proportions.

An apartment deep in the jungles of the city, undetermined time.

    A man had an idea. Not that original of an idea but he was going to work with this idea. Everything else was gone this was the one clear shot at the train out of this brutal reality. This man was a writer Nicholas Yoslava Romanov XXVI. From here on this man shall go by the condensed version of Nick. Nick, basically, is the hero of this tale legend thingy. "Note from author (have you ever realized that every sitcom in existence has a writer-type guy or a film-type guy. Because everything is, actually a narrative and people draw from themselves ((one of the easiest places to draw from)). In addition, I use ((when I am using (in a (." End authors note. I started this story in a relatively simple manner. I compiled a collection, which all human beings from natural birth are inclined to do. WE WANT MORE, all humans want more. More love, more money, more glory, more. This also inspires both greed and ambition but I'm not going to go Mr. Gecko on you now. I believe love is the only thing worth fighting over. Land, land is also good. Humans feel connections with the land, this is good. Later in life instead of collections we begin to relish free and original ideas. "Not all modern art is original.." Nick, the writer, who loved writing, wanted more in life so he began his idea.

    "An epic of mega proportions is what it will be. A fantasy epic of a tragic tale of a war-torn world and two star-crossed lovers would be splendendiforous (Yes, I did just add that to my own dictionary of awesome words," shouted the great writer Nick.) "This is going to be delightful," Nick thought to himself in a congratulating manner." He exclaimed so the people on the floor below him wondered curiously. He said "I will find something new and exciting."

    Obviously, he would look to his own experiences to find the ointment that would heal literature's wounds. He looked back. Nothing, a big spoonful of empty space with no adventure filled his mind. This did not matter, just like the lottery ticket in your pocket, this didn't matter. Still, this mattered a little and Nick needed a new plan. Suddenly the clouds of frustration lifted and the song of an idea sprang from the lighthouse that cut through the fog and delivered true inspiration. I'll take everything from other old dead guy's books. They can roll over in their graves if they don't like it. As Nick did his I'm a genius dance (I will not describe the humor of this dance at this time) he began to ask questions. A fantasy epic? What does one need? Companions!

    "Ah, I can see it! These companions' originality shall be plucked like apples from a tree. First of all, we need short dudes. All good fantasy epics have short dudes. They shall be stealthy and sneaky like. This shall give us characters and we shall give them emotional struggles between these many different characters. Okay, short dudes check. I will soon find names for them. "To find good names go to www.kabaiarians.com. It has every name in every language in existence. They have the coolest names. I figure this out from an author named Christopher Paolini who wrote the book Eragon. This is a great fantasy book and all fantasy lovers should really read that."

Yes, Hmmmmm. Dukhagjin (Kosovo) will be the short dude's name. On the other hand, maybe Cuana (Irish) would be a better name. Yes, Cuana will be the short person's name. All good adventuring companies eventually have a dwarf, this adds humor and a smith to the bunch. Hjamlur (Icelandic) will be his name. With every dwarf there must be a tall long haired arrow shooting handsome-looking elf. This allows for conflict between races of this earth. What shall this earth be called anyway? HHmmmmmmmm! I'll get to that while I'm actually writing the book. All adventuring parties need a big guy to help them out with swords and another big guy to use magic. The big guy needs to have something more though. He should be half-elven to cause inner turmoil in him. That would be good. Yeah, and then he could be battling in himself the human and elven portion of himself and not knowing who his parents are. "Good one," thought Nick "The magic guy cannot be too powerful or it wouldn't be any fun. I think he should be named Guibran (Gypsy names.) The magic would have to use up his energy or it wouldn't be fair. In addition, the magic itself. HMMmmmm. I have read about word magic before. In addition, it could be part of a secret language of the beginning of the world. Only some people would have the pure luck to stumble upon someone who knew it and then that teacher would spread the secret language." Thought Nick in his busy little brain.

"In the beginning part of the story we will start out with the human/elven guy, we'll name him Sunil (Sri Lankan) then these black-cloaked people will take his only family left, his younger brother, captive. All fantasies need black-cloaked people. You can't even see their faces. That's what is intriguing about them. Some things are essential in a fantasy. Shall we name them. Oh yes we shall. Here we go," said Nicholas

THE RULES OF FANTASY
The one and only set of rules
1. Companions listed above and descriptions.
2. Mean guys in black cloaks.
3. Mysterious traveling guy who can use magic.
4. Magical circular objects VERY IMPORTANT!
5. Beautiful elven princess
6. Mean guy who wants to take over the world.

"Personally, I like writing in the way I do," said Nick. "People may think that it's weird or ludicrous or something but I like it. The guy who wrote the mighty did that. He was a great author. Paul Zindel is like that, too. You just get a feeling of realism. If someone could incorporate that into a fantasy, I would be eternally grateful. Fantasy helps me escape," pondered Nick. Nick does that a lot. Nick ponders and rambles on in his mind. If he were talking, it would be rambling at least. He thinks of finer things and chicken wings; of cabbages and kings. "Cabbages and kings," Nick shouts to me from my own imagination. "That could be the name of our book," he says sounding fascinated by the idea. By the way, cabbages and kings is a line of the poem that Tweedle-Dee and Tweedle-Dum say to Alice in either Alice in Wonderland or

Through the Looking Glass. I like the way people act out caricatures of people's minds as if it was a tour of the subconscious.

"Yes," Nicholas exclaimed, "and Sunil can be a cabbage farmer who stands up to the evil approaching his homeland while the king simply ignores it. Then he can have his brother taken off by the black-cloaked figures and then Guibran can show up and lead him on a remarkable journey gathering companions as they go.

They'll be waterfalls, battles, monsters, beautiful cities, and beautiful elven princesses," said Nick. "She shall be named Zilia (Aragonese). Yes, that is an awesome name for an elven princess." Remarked Nick to himself.

"Well, I'll make things up as they come to my head," said Nick. "There isn't anything left to do but start. I guess every beginning must have a beginner. Here goes mine," Nick whispered.

"A man had an idea..."

Christopher Kozal Brennan
Age: 13

WHO AM I?

In the morning, I could barely breathe. "Graduation Day!" I thought. Nothing, nothing could express my squeal of happiness inside. I looked in the mirror. Then I filled with sadness. "Who am I?" I questioned myself out loud. Then I looked at Lucky, my beloved collie. His panting and deep, dark, trusting eyes seemed to say, "You are a person and I love you. I always will." I burst into tears then hugged my dog. I got dressed and felt truly relieved.

I got to the graduation. I had to say a speech. I did. I talked about leaving school and coming to Spoede. When I got off the stage, I felt like a huge weight was lifted off my shoulders. Whew! Afterwards, I had to sing a song. So I did. The words flew out of my mouth like they were part of my breathing. I saw the audience smiling at my words. I smelled the air sanitizer. It was really strong! I heard the sound of my voice. I felt the cotton fabric of my dress. It was rough. I was saying good-bye in my singing. I got off the stage. "Whew!"

After such a feast of food, once again, I had to go on the stage. This time, I had to receive an award. I went up to the stage again. A woman gave me a handmade piece of wood, engraved with gold, "Elena B. Mayer." It made me feel like I was in a dream. As I felt the smooth wood of the certificate, I realized I knew. I knew who I was. I was a humane person just like everyone else. Just like everyone else.

Elena Mayer
Age: 10

THE LUCKY COIN

Yesterday, Jon was walking to school, he saw a coin just laying on the sidewalk. It was gold with one tiny diamond in it. On the top it said Lucky! The diamond sparkled like a crystal. Jon imagined that he could use that diamond and sell it for lots of money! On the bottom, it said you can only use once! What in the world will Jon use his "Lucky" coin for?

When Jon got to school, his teacher told the class that they were having a test on everything they had learned so far in science. Jon remembered that he found a lucky coin. It was as lucky as a four-leaf clover. He decided that he was not going to study for his test, he was going to use the coin and see how well he would do. This was very risky!

Then he thought he could put the coin in the soda machine instead. A second later he remembered this wasn't just an ordinary coin, this was a lucky one! So he decided no way! His next idea was to use it on a rainy day. He would ask the sun to come out and the rain to stop. He remembered that the rain would stop after a while and rain was essential. So he was confident to drop that idea.

Then, Jon decided that he was going to just stick to plan A. That was the plan to just not study for the test and the coin would HOPEFULLY get him a great grade.

The next day the whole class heard "YES!" from Jon. The coin had got him one hundred percent but he usually got C's or D's. His teacher said good job to him but asked if he cheated. Jon said he didn't. His teacher was very suspicious, so that night he called Jon's mom. RRRIIINNNGGG!! The phone rang. Jon's mom had been in his room the day before cleaning and picking up.

When the teacher called, he asked if Jon studied and how hard he did because he got one hundred. Jon's mom said she didn't see him studying at all. She went to ask Jon if he had studied. Jon said he did.

The day after, his mom wanted to see what he was studying and what the materials were like. Jon finally acknowledged that he didn't study. He relied on a coin that might not have worked. He lucked out.

His mom was so baffled by him. When he went back to school, that day, he told his teacher the whole story. As it turned out Jon had to retake the test. As usual, Jon scored a C.

From that day on, Jon never relied on cheating or on any lucky coin!

Katie Corrigan
Age: 11

HOW OOBLECK CHANGED OBESITYVILLE

Once upon a time in a faraway land, the town of Obesityville was getting out of hand. All they did was eat and eat sugar plums and juicy meat. One fine day a man came along; he knew what the people were doing was wrong. Richard Simmons was the name; losing weight was his game. He had a substance bitter and tart, this was only the very start. He thought oobleck could change the town, and that is when his plan started to go down. The people did not agree with what he was trying to do. Why he was doing it? They had no clue! They liked how they were extremely fat, even Frederick the albino cat. The people of Obesityville did not like this weird man at all and the sound of his name it made them bawl. They knew they had to stop him, but how they did not know. They screamed and pleaded for him to go.

Richard was determined and would not leave them alone, even when they offered him a soft ice cream cone. Obesityville had enough, and they became severely rough. They went to the top of the highest hill, and were quite willing to plaster Richard with doughnut filling. Richard was furious, how could they do this? Not one inch of his body did they miss. Why wouldn't they give his oobleck a chance? Then they could fit into size eight pants! Their next plan to abolish him forever was to put him in a room and lock the lever. They filled the room with food so delicious, they hoped he would go hungry and become vicious. He would eat all the food and love it so much, low-fat foods he would not want to touch. This plan did not go through, Richard simply could not be untrue. They had one last plan, to send messy oobleck off to Japan. The problem was no one would touch it. They were all too afraid! What if oobleck changed what they weighed?

They let Richard go on his rants, while they bought bigger pants. He made commercials about weight loss, but the people said, "You are not our boss!" They liked going to Obesityville Buffet, and shoving food in their faces all day. It brought them comfort and made them content, so when they bought groceries they spent every cent. Richard was tired, but had to endeavor. He knew food would not make them happy forever. He made up fancy flyers that proved his product was effective. Although that did not change anyone's perspective. They ate fried green tomatoes, creamy mashed potatoes, drippy chicken wings, and lukewarm onion rings. Stringy, slippery noodles and thick buttered bread; they consumed food until their faces turned red. They ate until they felt ill; they ate against their own will. They didn't care what he had to say. They ate and ate the day away.

Richard couldn't take it anymore. Dealing with these people was such a chore. No matter how he tried, his efforts seemed futile. Their comments were incredibly brutal. He tried to convince them in everyway, but they would just laugh, and head for a bland café. Every day they ate something new, or sometimes everything mixed together in a chunky stew. They fattened up and ate it all, until they could hardly crawl. He had about given up hope, with their frightening attitudes he could not cope. He decided to try one last time. He himself would eat the green, gooey, slime. There was only one way people would believe him; he would eat it and become slim. He gathered a crowd, said a silent prayer, shoved it in his mouth, and watched people stare. They scarcely believed it; it could not be true! Richard became thin from drinking slimy, green goo?

Then feeling brave, little Ricky looked up. "Mr. Richard, serve me a cup. I don't want to live another second this size, I am sick of the fries going straight to my thighs." He looked at the contraption all bubbly and wet, as his forehead started to sweat. Then courageously Ricky lifted the cup to his lips, and instantly the fat went away from his hips. His stomach slowly began to disappear, and people all over started to cheer. In a twinkling people wanted to try some, and admitted being obese had made them glum. They did not want to confess they were living a lie, so they went on with life wanting to die. But now they could be happy, and play all day and never have to worry about how much they weigh. So the whole town celebrated this stupendous date, that changed the way they thought and ate. Richard felt proud and victorious, for the whole town was looking quite glorious. Obesityville lived happily ever after, and spent their days abiding in laughter.

Lori Wolfe
Age: 15

HAPPILY EVER AFTER

Once there was a princess named Catherine, who was to be married to Prince Simon. The whole town was bustling around trying to get ready. When the prince arrived the trumpets sounded and everyone gathered into the garden for the wedding. Upon seeing the princess, her beauty amazed him. After the celebration the prince and princess rode off. When they returned the king and queen had a wing in the castle for them. The prince and princess were very happy. A few months later a messenger arrived to tell the prince his father died. The prince reluctantly told his wife he had to return to Norway for a while, the princess was very upset, but he promised her it wouldn't be for long. After the prince left the princess found out she was having a baby. She couldn't wait until the prince returned so she could tell him. A man came to town a couple months later and told them the prince had been killed; the princess refused to believe. Seven months after the prince was presumed dead, the princess awoke to the sound of trumpets; she looked out and saw the prince riding toward the castle. She ran down to meet him and they embraced. They were joyous to be together again. A week later the princess gave birth to a baby girl who they named Emma. Then they all moved to Norway, to become King Simon, Queen Catherine, and Princess Emma and they lived happily ever after.

Kaitlyn McNamara
Age: 14

MY COLONIAL STORY

It is the year 1804 and I live in New Hampshire with my family. Our home is located in a town called Concord, which is the capital of New Hampshire. We live on a plantation that has a few marble and granite mines. My father goes to the mines and works very hard every day. He takes care of the entire plantation, including the livestock, horses, logging and helps with some of the planting. I wish he would bring all of my brothers and me with him to help with everything on school days but he doesn't.

Our house is big with an upstairs and a downstairs. We have five bedrooms upstairs and a big kitchen, dining room, sitting room, and playroom downstairs. The entranceway in our home is made of granite and marble that came from my father's mines. My family built our home from wood that came from the forest on our plantation.

On our plantation we grow our own potatoes, carrots, lettuce and other vegetables. We raise our own chickens and cows for meat, eggs, milk, cheese, cream, butter, and ice cream (my favorite). Deer and rabbit are also part of our meat resources. My father taught my brothers and me how to hunt for them at a very young age. We always had plenty of food so we never went hungry, but everyone sure worked very hard on the plantation and we always ate a lot.

We have a big family that includes two hunting dogs. There are a total of eleven people in our family that consist of six boys (including me) and three girls. My mother and father make eleven people in the house. I have a lot of cousins, aunts and uncles. They don't all live near us, but we do see them several times a year, mostly at family gatherings. My grandparents (my father's parents) live on our plantation in a smaller house than ours. They are at our home most of the time helping our mother and father. We always manage to get along and have a lot of fun.

Sunday is the church day. We go to church for several hours. It is the day of rest for everyone. After church the families go to the creek to throw in flowers in memory of their family members who have passed away. After we leave the creek everyone from church and neighbors, gather at our plantation for lunch. All of the families bring different kinds of foods and drinks. Everyone has a great time. We play tag, skip rocks at the creek, ride the horses and play hit the stone with a stick. It is a lot of fun.

The families in our town are hard working, generous and always helpful. Anytime my father has a problem with the animals the neighbors come to our plantation as soon as they hear something is wrong. He doesn't even have to ask them. My mother is always willing to cook and make them something to drink to show her appreciation for their kindness.

When we are not in school our father lets my brothers and me help him in the mines. If there is planting to be done my grandparents do it. My sisters do their chores in the house like laundry, sweeping, cleaning the bedrooms and doing dishes. They also help Mom and Grandma cook, sew and do some gardening. It sounds like we don't have a lot of time to play, but we do and we don't mind helping out.

School is only in session in the fall and winter months. Sometimes Father needs us to help out in the mines or on the plantation, so we don't attend school on those days. Father says it is important that we learn all we can about the mining because one day we will have to run the mines ourselves. The work around the plantation is important to us also, but the mining comes first.

I remember while I was growing up a war started. It was the French and Indian war. The French started to build forts, which were signs to the British. The British foresaw an attack from France and they were worried and so were we. The British got help from their Indian allies to make an army, a very strong army of course. The British had gotten the help they needed so they now had to defeat the French.

The British colonists and their Indian allies were involved in this war, which were the British Army and the Indian Army. The French Colonists and their Indian allies were also involved in this war and they were the French Army and the Indian Army. The Indians on each side were from different tribes. The British had won the war but it cost the king two hundred thousand pieces of gold. It didn't make him very happy even though they won the war. Then the king thought of something, he decided to make colonists pay back the two hundred thousand pieces of gold by taxing them. The gold paid to run the government. I felt real sorry for them.

The British government started taxing people without any explanation why or what they were taxing them for. They started adding taxes to everything they had to purchase including their wages. Some of the taxes they were taking went to the army and to the government funding. It was very costly to everyone.

Samuel Adams was a patriot and revolutionary idealist. I wanted to learn more about him. Samuel went to Harvard College and became educated in law. Samuel influenced the pre-revolutionary struggle against the British rule. He helped form the Boston chapter of the Sons of Liberty. It is a secret patriotic society organized in American colonies to oppose the Stamp Act. They enforced the policy of no importation, by which American merchants refused to import goods in British ships. Paul Revere was also a leader in this.

The boycott started because of the tariff. This made me so mad I just wanted to explode. The Boston Massacre has now occurred because of the boycott and I'm afraid what Britain will do next. It started by a redcoat who had gotten hit with a rock and fell down. He got up and opened fire. When he did that the other redcoats began to fire also. Five colonists were killed in the mob and sadly one was my cousin.

The government started taxing all people on imports and exports. Sam Adams led the Sons of Liberty, which led to the Boston Tea Party because of the tariff for the tea. The tariff also caused the boycott. The result of this was the Boston Massacre. This happened on the streets of Boston after the people became angry at the redcoats. This was a very sad event.

Now only the British company could sell tea without taxes. Although they were the only ones they put colonists out of business. They created a monopoly, which excluded colonists from trade. So they dumped their tea into the river.

Sam Adams rallied the colonists to stop ships from unloading tea. Since they were excluding them from trade. So the colonists dressed up as Indians. They got the tea and dumped three hundred and forty-two cases of it in the water, and that is how they did it. This didn't make the

British very happy. The colonists formed the Continental Congress, which is where all the colonies send representatives to have say. The congress agreed on certain rights and redeems they must have. Patrick Henry also created the saying "give me liberty or give me death." The colonists are also willing to die for freedom now. The war with colonists against Britain would surely happen now.

Now the king has sent British troops to Concord and Lexington, MA to find weapons that were hidden almost everywhere. They also went to find and arrest Samuel Adams. The colonists are beginning to take sides. Patriots (rebels) are the colonists against Britain Loyalists. (Colonist were loyal to Britain and its king.)

Paul Revere (a patriot) made his ride to Lexington. He rode to warn the Patriots to hide their weapons somewhere safe. He rode through all the towns, by horseback, shouting, "The British are coming, the British are coming!" Paul Revere was actually successful in warning them. Now the minutemen (army of citizens that formed their own militia) are waiting to fight and protect their weapons and fellow patriots.

The Patriots and British fought at both Lexington and Concord. The first shot was known as the shot heard around the world because it will have such great impact on our future. The American Revolution has sadly begun. The events that had followed changed the world in a way so that the British no longer were invincible.

The Patriots won the war and that is why the new nation, United States of America, is a world of power today. I feel the Revolutionary War was good for our country.

Michael Dean Speiser
Age: 11

DAD'S JOKE

I just got home from school and turned on the TV. The news was on. Newscaster Emma was saying stuff about a group of hunting dogs that had gone missing in the area where I live. She also said a number to call if the dogs were to be found. The owner showed a picture of his hunting dogs.

The next afternoon I went out to the woods. I had to collect things to make a nature diagram. My dad just got home from work. I gave a walky-talky to my dad and kept the other one. I went out to the woods to get my things.

I was about to pick up a pretty flower when I heard crunching leaves. Then I heard running. Suddenly I heard barking and growling. I didn't know what it was until dogs ran from behind a couple of trees. I ran in front of the dogs until I fell into a pit padded with leaves. They were soft, but it still hurt. I called my dad with my walky-talky. I told him about the dogs. He ran into the woods to get me. We ran in front of the dogs all the way home. We ran inside as the dogs stood in a crowd scratching the glass door. I locked the door as I yelled, "Mom!"

I ran upstairs and showed my mom the ripped up, smashed, ugly flower. We told my mom all about the dogs.

I remember the newscaster telling the number to call if someone were to find the dogs.

I thought of the number 896-5423. No, that was my friend's number. 477-0714. No, that was my old number. Finally, I thought of the number. I called it. The owner came to get them. I got twenty dollars for finding them.

The next day, I went to get my supplies for the project. I picked up a weird-looking leaf. I stood up and heard crunching leaves, running, and barking. I called my dad on the walky-talky. My dad walked out from behind a tree with my dog. I yelled, "Dad."

"I tricked you," my dad yelled back.

That was my dad's joke.

Meagan Leppien
Age: 10

MY GREAT-GRANDPA

My great-grandpa was born on April 23, 1882 in Alban, Germany. His name was Henry Baltizore Suttmoller. He was born to Henry and Mary Helen Suttmoller.

Great-grandpa was a twin. His twin was a boy. At birth both babies caught pneumonia. Great-great-grandma treated one of the babies with orange juice, but after she gave one the juice she got scared so she did not give the other baby the juice. The baby that did not get the juice did not survive. The baby that drank the orange juice, my great-grandpa survived. This was maybe a sign of how great he truly was. Henry Suttmoller, his father was a commander in Hitler's third Reich. To this day no one knows what happened to Henry Baltizore's mother and father when they came to the states. A priest took Henry Baltizore in, because he was an orphan and he lived with the priest until the priest died. When the priest died my great-grandpa was fifteen and he went to Bowling Green, Mo. and a farmer took him in. The farmer noticed my great-grandpa had a special trait.

Henry Baltizore married Lena and they had six children Mary, Anna, Herman, John Henry, Louise, and Angie Suttmoller. They had a farm in Bowling Green. They were very poor and lived off of the land. Great-grandpa was a very religious man. Every day Great-grandpa would kneel in his room and pray. When he went to church he would always give to the church all the money that he had on him, sometimes that might only be a quarter. Great-grandpa would always tell his children that they had to give to God, because God always provided for them.

My grandpa John would always talk about his childhood. He would tell my mom about Great-grandpa and how wonderful and special he was. To this day the family feels that Great-grandpa was blessed. Here is the story that was passed down from generations, about this man and the blessing that died with him.

Great-grandpa, Grandma and the children always traveled by horse and buggy. My grandpa would always say that he would notice that the farmers from around the area would always come over and ask Great-grandpa to come with them to their home. Great-grandpa would always leave with them. Grandpa didn't always understand because Great-grandpa would talk in German. So one day when a neighbor came over and asked Great-grandpa to come quickly, Grandpa asked if he could go along. What Grandpa saw was shocking. In the barnyard a cow lay dying, Great-grandpa walked over to the cow, knelt down beside him and started saying a prayer in German, with his hands holding the cow. Within what seemed to be only minutes to my Grandpa the cow got up and walked to the pastures. That is when my grandpa realized that his dad was special and what he was doing every time the neighbors came and had him leave with them. Grandpa also realized then why at a young age that his mother, brother, and sisters had to kill the animals on the farm and Great-grandpa never would.

On the way home from the farmer's house that he had just cured the cow at Grandpa asked "Dad, how did you do that?"

Great-grandpa answered "my son, this is a gift from God and someday I hope that I will be able to pass this gift on, if they are blessed from God and can accept the gift." After that day Grandpa understood some of the things that Great-grandpa did and why he did them. He also knew then that he could not complain about the chores and why he had to do them.

Then one night when the family were on their way to a church service, Great-grandpa looked over at Great-grandma and said "there is the light, someone in that house is going to pass tonight."

Great-grandma turned to the children and said "let all of us say a prayer for those people in that house." My grandpa looked at the house and tried to see a light, but could not see one.

Once again Grandpa asked "what light and why do we have to pray for those people."

Great-grandpa said "John I see a light above the house and someone will pass away there tonight."

Grandpa said "I do not see a light." Great-grandma answered "just pray John." The next day the neighbor came over to tell Great-grandpa that someone in the house where Great-grandpa saw the light, had passed away. My grandpa then knew that this was another gift from God given to Great-grandpa.

Grandpa would always try to understand the reason of why Great-grandpa was able to do and see the things that he did. Grandpa could also see that sometimes with these gifts, that Great-grandpa had a hard time dealing with the gifts, he would kneel down and start praying in German. Grandpa knew that Great-grandpa was asking for strength to carry on.

Grandpa grew up watching Great-grandpa continue his gifts. Grandpa also noticed that the children were growing up and none of them were showing signs that the gifts were being passed on. My grandpa got married and started having a family of his own. Grandpa was thirty-nine years old, when he was called and told that his dad was dying. Grandpa went to his bedside knowing that Great-grandpa was dying and with him was going the gifts that were given to him by God. My grandpa knew that he was not worthy enough to fill his father's shoes.

This is a true story about my Great-grandpa.

Megan Hallemeier
Age: 13

WHAT IT TAKES TO HAVE A DOG

Patience! Patience! Patience! Taking care of a dog is a big responsibility. Some of the responsibilities are feeding the dog, making sure it has water, making sure she is healthy, taking the dog outside, giving the dog a bath, walking the dog, getting shots, cleaning up after the dog, taking it outside, and taking her to the vet. Just like you have to make a house safe for a baby you also have to make a house safe for your dog.

Here begins the story of Holly and her new family. I woke up on Christmas day and I looked to see what presents were waiting for me under the tree. The biggest gift that caught my eye was a chocolate Lab sitting in its kennel next to the tree. I was so excited that I ran over to the kennel to see the dog. The dog would run between my legs, lick my face, and jump on us because she was so excited to have a family. During the night my mom and dad would take care of the dog, but one night I wanted to take care of the dog so I laid by her kennel. She whined all night, because she missed her mom, dad, and her brothers and sisters. After a couple of nights she became a little better at sleeping in her new home.

After a couple of days my dad came up with the name that everyone had seemed to like was Holly. The first couple of weeks Holly was so excited that she finally had a family and a name that she would follow us all over the house.

My mom, dad, and I would try to train Holly to sit, stay, and come. My dad told me it is important to teach Holly to sit, stay, and come so when she gets loose you can say "Holly come," and she will come. My dad said another very important thing is that when Holly tries to bite or jump on you, you have to tell her "NO!" I really didn't know why he said to tell her no when she jumps because I thought it was funny when she jumps on you. He later explained that when she gets bigger it won't be funny anymore because she might hurt someone.

A couple of weeks later Holly has learned the basics like sit, stay, and no jump. At nights no one has to lay next to Holly anymore because she has gotten used to us and our home.

The dog and I have become very close friends, but when I take the dog outside she thinks that she can run away from me. My dad said that I do not spend enough time training Holly. So, my mom and I spent at least a half an hour or more playing and working with her on tricks and behavior.

During the winter my family had to take Holly outside in the cold, when it was snowing, and when the wind was blowing. So my mom and dad were thinking of building a fence. When the weather got warmer my dad started working on the fence, with my mom's help while I was inside watching, and playing with Holly. My mom and dad said I was a big help by watching her while they were working on the fence. The fence took a lot of work and a rather long time to build. It took many, many, many trips to Lowe's to get all the lumber needed to build the fence. My dad worked for two months, but had to stop when the temperatures got near zero and when we had ice and snow. Since the weather has warmed up he has almost completed the fence except for one gate. My dad worked very hard and it is a very sturdy fence. Now that my dad has built the fence all we do is open the screen door and let her out and she does her business. It is so nice when it is raining or cold outside we just open the door and let Holly go. Holly is so happy to go outside and just run around, play with her toys, and dig in the garden.

When Holly first came to our house she had no idea what was going on, she didn't recognize all the sounds that were outside. Holly is now, after a couple of months getting used to all the noises and surroundings. I asked my mom why does it take Holly so long to get use to the smell and the sounds around our house. She said that Holly hasn't been exposed to all of the sounds and smells before, and this is all new to her. I told my mom and dad that I thought Holly was getting much better at doing tricks, some of the tricks she can do are fetch, down, sit, stay, and come.

Taking care of a dog takes a lot of responsibility, and also a lot of patience. When Holly first came home she was very excited to have a family. She also used to bite, bark, jump, and wanted constant attention. Once you train your dog not to jump, bite, or bark your dog will be your best friend forever. That's what happened to Holly and me. She knows that I will play with her when she wants to play with me. My dog and I have become best buds. If you want a dog you have to realize that it takes a lot of time and patience to train your dog. When you teach your dog tricks and she doesn't seem to get it the first time you just have to keep on trying until she does get it.

When I kept asking my parents for a dog they said are you sure you are ready for the responsibility. Now I know what they were talking about, she is a lot of work but she is also hours of enjoyment. Holly was the best present that I received for Christmas that year.

Chelsey Prost
Age: 13

A SEASON TO SPARKLE

The morning sun filtered through the slats of the barn roof, casting a shimmering glow upon the two-day-old filly, who nuzzled peacefully near her mother. Upstairs in the farmhouse, twelve-year-old Cassie stirred and stretched. Then her eyes flew open wide, for she remembered her precious new paint horse, lovingly named Sparkles. Flying out of bed, she quickly dressed, grabbed a piece of toast out of her mom's hand, and flew to the barn.

Leaning down to pet Sparkles' velvet nose, Cassie felt the familiar stiffening of her joints. Some days were worse than others, for Cassie had a case of juvenile rheumatoid arthritis. Sometimes she even had to use a cane to get around. Her wonderful parents encouraged her to do as much as she could to overcome the disease, for it could be managed with the proper medication and therapy.

In the near future, Cassie longed to ride her new prized horse. Riding was her life, after school and chores, of course, but because of her condition, it was hard and very frustrating, for it sometimes hurt to ride. The disease also caused rashes on her legs, and if she didn't wear padding in her breeches, riding could become uncomfortable.

Months flew by, and Sparkles grew, but so did Cassie's arthritis, although most days she could manage just fine. Her goal was to someday ride Sparkles with ease. She had ridden Sparkles' mother, Shine, her first horse, when she was younger, and together they won many ribbons from horse shows. Since Sparkles was still too young to be ridden, all Cassie could do was build her bond with her and watch her run gracefully and proudly in the pasture.

Cassie's ability to get around began to get worse. All of her dreams of riding Sparkles to stardom were fading from her mind, for she thought she would never be able to ride the same again. She began to think Sparkles might deserve a better rider. Cassie considered selling Sparkles or giving her to someone who could ride her to fame. She thought, "Sparkles shouldn't have a disabled rider like me for an owner. If only I didn't have this disease." Even with the encouragement of her parents, Cassie still could not bring herself to ride Sparkles.

One day, while shopping with her mother at the market, Cassie spotted a poster advertising a local horse show in two months. "By golly," she thought. "People can tell when a horse loves a rider, and Sparkles loves me. I'm going to sign up. Sparkles is finally ready to be ridden, so we need to get started with our training soon."

The very next day, she woke up stiff, but excited. Her father was waiting for her in the paddock for their first lesson on Sparkles. The beautiful paint had been "broken to ride" a few months earlier, which meant that she had been trained with a rider under her saddle. With a boost from her father, Cassie hoisted herself up onto Sparkles' lean, muscular back. "Yipee!" cried Cassie. "I have been dreaming about this for months!"

They walked a few circles, and then trotted figure eights over small poles on the ground. It was hard for Cassie to "post to the trot," so instead she remained in a sitting position. Then came the moment Cassie had been waiting for... her dad gave her the cue to canter. Gripping some mane to steady herself, Cassie gently heeled her horse into a faster pace. Cassie felt like she was flying with Sparkles' smooth gait.

At last, after weeks of training and practice, they were ready to compete. The show was a huge success, and everyone knew Cassie and about her disease, and admired her ambition to ride. Afterward, Cassie was exhausted but glowing. In her hand was a proudly-held blue ribbon, rewarded to Cassie and Sparkles for first place in the Dressage class.

As Cassie gently led Sparkles to the barn that night, she stroked her horse's soft brown ear and whispered, "Thanks, Sparkles, for making me a winner, too, in more ways than one."

Meghann E. Mollerus
Age: 13

TIME TRAVEL

A long time ago Jean Ann and Jessica were walking along. All of a sudden a big wave came and earth was covered with water.

Then they turned into mermaids. Everyone lived underwater! When they were underwater they could swim, talk, and breathe!

One time Jessica and Jean Ann were sitting down eating supper and a dolphin swam by and ate their food. So they followed it. The dolphin swam right into a cave.

"You go in," said Jean Ann.

"No, you go in," said Jessica.

This went on forever.

Finally the dolphin came out and said, "Do you want to be my friend?"

They both said sure.

They played, laughed, and sang together.

They were friends forever.

Jean Ann Gibbs and Jessica Clements
Ages: 11 and 10

THE SKELETON CURSE

Maria stared at the parched white bones of the skeleton. The hollow eye sockets seemed to stare right back at her. "Why did I get myself into this? Why had I been so stupid?" Maria asked herself.

So there she was, a girl staring at a dead skeleton that seemed to stare right back at her. She began to curse but stopped when something caught her eye. It was a glowing necklace with strange designs and patterns on it which hung around the skeleton's neck. She reached out her hand and gently lifted the necklace off the skeleton's neck. It was a necklace all right, but it had strange looking amulets around it.

Suddenly she recognized a resemblance between the necklace and the amulet she had found earlier. She took it out of her pocket and looked at it again. Her eyes grew wide and she gasped because it was a perfect match. She looked closer and noticed a tiny clasp no bigger than a baby's fingernail. She also observed that the center amulet was missing from the necklace.

Gingerly she attached the amulet to the necklace. She sensed something bad was coming so she quickly slipped it back onto the skeleton's neck. The skeleton began to shake as if it were in a violent earthquake. A blinding flash of light appeared so bright that Maria had to look away for a moment.

When she looked back, she gasped in horror, because the skeleton had come to life and was standing up rubbing its stiff bony legs. She backed up against the wall and managed to stutter in a frightened voice, "P-please don't hurt me."

Instantly a dry raspy voice like sandpaper rubbing on wood replied, "I would never hurt you in my life. My name is William Smith, but people call me Billy. What is your name?"

"My name is Maria," she answered. "If you're wondering, I was kidnapped by pirates, and put here to die. By the way, how did you get here?"

Billy thought for a while, and then he began. "When I was young, I joined the pirate crew that kidnapped you. I was put in here to die, but I had awakened a terrible curse, so even after my flesh rotted I was still alive. One day I lost an amulet off the cursed necklace I was wearing and died. When you placed the completed necklace back on my neck, I was restored, so I owe you my life."

"You're welcome, but we've still got to escape from this horrible place," said Maria. "I have a plan." She motioned to Billy, and the two bent their heads together to design the escape plan. When the plan was set Billy took off his arm, slipped it through the bars, and hooked the keys onto his arm. Maria took the keys off his arm and unlocked the door being careful not to wake the sleeping guard. She opened the door, and the two of them tiptoed quietly past the sleeping guard.

"Chicken eggs for sale..." the guard mumbled in his sleep as they passed. Maria held her breath until the guard went back into deep sleep. She silently breathed a sigh of relief.

They crept up the stairs, onto the deck, and then hid behind a barrel of rum. The crew and their bloodthirsty captain, Finn Scar, were drinking rum, talking loudly, joking, and laughing rudely.

At the perfect moment Billy leaped out from behind the barrel. The crew took one look at him and they all jumped overboard except the captain. He backed up against the side of the ship and fainted from fright. Maria and Billy quickly picked up the captain's body and hurled him overboard. Billy and Maria took control of the ship and rapidly plotted a different course. They sailed to New Guinea, where Billy stayed behind to live his life in peace.

Maria sailed for many months until she returned to London. There she sold the ship, "The Black Shark", and returned to her loving family at home. Maria never forgot Billy and was never afraid of anything even on the day of her death.

Caitlin Nancy Joanne Kropp
Age: 10

THE BIG DAY OF ICE

An icestorm caused me some problems. My name is Alex and my friend Tyler and I were playing a video game on the TV. The house got so cold from the ice outside that it froze the video game.

We went outside into the cold wintry day to fix the problem. Tyler went on the roof. Tyler fell off trying to fix a frozen antenna. Tyler got back up to heat up the antenna while I was looking for broken wires that might have fallen into the winter garden. I didn't find any wires but Tyler's idea worked.

We made an icy snowman. Then Tyler and I decide to have a snowball fight. Tyler beat me! We then went back inside to play video games.

Alex Winkler
Age: 10

PICAVICE PERIL

I had just finished breakfast and was walking into my room when I saw the steel machete glinting in the light. It rose ominously next to the head of President Baci.

"TRON! NO!"

My little brother ignored my woeful cries and the steel machete dropped viciously, slicing off his ear.

"Tron, that was my history project!" I screamed, rounding on him.

"Victory is mine!" he exclaimed, leaping victoriously off my bed. With a flourish and an evil laugh, he dashed into the hall.

Distraught, I trudged back to the clay figure sitting on my desk. Why? Why couldn't I have a normal little brother? Why was Tron so different? Actually, different was an understatement. Tron thought he was a pirate, one of those Earth sailors who stole money eons ago. Why he was so hyped on Earth history, I didn't know.

Earth was a dead planet. Nothing was there anymore. The few intelligent humans from the planet had escaped six hundred years ago when they built the Kywad Space Stay just past Neptune.

The population on Kywad was growing, which was why they had started construction on Fygoh Space Stay twenty years ago. It was almost complete and when it was ready, about half of the Kywad residents were being transferred there. Luckily, my family was staying here. My father was too important to the tech room to have him leave Kywad.

With a small sigh, I picked up the ear of President Baci, the human who had taken over Earth and eventually led to its destruction, and evaluated the situation. It was a clean cut and the ear was still in one piece. Just a minor setback, no real harm done. It was then that I noticed a small metallic disk on the lobe of Baci's ear. It didn't look like Tron's handiwork, so that left my other sibling: Cosmique. Cosmique was a three-year-old with no concept of privacy. She got into everything. She was born with a supersonic ear and could overhear pretty much anything she wanted to, including passwords and numeric codes used to block off-limit areas on the space stay.

Unfortunately, being three, Cosmique didn't understand that using top-secret information that she overheard was bad. So, she often ended up where she didn't belong with things that didn't belong to her.

Inspecting the disk, I deduced it was nothing more than a color chip used in games and computers to alter the colors on the screen. It probably belonged to someone's Gamer 8000. Later, I would ask around at study hall to see if anyone had lost one.

Pocketing the earring that my sister added to my sculpture, I quickly applied some Stik Again to Baci's ear and pressed it to the side of his head.

"Prota! Prota!"

"Tron? What is it?" I asked my brother as he ran into my room in hysterics.

"The oxygen level! It's dropped to twelve thousand Picavices!"

"What?" I asked alarmed. "Tron, this better not be your idea of a joke!"

"No, I swear! Pirate's honor! You can ask Mom and Dad! It's dropped!"

Twelve thousand Picavices? This was not good. Kywad operated on twenty four hundred Picavices of oxygen a day (one hundred Picavices an hour). That meant we only had five days before our entire oxygen supply was depleted, unless it was still dropping, then we would have even less time than that.

"Tron, how'd you find out about this?"

"It's all over the Poracle Network! They said there was a sudden drop. It went straight from the normal seventy-two thousand Picavice supply to twelve thousand Picavices."

"Is it still dropping?"

"No, it stabilized."

"What caused it?"

"They think something caused a breach, but it's closed up now."

"Stay here. I'm going to find Cosmique. And Tron?"

"Yeah?"

"Don't touch my project."

He nodded and I walked into the hall as calmly as I could to find Cosmique. No sense in losing my nerve until I confirmed Tron's story. Tron did have a sick sense of humor, but this was a little much, even for him. The hallway was madness. Everyone was declaring the end of Kywad.

"We'll never make it!"

"We're going to die!"

Guess Tron wasn't lying, for what comfort that would give. I really needed to find Cosmique. With her supersonic ear, she probably had one huge headache from all the screaming going on.

Keeping this in mind, I proceeded to the back of the stay, where it was quieter.

"Come on, Cosmique, it's Prota," I called gently. "Come on, Sissy's here to protect you."

"Pro-tah!"

I turned around to see an exuberant Cosmique dancing around. That was unexpected.

"Lookee, lookee," she giggled, displaying another small metallic disk.

"No! Bad! Bad Cosmique! You have to stop stealing color chips! Come on, you're going to take your nap and I'm going to see who these belong to."

"Nap nap!" she exclaimed happily.

I walked her to my room and told Tron to watch her. He reluctantly agreed, but only because I promised him that after my project was graded, he could play "pirate" and "kill" President Baci.

I walked into study hall and asked, "Anyone missing color chips to their Gamer 8000?"

"Gamer 8000? We're down to one hundred Picavices of oxygen and all you can ask is if someone is missing a color chip to their Gamer 8000?" Carpi demanded incredulously.

"What? One hundred Picavices? I thought there were twelve thousand," I backpedaled, trying to maintain my composure.

"No -- it just dropped again. We're down to one hundred."

"Sweet Milky Way," I breathed. "When?"

"Just a few minutes ago. See," she said, pointing to the poracle screen, where a solemn Captain Zykin was addressing the Kyward residents.

"As you all know, the Picavice level has dropped to a mere one hundred Picavices. We do not know how this has happened. The computers show no signs of a breach, although it is the only logical explanation. As you can see from our Picavice monitor, we have reached level red, the lowest level we can reach. I would just like to let you all know that it has."

"Wait. Can we rewind that footage? Back to the picture of the monitor?"

They backed up to the monitor part and froze the frame without questions. I looked closer at that Picavice monitor closer than I ever had in my life. It was a simple device. The top level was green, representing sufficient Picavice levels. The second level was yellow, showing moderate Picavice levels. We were on the third one, red; signaling little or no more Picavices left.

"Sweet Milky Way," I breathed.

They were ignoring me and had moved the screen back to Commander Zykin's farewell speech. There was pandemonium everywhere. People were crying, screaming, hugging, kissing, and giving their final farewells.

I, however, was reaching into my pocket, pulling out the two color chips. On closer inspection, I noticed one was a green color chip, and the second a yellow one. Happy and embarrassed at the same time, I groaned and started off to the east end of the stay where the Picavice monitor was.

"Prota! There you are!" my dad said, seizing me. "I thought I wouldn't get to say good-bye."

"Dad, I don't think you need to say good-bye just yet. Was Cosmique with you yesterday?"

"Yes. Remember, your mother couldn't take her to the cafe."

"Yeah, well, did she go near the Picavice monitor?"

"Why?" he asked suspiciously.

"Will you open it up for me?"

"Prota, I."

"Dad, just do it."

He gave a sigh before keying in the password. He stepped aside and let me look. As I had suspected, the color chips were missing. "Dad, I believe these are causing the oxygen drop," I said, handing him the two chips.

He looked at them, put them in place, and immediately, we saw the Picavice Monitor skyrocket to the "sufficient" Picavice lighting.

A silenced hush crashed upon the crowd outside of the tech room and then an ecstatic roar rose from all of Kywad and dancing, hugging, and cheers were all one could hear in the east end of the stay.

Commander Zykin's stout frame burst through the tech room door.

"Trapezius! What on earth just happened?"

"We found the problem sir. Oxygen levels have been replenished and stabilized."

"Trapezius, you are a genius!" Commander Zykin congratulated my dad.

"No, it just took a little ingenuity and a bit of tweaking. We found the problem and fixed it."

"Well, whatever you did, it's a miracle!"

"Thank you, sir," he said humbly, before ushering me back to my room.

To my amusement, Cosmique was lying on Tron's lap, snoring lightly. Having been both the cause of the disaster and the miracle, I found it funny that Cosmique, even with her supersonic ear, had managed to sleep right through it.

Jessica Platt
Age: 16

SAMMI IN THE DOORWAY

It was 11:00 on Friday afternoon and Khelo had no school because of conferences. But that doesn't mean that he didn't have work at home to do. Khelo had the job of cleaning out his closet. While Khelo was throwing his clothes everywhere he noticed a door that had never been there before. He slowly strolled over to the frightening door and opened it. As he looked inside something came up behind him and pushed him inside the door. He looked back and saw his stepmom's dog smiling at him as he looked away for a split second. His little sister Lola came in and slammed the frightening door closed. Khelo had no choice except follow the hall. When he finally reached the end of the hall, he saw a town that was not like any other town. There were dogs walking in and out of stores that said Bark Bones Pizzas, Race Dog Track. There were a whole bunch of other places, too. There were different kinds of dogs but one especially caught my eye. It was a puppy beagle all alone on the side of the street. Khelo slowly made his way over to the poor little puppy. As he moved closer the puppy moved closer. Khelo stopped at the side of the road and knelt down to see if the puppy would come near. After awhile the puppy did come and made itself comfortable on Khelo's lap. As the poor little puppy lay there helplessly Khelo slowly moved his hand back and forth down the puppy's back.

While he was rubbing the scratched up back, he looked up and saw a billboard that had a picture of the same dog that he had in his lap. He moves his eyes around the board and then finally stopped at a word that said Mimi. He knew that that had to be her name. But Khelo didn't like that name. It wasn't a name for a fantastic dog. So he decided to name the puppy Sammi. He thought Sammi was the perfect name for this very petite dog.

Khelo loved the dog so much that he wanted to keep it so he went to the door that he came through and tried to go through it with Sammi in his arms. But when he got to the door it closed as fast as the wind. Then he realized he can't go home and keep Sammi too. So Khelo went to the owner of the city. Prefer Poodle. Prefer Poodle was as plump as a plum and as round as an apple.

Since he couldn't go through the door with Sammi he was really hoping to have good luck with Prefers Poodle. Welcome to the Wonderful Land of Dogs was his first words.

Khelo asked very politely how he could get home. But all Prefers Poodle would say was go through the door you came through. Then Khelo explained how he wanted to take Sammi home too and that the door didn't let him go through with Sammi. And so Khelo asks how he can get home and keep Sammi. But again Prefers Poodle had an answer that didn't help. He didn't want Khelo to take Sammi because he was friends with Sammi and didn't want to lose him. So he said he couldn't help but also said that Khelo had a choice. And that no one or nothing could help him decide.

Khelo makes up his mind and decides to go home and leave Sammi behind because he has a family there and they're probably wondering where he is. Before he goes home he gives a good-bye to Sammi and says that he'll never forget her and that he will always love her no matter where she is. Now all Khelo had to do was walk through the door he came in from. As he walked he looked back to see Sammi looking at him too but only crying. And all Khelo did was keep walking down the long hall until he was home.

And now every week Khelo opens the same door that had led him to the Wonderful Land of Dogs. And every week he follows the long hall to find his little adorable fantastic puppy looking at him with joy. Sammi! He would say. And at one time in the year Prefer Poodle let Khelo take Sammi to live with him and he loved it and most of all Sammi loved it. Dogs really truly are man's best friends.

Maggie Knoedelseder
Age: 11

Welcome to my world. My name is Kaylee. Let me get you a chair and a drink and a seatbelt (to stay in your seat when you hear this).

Okay. Now that you're comfortable, you better listen up! One day I woke up to see snow outside my window. I ran into the kitchen and turned on the radio. Just as I turned it on, it announced that my school was closed!

"Yiipppeeee!" I shouted.

I rushed down the hall into Mommy's room, jumped on her bed and shouted, "SNOW DAY!" She told me to get down and go play in the snow. I rushed into my room and got my coat on and all my other snow stuff.

I noticed that my cat Cinnamon was not on my dresser. He usually lays on my bed if he's not there. I checked in my closet, under my bed, and then I went into the kitchen. I checked in the cabinets, by his cat food, and even in the fridge! He was nowhere! Maybe he went out in the snow, I thought. Everyone likes snow!

So I went outside and was greeted by a stranger. Mommy and Daddy told me not to talk to strangers, but this guy was so friendly. He said his name was Cinnamon. I said that was my cat's name. He also said that he loved to eat cat food. I thought he was crazy. But then it hit me. (Not a falling star!) He was Cinnamon!

I couldn't get myself to believe that. No cat could turn into a human! Just then I heard something. "Meow!"

"What was that?" I asked.

"Oh, that was a cat," said this guy who calls himself Cinnamon. I was starting to believe that this guy had swallowed Cinnamon! But why would he like cat food? I also remembered that Cinnamon had lots of fur so that guy would be coughing up hairballs by then! So he didn't swallow Cinnamon.

I was about to ask him when he said that he was the cat. Yup. That's right. HE WAS MY CAT! "How on earth did you get into this mess?" I asked him. That's exactly what Mommy says when I make a mess with my toys. But I'm only five years old! I'm supposed to make messes. Anyway, I'm off the subject.

"I'm MEOW Cinnamon," he repeated. Oh no, I thought. How will he turn back into my furry friend?

He told me that he woke up on my dresser and he had lost his tail and his other cat stuff. But one thing he didn't miss was hairballs. I thought, and thought, and thought. You know what I did next? I thought some more. "Well," I said. "If you woke up like that, then maybe a nap will turn you back." He agreed.

So, I tried to find something to hide him in so Mommy or Daddy didn't see him. He was a squirmy cat. (When he was a cat.) I took him through the side door close to my room. "What do you have in that sleeping bag?" Mommy asked me. I took a sleeping bag off of the clothes line and put Cinnamon in.

"It's a ummm a ummm sack of potatoes!" I answered. She didn't believe one word of that. But she let me go on.

I dragged Cinnamon up the stairs and into my room. He was nothing like a sack of potatoes. I didn't even know why I said that. As soon as we reached my room, he jumped out of the bag and hissed at me. I put him in my closet and snuck some cat food upstairs. He went right to sleep. When he woke up he was STILL a human. I thought and thought and thought again. Just then I got a bright idea. I ran to the bathroom and searched the medicine cabinet. I was looking for something that would change Cinnamon back.

To my surprise I found a bottle labeled CAT CREAM. I ran and put some on Cinnamon. He took a nap and then he woke up as a brown speckled cat. (That's why his name is Cinnamon.) I ran and hugged him. Just then two more cats strolled into my room. I realized THEY WERE MY PARENTS! I wondered what it would be like to change a cat to a human. What an adventure!

Alison Curtner
Age: 9

Intro

Hey! I got a short message for all who dream! Look, your life is your personal business, but after you read this, you will understand. So here we go... If you dream, be creative and don't worry what people say about your crazy dream -- just like mine! Be YOU. Just you. No one else. All right. We got the basics, but now we move on, okay? Listen carefully, now. If you take your dream to the limit, that silly dream could be a reality. Dare to dream BIG and do the impossible. Believe in yourself and do what is right.

Chapter One: The Present

For as long as I can remember, I have loved to sing and dance. It has been my passion to be a singer, to go out and meet people and do what I love for a job. Now that's what I call an awesome job! And now look where I am -- here in a studio with my band recording for a CD. But before I go too far, let's venture back and see how I got started.

Chapter Two: My Start

Well, I always loved to sing. It made me understand lots of things in life, and if you just listen to a song, you most likely will find a lesson somewhere, so that's why I like songs so much. Anyway, like I said before, I think this is an awesome job.

So, what else? Well, I guess I just plain old love music and feel compassion for it. Anyway, when I was young, I would stand in front of my room, turn on my CD player and sing my heart out! I felt like I wrote all the songs and I knew them by heart. I felt where they were coming from, so I could connect to songs and their meaning. I would sing so much I would get on people's nerves sometimes. I would find time somewhere in the day to sing—in the shower, in the car, in free time, and anywhere. I started to sing in my head, so I always sang. I didn't realize it, but I was on the road to fame.

Chapter Three: From Shower To Stage

So I progressed over from the shower to my church's stage. It all started when we started to rehearse for our Christmas play. First off, I got to know how to sing correctly, and I learned that warming your voice up can help. Secondly, it gave me the courage to sing on stage and in front of people. Thirdly, I learned I could really sing!

So the day of the play, I was so excited that I got butterflies in my stomach. When I got there, we played trivia and they had breakfast pizza waiting for us! It was awesome, with pizza and orange juice.

Finally the bell rang, and we put on our costumes, and I was the second one in line, so I had to be fast. Finally, it was time to walk up the aisle. We waited for the song, and before you knew it, the song was over.

After the play, I walked out, took off my costume, said great job to everybody, and went to the church's nursery, so I could still hear the sermon, but wouldn't interrupt it.

After the sermon when everybody was getting their coats, they stopped to tell us "great job" but not only did they tell me good job, but that I was a natural singer. Wow! What a compliment!

Next Sunday, the person in charge of our play said that people told her that they wanted me to sing any song I wanted to next Sunday on stage!

Chapter Four: My Big Break

Next Sunday I got all ready and picked a song "Shout to the Lord."

"This is my big day," I kept telling myself. "You can do this. This could be your big break." I had no idea how big. Well, when I got there, I thought, "No way! All this for me?" It was jammed-packed. It also looked as if a guy from a studio would be here. The church was all done up and prettied up.

I was right. A guy from a studio was here! He had heard about a small-town girl with a pretty voice and a strong girl -- me! Wow. Whoa!

I never in my life could guess that that guy from the studio spread the news around, and in two weeks, I got a call from Mike, the guy from the studio. He said that Billy Gilman heard about me and said he'd like to talk to me in person. So in three weeks, from singing at church, I had scheduled two meetings with two of my favorite singers -- Billy Gilman and Kenny Chesney!

In the meeting with Billy, I sang a song from his new C.D. "Heartsongs," and he said I was so good that I was eligible for his starter band.

In the meeting with Kenny Chesney, he asked me to sing a duet with him on Friday. I said yes to both offers, and Thursday I packed for my duet with Kenny. I was so happy! My life was turning for the best.

Friday night I was sitting with a big star and it hit me like a brick. "This is just great," I said. "I love this." And just like that, I started to cry. "Kenny," I said, "this is just too good to be true." The show was great. I wasn't scared at all. It felt natural up there on stage. Kenny hardly had to introduce me. I was a hit.

"Way to go!" Kenny said.

"Thanks," I said.

After the show, we did autographs, and it was so cool, and my friends were there and I was so comfortable.

"Bye Kenny," I said, and I went home.

Billy called an hour after I got home. He said that Sunday we were on at Nashville, North U. S. A.

"OK," I said. "Wait. What time?"

"4:30 for us," he said.

"Okay. Bye."

"Bye."

So, Sunday at 4:30 I was at Nashville North U. S. A., then at 6:00 I opened with the opening band. The band was really nice to me. So for a half an hour, I sang songs. Then it was Billy's turn. Whoa! He was so awesome!

After the show, we also signed autographs.

"See you later, Billy."

"See you tomorrow."

Chapter Five: My Choice

Later in the week, Mike called me and said other people from record companies wanted to talk to me.

"So, tomorrow morning?"

"Yeah," I said. "Sure. Bye."

I wondered what it could be over.

The next morning I got up extra early and got dressed and ate breakfast.

"Time to go," my mom said.

"I am kind of nervous," I said.

"Don't be. We are beside you 100%, and if this isn't what you want, just tell me and we'll go home, call those people, tell them to forget about it."

"Nah," I said. "I'm just nervous because they might ask me about my career choice."

"Well, if they do, you have what it takes to do it."

"Thanks," I said. "Better get out now," I said.

"Good luck. I know you can do this!"

"Bye!"

As I watched my mom drive away, I knew that if they did ask me, it would mean being away from my family a lot, even on holidays.

When I walked in, I said hi to Kimmy, the secretary, without noticing.

"Hello," I said as I walked in.

"Hello," she said professionally. Have a seat. Look, the reason we called you here is..."

Then I knew what they were going to say.

"We wanted to ask you about your career."

I knew it!

"Well," I said, "like what..."

"Like you being Billy Gilman in a girl's body," He said.

"Whoa, " I said. "Hold on. I am ten and that would mean being away from home, even on holidays."

"Yes, but this is a once in a lifetime chance. It's your choice."

My choice.. my choice... my choice.

"Well, I'll think about it," I said. "Excuse me," I said. "May I go home and think about it?" I asked.

"Sure, go ahead. I'll get Kim to call your mom.

"Thanks. Bye."

"See you later, kid," he called back to me.

When my mom got me, I said, "You'll never guess what I got offered."

"Wow, that's great, honey! Congrats!"

"Thanks," I said, unsure only.

"What's wrong?" she asked.

"Well, I would be gone, and I am still a kid, and... it's just so frustrating."

"Well, I thought you knew that."

"Well, I did, but I am just a kid."

"Well, it's your choice, sweetie. Let's go home and eat, and you think about it and we'll go from there, okay?"

"Okay. Deal."

That night, I called my grandma and told her my good news and also what was troubling me.

"Well, sounds like you are kind of scared of leaving home at such a small age," she said. "Now, do what you feel is right and trust your heart."

"Thanks, Grandma. I'll do just that. Love you! Bye."

So that night, I went to bed and asked God for some help. Also, later that night, I got a message from an angel. She said, "Be great. Do what you love to do. Go on."

So next morning, I called Mike and told him he's got himself a deal. So my mom drove me to Mike's studio and I signed some papers and, boom! Here I am!

Chapter Six: Look At My Accomplishments

So I progressed into who I am now: Tours, guests on concerts, on shirts, billboards, magazines, books. You name it, I'm on it. But I didn't get here overnight. Oh, no. It took years, but even though I had to be away from people I loved, it paid off.

My way of looking at a song is different than yours, probably. See, I look at words and meanings and the people who wrote the song and the people that sing it. If I were to listen to a sad song, it probably was not sad if you got the message right. So looking at different things and being strong mentally are not hard to accomplish if you don't look at the hard part, but the good part, what lies ahead, your rewards. So look at things differently and look at my accomplishments.

So, that's how I got started. If we take life and treasure every moment and look beyond what we can see or hear, you understand all questions and riddles in life. It matters that the world knows what you think, know, and feel. Don't let your chance to be heard go by. Say it. Say what you feel. The way you see life is your own color, so be unique. See as no one else has. Trust your heart and do as your instinct tells you. If you don't believe me, just look at my accomplishment. I did as I said to do. So be colorful!!

Marlie S. Bloome
Age: 10

ALL MIXED UP AT PETERSON MIDDLE

Hello, I am Miles Pritcher and I am here to talk about this one time when I switched schools. Okay, it all started when I came home from my old school one day with a big black eye from tripping on the playground. My mom, being the melodramatic she is, pulled me out of Lyle Migre Academy as fast you can blink. And about a week later, I was enrolled at Peterson Middle, and boy, let me tell you I did not know what I was in store for.

My first day I was assigned another student to give me the grand tour of the school. Well I was expecting a normal kid about my height, size, and build. Boy I was wrong, his name was Jones, Spike Jones, he had a blonde Mohawk, sleeveless shirt that read "Ozz-Fest 2002" across the front, more than three times my size, and looked like he could pile-drive me through a wall if he wanted to. He walked up to me.

"Ah, Ah, Ah, Are you M, M, Miles," he asked very frightened.

"Yeah, who are you?"

"Spike Jones."

Then a really nerdy looking kid walked up to me and ran in to my shoulder. His name was Melvin Crocker. He had taped glasses, a pocket protector, and a gelled comb over.

"Watch where you're going punk. You better watch yourself," Melvin boasted.

"Oh, sorry, I didn't mean to," I said.

Then a really nerdy looking girl was walking down the hall and tripped a really beautiful girl.

"Oh, sorry let me help you up, NOT!!!" Barb said, Barb was her name.

"Okay," Barbie said.

I just looked in amazement, wondering how any of this was happening. That day I was confused all day. The jocks getting swirlies and a whole bunch of stuff like that. That night at home I was talking to my mom about my day and she surprisingly did not care. The next day it was the same way. I put up with it for about a month until I took a stand.

"All of us stand up for ourselves and not let these nerds ruin our lives, what do you say!" I screamed.

"YAH!!!!!" yelled everybody.

From that day on the geeks tried but we would not let them find our goat, if you know what I mean. It was peaceful up until the geeks got together and decided that they would come up with the master plan to embarrass us.

"Let's get those dorks like they've never been got before!" Screeched Melvin who was the "cult's" leader. "Okay, listen up," I was outside the window listening to them but the rest I could not make out because Melvin was whispering.

The next day at school I told Brian, who was a big, buff jock and Spike what I had heard. They told everybody else. For about the next couple of weeks we were so neurotic it was not funny. It was kind of nice though, because the geeks were actually leaving us alone, I was guessing it was because they were planning their attack.

Then the day finally came when the first attack happened when Barbie dove into the pool and it was clear gelatin. That night I held a meeting at the Pritcher Residence.

"We need to retaliate against these attacks before another one happens. Poor Barbie here will have to wash her hair for a day straight to get all of the "Jell-O" out. Who knows what will happen next, maybe they will take Brian's clothes while he is showering in the locker room, or put glue in Spike's hair gel bottle. We need to take a stand before this gets out of hand!"

"Hey that rhymes!" Someone from the crowd yelled.

"I'm glad you caught that," I said sarcastically. "Any ideas?"

The whole crowd raised their hands. "You," I told a kid named Billy.

"How about we switch schools?"

I replied "No, that's exactly what they want!"

"How about we act like we don't care so they'll stop for good because we won't get riled up about it?"

"YAH!!" the crowd screamed.

"Miles, quiet down there, I'm trying to sleep up here!" Mom yelled.

"Yes ma'am."

The next day at school we did just that we ignored the "cult", oh by the way that is the name we gave the geeks. They would try as hard as they could to get us mad; one time they even stuffed my locker with cow manure. But all I did was get the janitor to clean it out and went on with my day. When I got home, I felt so accomplished because you could tell that the "cult" was getting mad. This was working for about a month until the geeks finally got smarter than us. They gave Melvin a wedgy up to his head and framed it on us.

"Miles Pritcher will you report to the principal's office, and yes you are in trouble."

I walked down to the office and on the way, I saw Melvin and the other geeks pointing and laughing at me. Then I finally reached the office after seeming as if I was traveling through the Sahara Desert. I walked in and the secretary looked at me as if I was the "unabomber". I walked into the office and principle looked at me. "Have a seat Miles," Principle Riley told me. "It's my understanding that you have given Melvin Smith a wedgy."

"What! That's crazy!"

"Well until you have proven you are innocent, you'll be serving detention every day for a month. Do you understand?"

"Yes sir."

That day at home, I told my mom the story and at first, she did not seem too thrilled, but she knew it was not me.

The next day I asked Principal Riley if we could have a hearing, to see if I was really, truly guilty. He said that would be fine, and it would be held on Thursday at 1:00 p.m.

Thursday finally came and it was time for the hearing. I was questioning Melvin. "Melvin where did this so called wedgy occur?"

"At your house, Pritcher."

"Where in my house."

"In your living room."

"Oh I see, right by the record player."

"Exactly," Melvin said.

"Oh, that would be kind of hard to do considering I don't own a record player."

"Melvin Smith, instead of Miles serving the detentions you will be serving the detentions, for lying." Principle Riley announced.

And from that day on the nerds did not bother us all the through middle school. Plus it just goes to show you, you do not have to retaliate to win. Oh, and I went on to being in the top 5% in my class in high school, and for Melvin, let's just say he's in the lower 5% in his class.

Dillon Shupp
Age: 12

THE THIEF OF SHARK'S EYE

Long ago when the land of Shark's Eye was a large and prosperous land there lived a thief who stole many valuable things. This thief's name was Goodarus. He had stolen many things such as the king's treasure and had kidnapped the princess and held her for ransom. If he traveled he did it by night and if by water on a private ferry.

On this excursion he traveled upon the sacred river to the Shark's Eye Temple. This Eye protected the land from evil when it wasn't disturbed but when the pupil was removed much evil would befall the land. Then the evil would destroy everything in its path. Goodarus planned to steal the Eye and hold it for ransom then retire to a faraway place. Goodarus chuckled, his plan seemed so foolproof.

Soon Goodarus and his ferryman reached the temple and paid the ferryman telling him, "Wait here until I return." With that parting command Goodarus entered the temple. For a long laborious month he looked for the sacred Shark's Eye but he couldn't find it. Then a day before the month's end Goodarus found the Shark's Eye in a secret chamber. The "Eye" was a bright blue with a pupil that was blacker than the darkest night. Inside there was a golden glow that gave off a sinister feeling. Goodarus put the Shark's Eye in his pack and left the temple.

When Goodarus got out of the Temple there was a crowd waiting for him to repossess the Eye. Goodarus was stunned. He wondered who told of his scheme. Then the ferryman told the people to get the Eye back. Goodarus ran for his life. He managed to escape for a week but then the King's Army captured him and brought him to a trial. The Shark's Eye was taken and put back in the temple. Then Goodarus was tried. Goodarus was sentenced to eternity on a distant mountain where a flock of bats would pluck out his heart and eat it. Then his heart would regrow so that he could suffer for all eternity. Goodarus pleaded to have the punishment taken from him but his pleas were denied. The army took him and chained him to the mountain where the bats came every day and dug out his heart and ate it. For five hundred years Goodarus suffered under this cruel unjust punishment. Then on the last year of the five hundred years a hero came. This hero called himself Killarus. Killarus broke the chains and killed the bats with the magic sword that was given to Killarus by his trainer. Goodarus was overjoyed that he was finally freed from his eternity of punishment. Goodarus then sang a song that was so joyous and loud that it shook the snow from the mountaintops. Goodarus then thanked Killarus for freeing him. Goodarus then asked if there was any way he could repay Killarus. Killarus thought about it and said that Goodarus could repay him by being his sidekick for the rest of Killarus's life. Goodarus agreed to these terms happily. For many years the fearsome warriors vanquished evil until their dying day.

Stephen Wade Peterson
Age: 14

I can't believe it. We did it. We won the war. I, John Sickles, defeated them all. I have to be the happiest man alive right at this moment. Here is how the story went and how I got to this amazing level. It all started one day when...

"Wake up maggots you have a long day ahead of you. Actually you are gonna have probably the hardest week of all of your lives. Wake up now, get dressed, and meet me in the galley at six hundred hours. If you aren't there at exactly six hundred I will have a severe punishment awaiting you," said our main lieutenant Jim Bagglet.

There I lay on my back in my bunk when my best friend Bill Aberchuck said, "Come on lazy lets get up, I have a feeling Jim wasn't lying." I am so lucky to have a friend like Bill because once we arrived we looked at all of the guys who didn't make the time, and I am glad that I wasn't late because they didn't get their breakfast (even though the food isn't that great, but what would you expect from a military camp galley).

During breakfast we heard Lieutenant Jim start to talk. Instantly everyone got quiet. He explained what we would do this whole week. "All of you will have to show hard work and commitment. This is why I asked you all to be here at exactly six hundred. Now I know which men," then a voice spoke out that said,

"Or women."

"Yes I am very sorry whomever said that." Said Jim. "Anyway as I was saying, now I know who will need to improve during this camp or they will not stay in the army much longer. Any questions?" There was a deep silence, "ok that's the way I like it. Ok good-bye and now meet in your groups, become friends, do whatever it takes because this may be the man who saves your life. That is all, dismiss and get ready for the training."

Finally, I thought to myself.

"All right let's get to our groups now," said Bill. "Ok, hey by the way what group are you in?"

"I am in group four, you?"

"I'm in group um seven I think."

"Don't think, know," said Bill. This is one of the reasons that I like him so much because he would risk his life for me.

"Alright I'll see you later then," I said.

"Alright I will."

If you think that Jim was joking around about the hardest week ever he wasn't. We had to work together and if one person got one thing wrong we all had to do the same drill over again. It was definitely one of the hardest conditions ever. I was very relieved though to have the comfort of my bed. Actually the beds smell really bad and they also have loose springs that cut you, but that's not the point. Anyway Bill and I lay side-by-side. I saw him holding something that looked kind of like a DVD player. I said, "Hey man what's that?" I happened to be right it was a DVD player. His parents sent it to him as a gift and sent him a DVD of what's going on in Hilton Head

Island, SC. Obviously that's where his parents and his younger brother live. We both just sat back and watched the DVD. It was pretty funny. They sent some of the latest comedy shows. That surely took my mind off of all my bruises and cuts. When it was almost done his parents said that they would send him a DVD almost every week just to show how they are all doing.

"Man I wish that my parents had enough money to be able to do that," I said.

"You never know, my family isn't all that rich either, but still managed to send me this," said Bill. "I'm sure they're all thinking about you John."

"Yeah maybe you're right," I said.

"No man I know they are," Bill said.

"Thanks that helps a lot," I responded.

"Alright let's go to bed now, I don't want to end up like one of those guys that didn't get food," joked Bill.

"Yeah you're right good night man," I managed to say. After all I was really tired and who could blame me for being tired.

The next morning was better. The screaming of our lieutenant didn't wake us. Actually just the slight sound of a trumpet in the distance. Man, I thought to myself, I could do this every morning wake up by the soothing sound of a trumpet not too loud. Actually it improved all of the men. No one was late for breakfast that morning except for about four or five men. I recognized them. Yet I still couldn't remember who they were. Then I remembered, they were the men that were in my group yesterday. They all looked really alert, which is what confuses me the most. How could you be late to breakfast if you are that alert. Anyway back to breakfast, it wasn't that bad today. They cooked something that smelled kind of like pancakes. Almost looked like them too. After breakfast it was a more slow day. We weren't rushed quite as much. That didn't change the exercises though and the drills. It was amazing what we had to do. We had to climb a wall, after we made it down we had to do fifteen nose touching pushups with your hands clapping. Then after that we ran one mile and did twenty nose touch clapping pushups. Then run the mile back to the wall. Twenty more pushups. Climb the wall, and then do an obstacle course with no breaks. Yet it still didn't bother me all that much. For some reason I almost enjoyed it. It seems funny too because I am a fighter pilot so I don't really need to be the fastest runner or the man in the best shape.

After the training ended early for my group one of the lieutenants pulled me aside and asked me to follow him. He took me to this amazing hangar where all of their planes were. He asked me, "You know how to fly right?"

"Um uh yes sir," I said stumbling on my words.

"Alright I want to see your skills."

"Sure," I said. When I got into the hangar I saw Bill there. "Alright Bill, you and I might get to fly side-by-side!"

"Yeah, that would be really cool," he said. We both suited up and picked out a plane for each one of us.

115

"These have to be the most expensive planes ever!" I stammered. Next thing I knew he and I were on the runway side-by-side starting to take off. The speed felt awesome tearing down the runway going really fast. "Man these planes are awesome!" I exclaimed catching a small breath. For some reason though Bill wasn't talking. I looked at his plane and I seriously thought that it was someone else. He had so much concentration. "I guess I shouldn't fool around." We both made it successfully off of the ground and maneuvered in and out between each other. It had to be the greatest feeling in the world.

When we landed the lieutenant came our way and said, "Boys you were great. I think we are planning a war over the Pacific Ocean and we are in need of two more fighters. How would you two like to join?" We were both speechless.

I finally managed to say, "Yes sir it would be an honor."

"Good we need you boys, now go and get some sleep and I will tell you two your mission. Just a warning though we might even go into war tomorrow so we need you guys ready."

"Yes sir," we said at the same time.

That night we got a new DVD from Bill's parents. It was very sad. It turned out that his little brother died. A drunk driver hit him. It was a tragic death. It really made Bill sad. I was really confused though because he got straight to sleep. I just don't know.

The next day war was declared, and we were sent to the hangar first thing in the morning to run some quick patterns really fast so we would be ready. I went up to Bill and said, "Are you all right?"

He responded, " I'm not so sure. This fight is definitely for him though . I don't care if I die I just want to fight for the sake of my little brother." We all suited up. I was really nervous. Yet very determined to fight and win this war. The plan was to fly overhead then drop a surprise attack on them early so we could get a fast lead. Everyone got into their own plane, put on the headphones, and we all introduced each other. Bill Aberchuck; first plane. Kenny Roberts; second plane. Then came my turn. John Sickles; third plane. Rick James; fourth plane. That was our line up. After introduction it was time for take off. We soared into the sky almost as fast as lightning. We flew for a small distance before we spotted a ship.

"All right," said Kenny, "Who's going to go first?"

At the same time Bill and I said, "I'll go."

"Alright you two go ahead and Rick and I will back you two up. The other planes are flying really close behind so you get into trouble back out until you think you're ready again." We did a nosedive straight down until we were out of the clouds then Bill and I fired the first shot. BOOM. A direct hit right on their deck. A few more shots and that boat was down. I was flying really close to Kenny when I saw one of the enemies planes take off. Right as it made it off of the runway I shot it down.

"Watch out," said Rick. Right as I looked back I saw a big explosion. All of the sudden I hear a voice scream, "I'm Rick James. No one hits my partner."

"Thanks Rick I owe you one," I said in relief. The war lasted for a long time and I realized that I was untouchable.

Everything was going great until I heard Bill scream, "I'm hit. I'm falling straight down. I know what I'll do, I will crash into one of their ships and blow it up." Right then I noticed that the plane was heading straight for the ground.

"No, don't do it Bill."

"I have to. It's for our country." After he said that, I heard a funny noise that sounded like when you hit your hand on the end of a pole how it has that pop noise. All I saw after that was the biggest explosion I have ever seen.

"No," I screamed. "No it can't be." Right then and there I grew furious. Nothing could stand in my way. I am going to destroy everything. John blew up twenty-four planes and sank three ships after what happened to Bill. The rest of the crew returned home safely after the war.

"When I landed," said John; "everyone was waiting and cheering for us. I wasn't very happy though. My best friend died for his country, and I had no chance at stopping him. There was a big ceremony celebrating our win. It did make me happy though when I received the Medal of Honor for destroying the most planes and for showing so much bravery.

Later that night when we were all in our cabins we all heard a funny noise. It sounded like a whistle. It almost sounded like Bill whistling. I could tell it was getting closer. Then all of a sudden Bill enters the cabin completely wet. "Bill! I thought you died. You should have seen me. I sank three ships and shot twenty-four planes. It was awesome. Why did you scare us all like that?"

"Didn't you hear that popping noise? That was me using the ejection seat. I remembered it in time." explained Bill. "I landed safely in the water and swam home. I am so lucky we had those swimming lesson training camps."

"Ha, now is not a time to joke around Bill. We all thought you were dead," I stammered.

"Nope. I guess I'm not dead," said Bill.

"No you're not dead," I thought, "No you aren't."

Jeff Simpson

The two guys sitting behind Tess kept shooting her mean looks whenever she turned around. Obviously they didn't want her in on their conversation. The men both wore sunglasses and leather jackets looking like spies from a movie. Skye's voice dragged her back to the present.

"So, Tess, are you going to the mall with us?" she questioned her. Tessa's answer was interrupted by the waitress bringing their food.

"Do you need anything else?" she asked as her striking red hair bounced around on her shoulders. She flashed a smile that showed all her glittering white teeth.

Sydney looked around at each of us and said, "Nah, I think we're good," as she let her dark brown hair out of its pony tail. The waitress nodded and walked to the table behind us and started an earnest conversation with the two men. Something about her she didn't like, but Tess shook it off.

"So are you?" Skye asked as she stared at her inquisitively.

"Am I what?"

"Going to the mall with us Sunday?" she asked anxiously.

"I guess," she answered shrugging her shoulders.

"Thank you! Getting a straight answer out of you is like trying to keep my little sister out of my room. Impossible," Skye explained as she heaved a big sigh of exasperation.

***

A little while later as we started walking out Tess felt the hairs on the back of her neck stand on end. She chanced a quick look over her shoulder.

A few booths back an old couple sat chatting away. A few tables behind them a man, probably in his forties, sat reading a newspaper.

"Oops! I forgot my purse!" yelped Mandy as she ran back to our booth. Tess turned around. There, behind her, were the same two guys she had been staring at earlier. With them was their waitress. They sat there staring at her.

She quickly ran out the door.

***

"Ring! Ring! Ring!" Kathryn picked up the phone in her country-style kitchen.

"Hello. Moresby residence, may I ask who's calling?" she answered politely.

"Tess has been kidnapped!"

"WHAT?"

"Yes, but don't say anything to the police about kidnapping because they just think she ran away. But she didn't! I know my own daughter better than that!" Liz said stressfully.

"Hang on Liz: I'll be over in a tick." In one swift motion she grabbed her keys, unplugged the toaster, and locked the door.

***

Grandma Kat drove up to her daughter's ranch home. The door was open. She walked inside.

Sitting on the sofa was Mrs. Johanson, (Liz), with big, red, watery eyes. Next to her stood a police officer, holding a small notepad, with bored written all over his features.

"Ma'am, really, it's nothing to worry about. This happens all the time with teenagers. You did say you had a fight before she left to go meet up with her friends," he asked her pointedly.

Liz sniffled, "Yes, we did. But it was only about her not going to her father's house so early. We're divorced, and she wanted to leave a day early but I wouldn't let her. She would never run away!" she added determinedly.

"Just let us do our job," he spoke softly.

"Okay , thank you, give us a call if you find her," Liz requested as she wrote down her phone number. Grandma Kat saw the gleam in her daughter's eye and knew this wouldn't be the end.

As soon as the officer left, Liz burst out, infuriated, "She did not run away! If one person tries to convince me of that I will scream!" Suddenly realization hit her. "Grandma Kat! You're a retired investigative reporter! Why didn't I see it before! You can find her! This is what I used to do for a living! Ohh, please! Find her!" she begged.

"Actually, uhh, that's not what I did for a living." She was incredulous. "My job was to figure out stuff like when a certain actor stops dating a model." Kat said doubtfully. But when she saw the look on her daughter's face she gave in. "Fine," they both sat down on the couch. Where was Tessa when you last saw her?" she asked, notebook in hand.

"Friday night. She was with Skye, Mandy, and Sydney. I'll give you their addresses if you like, but they'll probably be at Whataburger. It's where they normally hang out."

A couple of minutes later Kat was driving down the road.

***

"Don't struggle or I'll shoot." The man leveled a gun at Tess' head. It was the men from the restaurant. She had no trouble believing him.

Another guy stepped up behind her, and tied Tess' hands against her back. She was in the back parking lot of Whataburger.

"Now, get into the car," he pointed towards a white van that had Ron's Roofing painted on the side as soon as they got close enough he opened the door, shoved her inside, and locked it.

It took Tess only a few seconds for her eyes to adjust to the dim lighting. She looked around. There were about fifty boxes of shingles stacked around her. Tess stood up, which was extremely difficult having her hands tied behind her back.

She slowly walked around the van. Near the back, was a small built-in shelf, which she normally wouldn't have noticed. Sitting on it was a long, red toolbox. She turned around and grabbed for it. After five minutes she managed to drag it onto the floor. Tess pushed the box open and looked inside. On top there was a saw-type thing. She turned around, visualized where it was, groped for it, cutting her finger in the process. As carefully as possible, she sliced and sawed through the bindings.

Finally free, Tess vigorously rubbed the feeling back into her arms. She knew the men had walked away because she couldn't hear them talking anymore.

Half-heartedly she tried the door. Of course, as she expected, it was locked. Just noticing her purse, she shrugged it off and dumped out the contents. Some lip gloss, money and her tape recorder. Being on the school newspaper staff she needed a way to remember her ideas.

Tess turned it on, expecting to hear her voice come billowing out. But it wasn't her voice. It was the conversation she had had at the restaurant with her friends. She had probably left it on from her last recording. As she listened she could faintly hear the sound of men's voices in the background. Turning the volume up all the way, the conversation was as clear as day.

After a few minutes she shut if off with a gasp. She couldn't believe it. That's why the men had kidnapped her. They thought she had heard them talking! They had been conversing about smuggling elephant ivory across the border from Kenya, Africa. Definitely illegal. She had to get out of here and catch the men before they could leave the country! Those poor elephants! Pounding and shouting, she slammed her fists into the side of the van.

***

Grandma Kat turned into the parking lot of Whataburger. The place was packed with teens. All the parking spots were taken. So she drove around towards the back. It too, was really crowded. There was an open slot sitting next to a white van that had Ron's Roofing on the side. She slid her car into the space and got out. Right away she heard thumping and yelling coming from the back of the van. Wondering what was going on, Kat reached for the handle, but the faint word, "Help", kicked her into gear. She turned the knob quickly, knowing it was locked, and reached into her purse for a hairpin. Finding one, Kat bent it straight and stuck it in the lock, twisting and turning. Finally she heard a small click.

***

Tess was huddled in the corner, behind some boxes, thinking the men had come back for her. She grabbed for the saw-type thing and held it in her hands like a bat ready to whack anyone who came through the door.

A second later it opened. Tess had to stop in mid-swing to keep from hitting her would-be attacker. She recognized the person.

"Grandma Kat!" Tess ran over and hugged the woman..

"Oh, Tess!" Kat yelled back.

"What happened to you?"

"No time to explain. We have to get this to the police, ASAP!" she said reaching into her purse and handing her the recorder.

On the way, Tess told her grandma everything she had heard on the tape.

Reaching for the door to the police station Kat said, "Well, aren't you just the picture of an investigative reporter, nothing like me though," she joked pointing to herself.

"Actually Gran, I've been thinking more about focusing on the investigation part. You know, detective work."

"Oh."

"You see, I'd like to picture myself as Sherlock Holmes, rather than you. Besides, I think he sounds cute."

"Cute," Kat said flatly.

"Yep, very cute."

"So, you'd rather be cute and clueless like Sherlock what's his face, than intelligent and quick thinking like me," she said doubtfully.

Tess walked through the door, turning back she replied, "He is not clueless. Oh, and you left out old on your list, Gran."

Huffing after Tess, Kat mumbled, "I'll give you old."

Lauren E. Halbert
Age: 12

LIL HOMIE'S SPRING BREAK

You are probably wondering what this story is about. I mean what kind of story is called Lil Homie's spring break, right. Well let me tell you, first I am Lil Homie and you can guess this story is about me. Let me describe myself to you. I am white and furry; I have a pink nose, pink eyes and a tail. Oh, I am a mouse too. Now you are thinking eww how gross a mouse; well my owner thinks I am cute. Her name is Emi. She is about five feet eight inches with dirty blond hair, hazel eyes and kind of a punk.

I live with Emi at school in a dorm room; well I live in a cage, of course I don't stay there all the time. I also have a little ball I can run around in it. Emi's room is big at least to me. She also has another roommate named Mel.

People think just because mice are small they are not smart. Well guess what they are wrong. I am very smart and I can figure out things. The day Emi and Mel started to pack I knew something was going to happen. I just didn't know what. Emi and Mel were laughing, talking and listening to music. They were also pulling clothes out and throwing them into a bag. Then that is when I heard it, Mel asked Emi "What are you going to do with Lil Homie when you're gone?"

"I don't know," said Emi. That's when I got scared. Who is going to feed me? Give me water? Play with me? I was freaking out.

"Are you going to take him on the airplane? Will they let that happen?"

"I don't know," said Emi. "I guess I will have to call."

She left the room, and I was hoping the airlines would say yes. However, what if they said no? Please say yes. About two minutes later Emi came back, "The airlines said I could."

I was so happy to know that I was going to go home with Emi. Then that night it crossed my mind I had no idea what an airport was, was it scary? Will they hurt me at the airport? What are they going to do with me? I didn't sleep at all that night. The next morning Emi got up early and woke me up. She took me out of my cage and put me in my ball. She then started cleaning out my cage. When she was done, I was put back in. Later she came back, grabbed her bag, then put me in a new cage that was smaller with a little screen window. It was nice and comfortable so I decided to go back to sleep.

I slept for an hour but then I was woken up by strange people talking. Emi then told me I was OK and not to worry. Emi started to walk, I heard Emi telling a strange man that she had a live animal. Duh I was alive. Did they think I was dead? Then a guy's voice asked her to step aside, my cage opened and a strange person looked in. I got scared and ran and hid in the corner. Then Emi got up and walked outside. I looked out and saw this big metal bird I got scared. Emi then got on the metal bird. She sat down in a seat and put me on her lap. I was really scared. A few minutes later another strange voice told Emi I had to go under the seat, so she told me I would be ok and put my cage under a dark tiny space. Then I heard the big roaring noise and I felt a pain in my ears. There was a strange feeling in the pit of my stomach making me wish I hadn't eaten my breakfast. It was like that for an hour. Then there was a big thump and I bounced around in my cage. Thankfully, Emi picked me up and we got off the scary metal bird.

We walked into another big building with more people than the last one. I heard strange people talking all around me. I didn't know what to do. I was starving. It was really bad because I could smell the food and my mouth started to water. Emi went up to a counter and asked for some bizarre things called fries and a cheeseburger. She then sat down and put something in my cage, and said it was a fry. I tasted it, kinda soft and salty, and it filled my stomach quickly so I felt better.

After we ate Emi got up, I knew Emi wouldn't make me go on another metal bird. It was bad enough once but to do it again I don't think so. That's when I realized Emi was sliding into another dark space and the strange feeling came back. I realized I was on another metal bird. It seemed like it lasted forever but when there was another thump and I felt better. Emi walked to another huge building. Emi and I sat for about thirty minutes. I fell asleep. I woke up when Emi picked up my cage and I had another strange feeling in my stomach as if I was on another metal bird. Emi opened the cage and put my water bowl in. I was happy I was really thirsty. I drank a lot and felt a lot better. A few minutes later, there was a big bump. Emi then told me it was all over for today. Emi walked for a few minutes through some doors and there was a man there to meet her. He was a tall guy who turned out to be Emi's dad.

Emi said "Hi! How are you doing?"

Emi's dad said, "Good is that your pet mouse?"

Emi replied, "Yes isn't he cute?"

Her dad looked at me and said, "He's very interesting Killer will be happy to see him."

We headed out to Emi's dad's car. All this time I was wondering who this Killer dude was.

The car ride to Emi's other house was long. When we got there, I was happy to get out of the car. I think I was getting car sick, that fry was not feeling so good. We went inside and this woman came up to Emi and gave her a hug. "Good to see you," she said.

It turned out to be her mom. She looked at me and said I was also interesting and Killer should enjoy me. I kept thinking who is this person and hopefully this Killer person is nice. Just then, her brother came and picked me up out of my cage he looked at me for a little bit then put me back in my cage. He then said, "I am going to go get Killer." I was excited I finally get to meet this Killer dude.

A few minutes later Emi's brother came back with a cat. What was he doing with a cat? Cats eat mice like me. I thought he was going to get the dude named Killer. Why did he bring a cat? I surely thought my life was over. The cat came to my cage and started to bat at the screen window. Emi said "Killer stop batting at the cage!"

I was confused; this monster was Killer. Killer stopped batting at the cage. How could Emi forget to mention Killer was a cat? Emi then said she was tired and was going to bed, so she picked me up and took me down to her room. Killer followed her she put me up and told me it would be OK. She then went to bed with Killer at her feet. I sat there for a bit thinking it might be a good time and Killer and I will get along as I drifted off to sleep.

Emily McCollom
Age: 18

123

FAITH LIKE A CHAMPION

Many years ago, before you and I were born, Jeremiah ran from his mailbox towards his home.

When Jeremiah went to the mailbox to get the mail he discovered it was finally here. "Thanks Mom!" he yelled as he ran into the house with his new Gene Autry comic book. He had been waiting for that book for what seemed like forever.

"You're welcome," his mom said as she took the other mail from him. Jeremiah couldn't wait to see if Gene Autry captured the bad guys and if so how he would do it. Jeremiah read the comic book in no time flat and discovered that Gene Autry saved the day again. He then began to read it once more because it was so intriguing. Later, over the weekend Jeremiah's parents took him, his brothers, and sister to see a Gene Autry movie at the theater in town. This was a huge event because Jeremiah and his family lived on a farm far away from town. He thought the movie was great!

"Thanks Mom and Dad, I really enjoyed it!" He told them on the way home from town.

"Yes, thank you," chimed in his younger brothers and sister.

"You're welcome," said their parents.

Even though the whole family enjoyed it no one liked it as much as Jeremiah. He especially liked the end. Not only did Gene Autry capture the criminals but he did an awesome trick. Gene Autry made his horse, Champion, stand on its back legs as he waved good-bye with his cowboy hat.

Sometime later, for Jeremiah's eleventh birthday he received a horse. The horse he received looked just like Gene Autry's horse; it had a light brown body and a white stripe down its nose. Jeremiah loved the horse very much and he named her Champ after Champion, Gene Autry's horse. Jeremiah thought, "I have a horse like Gene Autry now all I need to do is get a white hat like his. If I do that then I'll look just like him." Every day after school and after he did all his chores, Jeremiah took Champ to an enclosed pasture on his father's farm. There he would ride Champ around. One day after school Jeremiah got an idea. He was going to take his black cowboy hat and spray paint it white to look like Gene Autry's. Jeremiah was thrilled when he had finished painting the hat and it was dry. Now he was even more like his hero.

One day as Jeremiah was riding Champ he decided to try the trick he had seen in the movie. As he got Champ to stand on her back feet he took off his hat and began to wave it. That's when things went wrong; they lost their balance. The next thing Jeremiah knew he was on the ground with the horse in his lap. The horse was fine, she got right back up and started to look for a place to graze. Unfortunately Jeremiah could not move or feel his legs. All Jeremiah could do was lie there and scream for help in hopes that someone could hear him. For a while when no one was coming he began to lose hope so much that he was almost to the point of tears. Jeremiah closed his eyes and said. "Lord, please let someone hear me." When he opened his eyes he saw his mom running toward him with a panic stricken face. "Man, prayers really do work!" he thought.

When she reached him she frantically asked, "Are you okay? What happened?"

"Well, I was trying to do the cool trick Gene Autry did in the movie where he made his horse stand on its back legs as he took off his hat and waved good-bye. I got Champ to stand on her back feet but as I took off my hat we lost our balance and fell over backward. Champ landed in my lap and now I can't feel my legs," Jeremiah told her.

"Oh dear. I'll try and move you to the house." She slowly began dragging Jeremiah towards the house. This was very difficult because Jeremiah was not a small eleven-year-old. When they finally reached the house Jeremiah's mom got a quilt and laid it on the floor of the screened-in porch. She then put Jeremiah on it and said, "We'll wait until your dad gets home and see what he says to do. In the meantime you better rest. I'll go get you some lemonade." When his mom came back she said, "I guess you won't try that trick again will you?"

"No I won't," said Jeremiah as he sipped the cold lemonade. He was grateful that his mom wasn't mad at him, but how was his dad going to take it.

When Jeremiah's dad arrived home from working in the fields Jeremiah's mom told him what had happened. Jeremiah was relieved that he didn't have to tell his dad. His dad walked onto the porch and said, "If you can't walk by morning we'll take you to the doctor in town." The family lived far from town and they didn't want to go to town if it was unnecessary. He went on, "Your brothers can do the rest of your chores for tonight but don't ever try to do that trick again you could have been seriously hurt."

"Okay Dad," Jeremiah responded. He was glad he didn't have to do his chores that night.

About an hour or so after Jeremiah's dad had arrived home Jeremiah began to have feeling in his legs again. He decided he would try to get up and walk. Jeremiah slowly got off of the floor. He was so excited; he could stand up! "I can do this," he thought to himself. Then he slowly but surely picked up his right leg, put it in front of the other and began to walk. Everyone was thrilled when they saw Jeremiah walking around. They danced and sang praises to God.

"Thank You, Lord!" his mom said when she saw Jeremiah.

"Amen to that!" agreed his father. God had surely worked a miracle for Jeremiah!

Jeremiah was saddle sore for a month or so after that, but he was able to walk! Although Jeremiah rode his horse, Champ, many times after that he never tried the Gene Autry trick again. He decided he would leave that to the professionals.

Kate Bocklage
Age: 13

Hearing the hum of the boat engine was soothing in the hot sticky July month. "John, did you pack enough soda?"

"Yep", said John.

"Enough for three days", I asked.

"I said yes now stop worrying and just relax", replied John. "I need to find that fishing spot that Jerry was talking about", said John.

I decided to go inside our houseboat and watch TV when I heard a loud boom, I went outside and saw John lying unconscious on the deck, and then I saw the rushing water pouring in with rage. My mind was spinning. I knew that I had to get us to safety. Finally I thought of life jackets. As I was buckling the life jacket on John, a wave of water came in and swept it out of my hand, so I had to grab onto John's life jacket. I saw a point land to my far east. I knew that I was done for when I saw a hammerhead shark and jellyfish about fifteen feet below me. The only instinct that I could think of was to stay still no matter what. As the jellyfish grew nearer the shark submerged into the navy blue ocean.

As it grew darker my body was limp and John was still not awake. All that I have to do is get to that point of land and then worry about food and water. The point of land looked about five miles away. I guess that we drifted a mile or two. "Keep awake, keep awake, keep awake," I kept telling myself. If we drift away from the land then we should just consider ourselves dead.

In the morning as I was floating there just looking at the beautiful horizon when my foot sank into some sand. All of my attention was directed toward my thirst and hunger. It took me a while to realize that I touched land. When I became fully alert to what had happened I was bewildered. Maybe we have a chance just maybe, I thought. But John had still not woken up. I was terrified for him, but first I must get food and water for both of us. Our island was rocky and wooded so it shouldn't be hard to find coconuts and then I might find a puddle or a stream for some fresh water. I hit the jackpot with a stream but I had no luck with food.

When I walked back to where I had left John he was sitting up wide-eyed, I explained to him what happened and he sat there dumbfounded.

"How long have I been out?" asked John.

"About two and a half to three days." I replied.

"How did we make it?" asked John.

"Well it's a long story."

As he lay spellbound I left to go and get some leaves off of a low tree branch. When I came back John asked "Are we all alone on this island?"

"Yes." I said, "but I can check again." I said.

"No, there is no point of circling the island again." said John.

We ate our leaves and water in silence; I went down to the beach to look for a sharp rock. I thought that we would need some kind of weapon in case of animals. We decided to stay on high land by the gurgling stream. "How will we ever get off or be found?" John asked in a serious tone.

"I have no idea, but if we are not found by tomorrow, we have to build a shelter in case of storms."

As the silence of night droned on I clutched the rock in my hand like a child holding his teddy bear at night.

I awoke in the morning limp and numb as if I were in a dream. John was already up he was carrying tall reeds and timbers. When I was wide awake I asked "What are you doing?"

He replied, "I am building a shelter. Audrey can you weave these reeds into a mat for our doorway?"

I said "Yes." My stomach felt like knives were cutting my flesh into pieces so I left to go and get some leaves to eat. I still had my rock but no weapon. To my surprise, I found some crabs roaming along the beach I gripped the rock and smashed it against the crab it flinched, but then it was dead I thought. When I finally reached the stream John had our shelter done. I was glad because the sun was setting.

That night John and I ate the crab meat raw but it was better than nothing. "How will we ever survive? We have no food, we will never make it." John said.

"Yes we will, if we keep trying, we will survive," I said, "But we need a good night sleep."

When I woke up in the morning I heard drumming on our roof, it was the rain. The mosquitoes were horrible. But with all of my time on my hands I figured out where to carry my water, in the crab shell. John was up by this time. The winds were increasing but we had much bigger problems to worry about: we needed fire. But as the winds grew furious I began to worry the next thing I knew fifteen-foot waves were crashing about our roof. Our roof was being torn away with fury, and all that we could do was to grasp onto something. John and I were holding onto a tree but the wind and water seemed to be getting enraged. I could not hold on any more, the wind took me away. I landed on a ridge of flat rocks, I looked up and saw what was coming. I dragged myself to some brush, but nothing could protect me from that last wave that could end everything. The wave swept me into some corral reef. I lay there gasping for breath with blood gushing from my back to my legs. Struggling for a breath of air, another treacherous wave came and took me back to the bay.

I blacked out for an hour or so I am guessing, but whenever I woke up I had sand in my mouth and my body was stinging. I looked at my arm it lay there like a limp flower. I tried to drag myself to the shelter, but I couldn't. After a couple of hours I managed to get to the stream to wash out my cuts and to drink. I couldn't see John anywhere. I was trembling with fear when I saw drops of blood around the bush. I scooted over there and found his bruised and bloody body. I was hysterical why couldn't I die instead of him? But then his arm flinched and his eyes were bleeding. I was so thankful that he was alive. After John washed up his cuts, we had some leaves to eat. I was now more determined than ever to get off this island.

We took a day to rest. I woke up early the next morning to make a fire. I gathered some dry shrubs and my sharp rock and some wood. Next I started striking the rock against the wood my first strike to the log was not hard enough but the next time it was perfect and a beautiful stream of sparks showered my shrubs and it was an amazing sight. I screamed to John, he came limping and his sad eyes were now filled with hope. "What if we are spotted by a plane?" asked John.

"That would be a miracle." I said.

He was searching for a new spot to rebuild the shelter he found a perfect spot and it was done by nightfall. In the morning, while I was feeding my fire, I heard a loud buzzing noise. I looked up and saw huge red and white blinking lights I realized that it was a helicopter. I ignited a stick with fire and started waving it around wildly and screaming to John to come over there. The helicopter started hovering over my island and then dropped slowly. My heart was pounding so hard I thought that I was having a heart attack. Three men got out of the helicopter and rushed out towards John and I. Everything was such a blur that I might have passed out. As I was sitting in the helicopter, I realized that we were finally going back to the lives that we left behind.

Andrea Boerding
Age: 12

THE MISSING HORSES

There were two girls named Sydney and Rose. They loved dogs, horses and cats. Sydney had three dogs and one horse. Sydney had to share all her animals but she did get her own horse named Pepper. She named her Pepper because she was reddish brown. Rose had one cat, two dogs and one horse. She got to choose her cat and her horse. She named her horse Spirit because she was all white.

One day, Rose's horse was gone. She told Sydney about her horse. Then Sydney told Rose that her horse was missing too. Rose and Sydney had brothers and sisters who wanted horses. Their friends wanted horses too.

"Where would they put the horses?" asked Sydney.

Rose said, "There was a man who walked down our trail to see our horses. Maybe, he has a barn and he took the horses."

"I don't think so," said Sydney. "There was that one girl and that one boy who kept asking if they could ride our horses."

"Why do you think they did it?" asked Rose.

"Because they have a barn and they kept asking to ride the horses."

Rose asked, "How could someone break in the barn? There were locks on the barn."

"Only our brothers and sisters know where the key is," said Sydney. "We need to go see our suspects."

"Okay!" said Rose.

Sydney and Rose went to the boy's and girl's house. They told them to go look in their barn. The horses were not there. Rose asked them if they knew of any other barns in the area. They said no.

The next day, they went to the man's house. He said that he liked to look at horses but not to touch them.

"Can we check your barn?" Sydney asked.

"Okay" said the man. Sydney and Rose found nothing in the barn.

"What are we going to do?" asked Rose.

Sydney said, "I don't know."

Rose went home and found a note in her room. The note said that the horses are in Shadow River Peak Field. The horses are in a barn. So Rose called Sydney and told her where the horses were. Rose and Sydney went to the barn and they found their horses safe and sound.

Sydney figured out that it was her sister who had taken the horses. She remembered seeing her sister writing a note. Sydney found out that when her sister went over to Rose's house, she put the note in Rose's room.

Sydney and Rose took their horses home. They both got another horse.

Kendyl Blanke
Age: 9

VANISHED INTO THIN AIR

Nancy Walker was in the eighth grade at Newman Junior High School. Nancy was an amazing athlete and played select soccer, basketball, baseball, and volleyball. Her best friend was Libby Richardson. Libby wasn't a big athlete and she was plump and had a bunch of pimples. Much of the time the boys would call her "Swamp Monster". After a while Libby got used to the names and she would just call the boys "big fat slobs" right back. Nancy thought of Libby as the coolest person in the world because she went to all of Nancy's practices and was very supportive of her.

On Friday, Nancy and Libby were walking to school as usual and talking about how Matt Spencer was a jerk for taping a sign to Libby's back which said "Kick me I'm a swamp monster." Suddenly, a white Suburban SUV sped by and got mud all over the two girls. When Libby and Nancy arrived at school Matt Spencer and a few other boys shouted, "Hey look, Nancy must have fallen into a swamp and brought out a monster named Libby!" The whole school was cracking up laughing.

Nancy couldn't take it any longer. She punched Matt Spencer in the lip and it burst open. Right then and there Nancy was glad her father had taught her boxing. Too bad she got detention for her good deed.

Libby said, "I'll wait for you after school Nancy. Thanks for sticking up for me."

"No problem Libs. I have always hated that brat. It felt really good socking him," said Nancy. The two girls laughed.

"It would even be funnier if you didn't get a detention, but it will only take an hour and I will see you when you are finished," said Libby.

When Nancy's session was over she went outside to find Libby, but Libby wasn't there. She called Libby's parents with her cell phone, but Libby wasn't there. Mr. and Mrs. Richardson called the police to start looking for their daughter.

Nancy ran home afraid that she would be the next to be kidnapped. She was welcomed by a police officer. "I am Officer Andy. I want you to answer a few questions, okay?"

"Okay," answered Nancy.

"Was Libby upset about something today?" he asked.

"I can't think of anything except the fact that when we were walking to school a white car sped up in a huge mud puddle and we got splashed so people were making fun of us," said Nancy.

"That's it. Case closed. She ran away. We will have a search team look for her," said Officer Andy.

"Officer, I know that Libby would never even think about running away!" exclaimed Nancy. Officer Andy ignored Nancy and said good night and then went out the door. Nancy knew then that she would have to solve this case by herself.

The next day was a Saturday and Officer Andy came back. The search team had found Libby's glasses in the Cobblestone River. He said that Libby had obviously drowned. Nancy knew that could not have happened because Libby was too mad to drown. Nancy told her parents that she was going to go shopping, but instead she went to the Cobblestone River where she found a note in a tree that said:

"Robert meet me at the Collinson Hotel at 7 p.m. sharp. My room is 278, their best suite. Jacob Peterson.
P.S. Meet me on the 2nd of March. I have Libby Richardson with me."

Nancy was astonished. March 2nd was tonight! Nancy knew that she couldn't do this alone anymore. She needed some help so she decided to call Erin, her second best friend. Erin said she would arrive at the hotel at about six p.m. so that they would have time to find a place to hide and set up cameras.

Nancy had a huge knot in her stomach all day, but she still went to the Collinson Hotel. The two girls met. Erin brought a huge ladder that you could fold in case of a fire. "Jacob isn't here yet," said Erin. "At least I don't think he is. I bet we can get through the window of his room."

"No one would be so stupid as to leave their window unlocked when they are gone," said Nancy just as Erin climbed up the ladder, opened the window, and jumped right into room 278. Then Nancy heard a blood-curdling scream! It was Erin! Nancy saw a man grab Erin and force her into a closet and lock her in. Nancy knew she had to run, but before she could make any other movements a tall, powerful, and strong man grabbed her and put a handkerchief with a certain formula right in front of her nose. Nancy tried hard not to breathe, but it was too difficult. She breathed in the formula and fell into a deep sleep.

When Nancy woke up she was not home and she did not see Erin or Libby. She was in a cabinet. Nancy's hands and feet were tied and there was a bandana stuffed into her mouth. Nancy rubbed her mouth against her arm and to her surprise the bandana came off. In the cabinet there was a knife that Nancy leaned against to cut the ropes on her hands and feet. She was free! Now all she had to do was to find Libby and Erin.

When Nancy looked at the clock she saw that it was four a.m. and she was in the Collinson Hotel. She looked all over the hotel and finally found Erin in a closet under a bunch of clutter, and Libby in an empty trash bag in a trash can. It was hard to tell that it was Libby because her hair had been dyed and cut short, and there were scars all over her body. The three girls hugged.

"What happened to you?" asked Nancy.

"Why do you have so many bruises and scars?" asked Erin.

"I was sitting on a bench outside of school waiting for Nancy to leave detention when suddenly a man grabbed me!" exclaimed Libby. "He knew that my family is rich so he has left them a few messages saying that he would only give me back if they paid him a certain amount of money. When he found out that a search team was looking for me he dyed and cut my hair. I tried running away, so he beat me and didn't feed me for a day. I think the man's name is Jacob. He has a friend named Robert who also beat me and hid me in different places that were very uncomfortable."

"Great story, but I think we should get out of here now!" Erin said harshly.

The girls opened the door to get out and there was Jacob. They turned around to run, but there was Robert who grabbed Nancy and Erin, while Jacob grabbed Libby. Robert gave the three girls a good beating and threw them in a shed outside of the hotel and locked the door. The three girls were crying.

"We will starve to death if we don't get out of here," said Erin.

"Are there any shovels in here?" asked Nancy.

"There are four shovels in here," answered Libby, "and if we start digging we can make a little tunnel for us to squeeze through. Get the shovels and let's get going!"

The girls worked for four straight hours without a break and finally they were able to squeeze through the tunnel to the outside. "Run! Jacob and Robert are out here and they see us!" yelled Erin. The two men chased the girls, but they couldn't catch them before the girls reached the hotel lobby where there was a security guard. The girls called the police while the two criminals tried to escape on foot. They were not fast enough. Before they could get away the police had surrounded the area and arrested them. Officer Andy said, "You're under arrest for kidnapping these three young ladies and for child abuse. You will spend the next fifteen years in jail." Robert and Jacob were led away in handcuffs.

The girls' family members rushed into the hotel and hugged and kissed all three girls like they had not seen them for years. Everyone was crying tears of joy and Nancy, Libby, and Erin knew then that they would be best friends forever after this adventure!

Monica Macheca
Age: 10

THE GHOST HOUSE

It was a cold day in the small town of Novinger, MO. Mary Jo had just moved into a house off of west Missouri Street. She had just moved there from Kirksville and had heard that teachers there were so mean that some kids had never seen the sixth grade and were seventeen. But when she had heard that there were some really cute boys there, she said that she would stay.

When Mary Jo got into her room, she thought it was kind of strange because it was painted black and had red names all over it.

On Mary Jo's first day of school, she met a guy named Brian and then she knew she was going to like it there. But when people started to tell her that the house she lived in was haunted, she started to get scared.

Later that night when Mary Jo was sleeping, she heard something and went to the living room, and saw a ghost. She screamed so loud that she thought that the whole world could hear her, and then the ghost screamed, too. Mary Jo asked if the ghost was OK. The ghost said, "I'm so sorry, I did not mean to scare you. I thought you were my mom and dad."

Mary Jo did not know what to say. Then she asked what she meant when the ghost answered. Her mom and dad had killed her and that they hid her body under the house. They said that they were going to come back and get her body so she had been hiding it every night just in case they did really come and get it. She hoped that some day someone would be able to tell the police, and that they would get put in jail. That day had come. So the next day, Mary Jo told the police and the ghost was able to rest in peace. Mary Jo hoped that that would never happen to her again. The red names were the ghost's friend's names that had died also, and whenever one would die, they would add their names.

Samantha Elms
Age: 12

WHY ME?

My name is Camden Yager; I was ten years old when the Nazis started to invade Denmark. It was 1940, at that time I lived on a small farm. Although my family was not rich, neither were we poor. Our small farm met all our needs. My father's name was Jacob he was a butcher. My mother's name was Ellen she was a schoolteacher. As far as I knew, I was the only child in my family, which at times caused me great sorrow. However, I had many cousins who lived nearby. I had just turned ten on September 16, 1940.

Our life had been peaceful for most of my existence. Until, one day when I was walking home from school I saw a German soldier. He started toward me so unwisely I started to run. Once I was home, I told my mom what had happened, she laughed. She told me that he probably was going to ask me for directions. Looking back, my mother probably knew what the Nazi was doing, but she didn't want to tell me, because I was too young. Consequently, each day as I was walking home, the number of soldiers on the street and corners increased. Vaguely, I remember how cold the winter of 1940 was; at least it seemed to be a very cold walk.

One day, when all of my classmates were in their seats three German soldiers walked into the classroom, they talked to the teacher for about ten minutes. When she stood up she looked very scared and kept glancing at the soldiers. Then she said, "Will all of the Jewish children please raise your hand?" One of my best friends sitting next to me raised his hand. The soldiers went to every one of those children. I did not raise my hand. My mother had warned me not to do anything or say anything that would indicate I was Jewish. After school I asked Johanna about the soldiers. He replied that they wanted his name and address. Three days later my best friend Johanna disappeared. We lived pretty close to Johanna so unknown to my parents I walked to his house. When I arrived, I found that his front door had been knocked in. It was then that I began to realize that maybe things were different than they seemed. Perhaps the German soldiers were in my country for different reasons then I had been told. Upon viewing the destruction in Johanna's house, I ran as fast as my legs could carry me. When I went through the door, I began to holler.

"Mom, Johanna is gone his front door has been knocked in."

My mother was crying, "I know I saw it all from the window." The Nazis came in a truck, six German soldiers broke the door down. All of the soldiers from the truck ran inside and grabbed the Link family. My mom said she heard three gunshots. Then the soldiers pulled out three limp bodies and threw them into the back of the truck." As my mother recounted the story, I became very scared.

My fear increased when I went to do my farm chores. While I was putting on my boots my mother started to talk to my father. Their whispers were so low I could not hear their words clearly. However, finally I heard my father say he had to go. My mother started to cry and sob no over and over again. While I was doing my chores, I thought about my father's words. Hurriedly, I finished my chores and returned to the house and the safety of my parents. At that time little did I know that it would be one of the last times I would see my parents together.

Soon after, in early January my dad looked up to the sky and said, "There is a blizzard coming tomorrow." There was a huge snowstorm. My mother caught pneumonia in the blizzard and she passed away six days later. It was now January 28, 1941. It was as if my mother's death forced my father into action. Early the next morning, my father and I set out upon our journey. While I questioned where we were going, my father simply kept walking. As we moved farther and farther away from our farm, my questions increased. We would find somewhere to sleep during the day and proceed during the night. Left without answers, wondering about our abandoned farm, my father and I walked to the coast.

My life would never be the same. At our journey's end, my father paid a fisherman to hide me in a boat. Ordered onto the boat and concealed beneath the deck, I complied. As I boarded the boat, my father started to walk away. Once he stopped and looked back at me. I popped my head from below the deck his face was red. I started to get off the boat and this giant man around the corner had grabbed me. I fought this man with all my strength and screamed "Father". This man picked me up with one hand and in a deep voice said, "Quiet." He put me under the deck and said, "You will respond to Hank." I sat down in the corner and tried to get as far as I could from this man. Later, when the big man came back, he gave me a bowl of fish. I asked him his name and he said in a deep voice Mikkel, I am a fisherman. His orders were clear, be quiet in the day and move a little bit at night. I asked Mikkel where my father was. He didn't answer.

I started to forget the days. It had been a long time since my father had left me. We traveled for at least seven days. I was tired of eating fish and still very scared. Finally, we arrived. At first, my legs would not carry me. But Mikkel urged me forward.

We walked to this small farm about eight miles away. He knocked on the door and four children answered. Mikkel walked inside and kissed the woman. Once again his orders were clear. This was my new home, I was to stay downstairs, follow the children. The place was small and had concrete walls.

Once again I am alone among strangers. Later, I overheard the man explain my position as a Jewish child. As he talked to the woman, he explained how my father paid him to bring me to Sweden.

My memories are faint as to the length of time I stayed with these people. Mikkel returned often. Horror stories about the concentration camps in Europe came with him, as he was my only link to my homelands.

One day when we were working we saw soldiers waking up the road. Having been enmeshed into the family situation, I began to be afraid. Although these soldiers looked different than the Nazis, any uniform made me afraid. Later, I found out that these soldiers were part of the Allied forces the war had ended. Once Germany was defeated, life at first did not get any easier for me.

Fortunately, Mikkel worked with the partisans to help me. At this point, I found a job and began to make inquiries about members of my family. Then one day a man walked up to the door and asked if Levi was there. I did not know who he was talking about then I remembered that was my name. He looked just like my father. I said Father. Sadly, he told me no, but I am your long lost brother. I didn't understand what I had just taken through my head. I said I am an only child. He said his mother and father only saved up enough money to send me away. I asked him why they didn't send me. He looked at me. I walked up to him and gave him a hug. I asked if Father was alive. He looked down at his shoes and did not talk.

As I matured, I kept thinking "Why me?" Why was I one of the lucky ones to survive the devastation of the Holocaust? It is a question that remains unanswered.

Cody J. Youngman
Age: 13

FOOTBALL

Once upon a time in the town of Fosse, there was a boy named Kidd. He was a boy at the age of seventeen, the age you could start to play sports in Fosse.

Kidd had two brothers, one older than Kidd and one younger. The older one was nineteeen-years-old and his name was Lexis and his younger brother Nix who was fifteen-years-old. They had played football and soccer in the backyard ever since they were old enough to understand the game. They played basketball too. Every weekend Lexis, Nix, and Kidd had two friends over for the weekend. They would play all of their favorite sports together. Then they would go to sleep and go back home the next day. Eventually it was spring and that meant that football season started in Fosse.

"Come on Lexis, we have to get to football tryouts!" Kidd yelled anxiously at Lexis. Kidd was very eager to get to the tryouts because this was the first year he could play football.

"Hurry up Lexis! We'll be late!"

"I'm coming Kidd, hold your horses!"

"I'll be in the car Lexis."

"I'll be out in a minute; do you have a water bottle?"

"Yes Lexis!"

"I'll be in the car in a minute Kidd."

"OK" When they finally got to the tryouts they discovered that the were not until tomorrow. So Kidd and Lexis went home and practiced as hard as they could. Kidd trained and trained, while Lexis watched TV and slept.

Then came the day of the tryouts. Lexis had no clue how to do some of the drills, because he didn't practice. Kidd, on the other hand, who had practiced his heart out, did excellent. They eventually got done and went home. Three days later they got a note in the mail saying that Kidd made the team. So Kidd practiced even more and put all of his effort into games and practices. Kidd scored at every one of his games since he had practiced so much, and at the end of the season he made the All-Star team. It had some of the best people all over the United States. They went to Korea for their first game. The people in Korea weren't that good and the U.S. All-Stars won 52-3. Soon the U.S. team was announced the best football team. So since U.S. was the best football team each player got eight hundred dollars. Kidd spent most of his share on buying things to help him in football. Soon Kidd graduated from college and played on the Kansas City Chiefs professional football team.

Ben Matthews
Age: 11

137

THE KEY

As David hurried up the stone steps to his new school in Connecticut, he thought back to the day before. His dad had to go to Connecticut for his new job, so today would be David's first day at school in the fifth grade.

When David looked at his watch, he realized that he was late for school. As he ran through the halls, trying to find his way around, he was thinking about his new teacher.

The kids all said that he was the toughest teacher ever. Mr. Clark was very strict, and in the few months he had been there, it didn't take the kids long to find out!

Finally, David found the right door. It said 207, David's room number. He opened the door and quickly slipped inside his room.

For the first time he saw Mr. Clark. Mr. Clark had dark black hair and seemed to be in his thirties. Mr. Clark slowly looked up from his papers. The students turned to look. "You're late," he said in a loud deep voice.

"I got lost," David stammered.

"You have a tardy slip and a detention on Monday."

"But it's my first tardy!" David said angrily.

"Sit down," Mr. Clark said. Angrily, David walked to his seat. David didn't like Mr. Clark at all.

Late at night, when he was asleep, a storm woke him up. When he looked out the window, David saw something strange. There was someone on the edge of the woods that overlooked his house. He was wearing a long overcoat with a high pulled-up collar on it to hide his face.

Then he took something very small out of a pocket inside his jacket. It was shiny, but David couldn't make out what it was.

Just then the stranger turned, looking straight up at the window. David couldn't see his face in the pouring rain. Then the stranger turned, and ran straight into the center of the woods.

When David woke up, he was very tired. He couldn't get any sleep from the night before. When his second school day was over on Monday, he had to go to detention. He still didn't know his way around the school, but when he came to a door, he thought it was the right one for detention.

When he opened the door and saw what was inside David's heart leapt. It was all familiar. There were the same overcoat, boots, and gloves that he had seen on the intruder the night before. Then David remembered the small, shiny object the man had taken out of his pocket.

Suddenly, he started to search the pockets of the long overcoat. There was nothing there. The only thing he could do was to search the woods.

When David got home from his detention, he set out into the woods. He had to find out what the shiny, small object was and why it was so important. It was starting to get dark. As he got deeper and deeper into the woods, he was about to turn back, thinking it was hopeless to find out where it was.

Just then, he heard a low growling, getting closer and closer behind him. It was completely dark now and all he saw were two glowing eyes. David saw that it was a big, snarling wolf and started backing up slowly. Every time he stepped back, the wolf would step forward. Suddenly, it lunged forward at David. David ran as fast as he could to the nearest tree and jumped, his arm grasping a low branch. He was just about to cling on with his other hand, when he felt a sharp searing pain on his leg. The wolf had bitten him. Then, with all his strength left, he kicked the wolf with all his might. David let go of the branch and fell to the ground, his leg aching with pain.

He started to run again. The wolf was already starting to get up. Then David fell, rolling down a big hill. When David got to the bottom, there was a hole in the ground. He tumbled into it and realized it wasn't a hole, but a tunnel. Then something caught David's eye. There was something shiny, barely sticking out of the ground. He started to dig with his hands until he pulled it out. It was a small key. David knew at once it was the same thing the stranger took out of his pocket during the storm.

He grabbed the key and ran home as fast as he could with his hurt leg. When he got to his house, he climbed in through the window so no one would notice. He went to his room to look at his leg. It wasn't a bad bite, but it still hurt. David wrapped it up and looked at the key. It was an old-fashioned key and looked very old. David hid it in a drawer and went to sleep.

When he went to school, he put the key in his pocket. He walked with a small limp because of his leg. David wanted to explore the small closet again where he had found the stranger's things. In the classroom, Mr. Clark noticed his leg. "What happened?" he said.

"Nothing," David replied quickly, too quickly.

"Let me see your leg," Mr. Clark said.

"This is a bite," he said.

"How did it happen?"

"I was hiking in the woods," David said, unsure whether to trust him or not.

"You were?" he said. He suddenly seemed concerned, or even worried. Mr. Clark was about to turn away when his eyes widened. "What's that?" he said.

"What?" David said.

"That," said Mr. Clark, pointing at David's pocket. The edge of the key was just sticking out.

"It's my house key," said David.

"That's not a house key," said Mr. Clark. "I'm going to have to keep it."

"But...," said David.

"Give it to me," said Mr. Clark. David reluctantly handed the key over. He had to get it back. When school was over, he went to find the secret closet.

He was at the door now. He opened it and stepped inside. He started to move things around and see what was inside. After a while, he found something that he was sure had something to do with the key. There was a tiny keyhole in the very back of the wall in the same shape of the end of the key. David heard footsteps and quickly dived into the back of the closet where no one could see him.

Just then he heard someone turn the doorknob. He stayed very quiet, not daring to move. The door opened and he saw a pair of boots. Someone was looking around. Then the person turned and closed the door. David waited a while before he came out. He went home and thought about how he was going to get the key back.

He decided that he had to go right back at night. Mr. Clark never locked the windows and was on the first floor. When it was midnight, David ran to school. Luckily, the windows weren't locked and he climbed through. He searched Mr. Clark's desk until he opened the right drawer. Mr. Clark forgot to take the key home with him. He grabbed the key and ran out of the room. He got to the closet and found the keyhole in the wall. He inserted the key into the hole and turned.

Part of the wall slid away revealing a secret staircase. He climbed the stairs until he got to another door at the top. There was another keyhole. He put the key through and opened the door. He stepped through without looking and realized that there was no place to go. He was falling down and going very fast.

When he hit the bottom, there were mats and stuff stored all around him. The wind was knocked out of him, and it took a while for him to get up. When he got up, he was trying to search for a way out. He looked up to the high ceiling and saw the door up in the wall. Then he saw a big rock beside the wall. He moved it with all the strength he had left. It was very light.

When he had moved it, there was a hole in the wall just big enough for him to fit through. When he stepped out on the other side, it was completely dark. When his eyes got used to the darkness, he saw a dark figure standing in the shadows.

"I was expecting you," he said in a cold voice. He stepped out of the shadows and finally David saw who he was. He couldn't believe it. It was Mr. Clark!

"Mr. Clark, it was you!" David exclaimed.

Then his teacher said, "There is no Mr. Clark and there never was."

"I was the one who hid the key. I knew that you would try to figure out what it was so I took it from you. Then you found my hiding place where all of my things are kept."

Just then, David looked around. He hadn't noticed it since he had seen Mr. Clark. There were treasures and stolen things everywhere. "How did you get here?" said David.

The robber pointed to a tunnel in the wall. It was the same tunnel that David found in the woods, and Mr. Clark had tried to hide the key there. David ran towards the tunnel, but the man was too quick for him. He blocked his path and pushed him back. David fell to the ground and then thought up a plan.

He saw that there was another big rock by the tunnel. David picked up the treasure and stolen goods and threw them far away from the robber across the room. The stranger ran toward the things while David ran toward the tunnel. He got inside and pulled up the rock as hard and tight as he could. Then when he climbed out a long ways, he buried it up with dirt that was surrounding it. The robber was trapped.

David went home. The next day, he went into the secret closet and locked the door in the wall. Then he went home and threw the key into the lake where it would never be found again.

Joshua David Avery
Age: 11

140

THE NEW KID

Once upon a time there was a school that had just opened that year in 2004. There were only a couple of children that went to that school. When people started talking about it, more people would start to come to the new school in town. The people who own the school didn't have a name for the school. When more kids started to come to the school they came up with an idea for a name for the school. They wrote it down on a piece of paper, then they put all of everybody's vote in a box. The principal didn't like any of the suggestions that the students had made. When more people started to come, they would get more votes. In a couple of weeks they didn't have a good name for the school. When the next week came there was a new girl who wrote down a name that was very clever. When the principal saw this name she was very impressed. The name she wrote down was St. Elizabeth Cathedral School. The children took a vote on the name. There were about ninety percent that liked the name that she had come up with. She was a very mysterious person. Her name was Mary Ellen. She was good at everything. She was smart, good at sports, and she was the most beautiful girl anyone had seen in their life. Everyone was playing with her because they thought that she was cool. Mary was really shy. It was kind of like she didn't like all of the attention. Every day she would just go off on her own. After school every day she goes and she walks off all alone. One day I followed her to her house. On the way there it was dark and had a lot of trees around that area. When Mary Ellen reached her house I saw a huge house it was probably ten times the size of my house. I had never in my life seen such a big house. There were beautiful plants all around it. It was awesome. When I got home I called all of my best friends to let them know about her house. I told them that they could not tell anyone, because I didn't want Mary Ellen to know I was spying on her. If Mary Ellen found out that I was spying on her she would think that some of the kids thought that she was weird. I didn't want her to think that. Then she might want to leave our school because she thought the kids were making fun of her. The next day at school I had to tell her because it seemed like she was feeling really left out. So during recess I went over to Mary Ellen and I told her that I followed her home after school one day to see where she had been going every day after school. She started laughing when I told her that. I didn't know why she was laughing, but then she told me that she baby-sat at that house every day after school. After she told me that I started laughing too. The next day at school I asked her to play with my friends and me. We played together all through grade school and high school. We were best friends.

Allyson Bradshaw
Age: 11

SIR RAMSELY'S ADVENTURE

Sir Ramsely was a kind man and he never got in trouble with King Arthur. In fact he and the king were friends. That soon ended.

While Sir Ramsely was chopping up wood, a messenger and some knights on horses came up to him. "Sir Ramsely, King Arthur wants to see you," said the messenger.

"Why does he want to see me?" asked Sir Ramsely.

"I'm not sure he just told me to come and get you, put you on a horse in cuffs and bring you to him." said the messenger.

"But I refuse to go with you especially in handcuffs." said Sir Ramsely.

"Fine if that is the way you are going to act, I'll have to let the knights arrest you," said the messenger. "Go get him!" ordered the messenger.

After the long ride to the castle the knights took him and brought him into the castle, Sir Ramsely soon realized that something was wrong.

"So where is King Arthur?" asked Sir Ramsely.

"Actually, he isn't here. He is dead and when we found out that you were a close friend, we wanted to lock you up without food until you die." said the messenger.

"You tricked me!" exclaimed Sir Ramsely.

"Sure did, so down you go into your jail cell." said the messenger.

When Sir Ramsely got in his jail cell, he realized that the jail cell had a fire going in the corner so the prisoners wouldn't get cold. It had a large window and the jail cell looked like it hadn't been cleaned for weeks. But the best thing of all was that he wasn't going to be alone in this jail cell. The person that was already in there was his friend that he hasn't seen in a while. "Sir Gilbert, how did you get in this place"" asked Sir Ramsely.

"Last week people came and told me that the king wanted to see me so I came. Once I got here, they threw me in this jail cell." said Sir Gilbert.

"So they did the same thing to you that they did to me. This is what I'm going to do. I brought my knives with me so we are going to try to chisel our way out of here." said Sir Ramsely.

"Well, sounds good to me but we might want to start at night so that they won't know we left until after they check on us in the morning." said Sir Gilbert.

After waiting until dark, they started to chisel their way out of their jail cell when somebody came knocking on their door.

"What are you guys doing in here because if you are trying to get out of here there will be consequences." said the guard.

"The only thing we are doing in here is trying to stay warm by the fire." said Sir Gilbert.

Then Sir Ramsely showed Sir Gilbert the fireplace and that he has another idea to get them out instead of chiseling our way out.

Then Sir Gilbert asked the guard if he could come and put some more wood in the fireplace since the fire was starting to die down. The guard agreed and went to get some wood. During that time, Sir Gilbert told Sir Ramsely the other idea that he had to get out of this place. "This is my plan. When he comes back with the wood you will go up behind him and knock him out. Then we will take his sword for protection and get some food to take with us on our way home." said Sir Gilbert.

At that moment, the guard came back and started to work with the fire. When the guard bent down, Sir Ramsely came up behind him put his hand over the guard's mouth so that the guard wouldn't scream for help and knocked him out. After that, Sir Gilbert took the guard's sword. While Sir Gilbert was busy with the guard Sir Ramsely shut the door but didn't lock it so they could go out to get some food.

Once they were ready they left their cell to get a couple of days worth of food since they didn't have any to take with them back to their homes which was a couple of days ride on horseback.

They went out into the hall and went to the kitchen without anybody seeing them. But when they were leaving the castle, they saw a guard and they hid in a room until the guard passed. When they started to walk past the cells, Sir Ramsely thought of something.

"Hey, Gilbert, I just thought that what if we aren't the only ones who have been thrown in here for no reason at all." said Sir Ramsely. "Well let's go see if anyone else is in here and get them out." said Sir Gilbert.

After they had looked in all of the cells, they realized that they were the only prisoners in the castle. Then they continued their way out of the castle with the food.

Once they got out of the castle they went to the stables to get their horses. When they got in there they found a guard. So they snuck up to him and did the same thing that they did to the other guard. After they had knocked out the guard they hid him in some hay and then went to search for their horses. Once they stole some horses they set off back home. They found a place to camp shortly after they began the trip back to their homes. When they woke up they realized that it was going to rain pretty hard today.

"Well I guess that now we are going to have get to our house fast and send a messenger to King Richard to tell him that King Arthur has been murdered." said Sir Gilbert.

They left to go to their homes and to send a messenger to King Richard. But when they got there they realized that they wouldn't be able to do their plan as easily as they had planned. What they had realized is that the person who is the head of the castle put guards around their whole entire village. So Sir Gilbert came up with a new plan. "Okay here is my plan. At night we sneak into the village, get some money and someone to deliver the message to King Richard." said Sir Gilbert.

At midnight they left to go to their house and found that it was pretty easy to get the money. So they went around all the tents to find someone to take the message to King Richard. Right when they were about to give up all hope they found someone to take the message and the person left right away. Well that was pretty easy thought Sir Ramsely. Later on that same week a messenger came and gave them a letter from King Richard. The note said that he was grieved by the loss of the king and also thanked them for bringing it to his attention. The king also said that if the king didn't have a will then he would take over the land, and that he was going to send troops over to arrest the people who had killed the king.

One Year Later....

King Richard took the land that belonged to King Arthur and imprisoned the people who had killed King Arthur. The final thing he did was to make a proclamation awarding Sir Gilbert and Sir Ramsely gold and land for their bravery and good deeds.

Dan Vogt
Age: 12

ONE SCARY NIGHT

A long time ago there was a couple; their names were Bob and Janet. They were a happy couple. They got married and had little Boppet. After they had the baby, things started to become different. Bob and Janet heard things at night and they just thought it was the wind.

Until one night they heard something banging like pots and pans. Janet got up and she walked in the baby's room to see if the baby was okay; she wasn't there. So Janet ran to wake up Bob and they started to look for Boppet. They found her in the kitchen sleeping. Everything seemed fine with her but, they couldn't figure out how she got out of her crib.

They took Boppet to the doctor who decided there was nothing wrong with her. So Janet and Bob went home. They still didn't know how she got in the kitchen or the banging pots and pans.

A week later they still heard things at night and still found the baby in the kitchen. So one night Janet stayed up all night and she saw Boppet climb out of her crib and play with the pots and pans so all along it wasn't a creatures it was beautiful baby Boppet. Janet and Bob built the crib to the ceiling so that baby Boppet couldn't get out at night and so Janet and Bob could sleep again.

Sara Webster
Age: 14

MY FAMILY

I have a very big family. I have a real mom and dad and a stepmom and stepdad. I live with my real mom and stepdad, but I see my real dad and my stepmom all the time. I love them all very much. The good thing about it is that all my parents get along great with each other.

At my real mom's house I am the only child, well at least Momma says she has two kids counting Daddy. It's not that bad being the only child, not having anybody to play with. You can always play with Daddy. I have a golf cart and I ride it out around the field, it keeps me busy most of the time.

At my real dad's, on the other hand, I am not the only child. I have two sisters, Caitlyn and Sarah. There is also Keli, my cousin, who is also like a sister to me. There is never a dull moment at my dad's house. We also have a swimming pool at my dad's house which we use a lot in the summertime. We are always doing something at Daddy's.

That is my family for you. I love them all very much and I know they love me too.

Tessa Springer
Age: 11

Me, Justin, and Hunter met with each other at school. All of a sudden Nathan, Tyheim, and Collin challenged us to a basketball game. We accepted their challenge, and at recess we started the game. Nathan passed it to Tyheim, and Tyheim was guarded. He saw Collin wide-open but instead he passed back to Nathan. However our team passed it to each other every time. Recess was almost over and the score was 0 to 12, us having 12, and Collin hadn't had the ball all recess. The recess bell rang and we won by fourteen. So it goes to show you if you pass and share the ball you can accomplish much more.

John Wesley Young
Age: 9

SMALL MAN TO BIG MAN

One day a kid named Jacob went to school. He was very thin. He had a lot of friends. He was smart, cool, and handsome. He only weighed about eighty-five pounds. Yep, he was really popular but even thin kids can get fat just be eating a little bit of junk food.

It was the last day of school and the kids were eager to leave. "Okay class today we're going to have a pop quiz."

"Ahh man!" Jacob said in an unhappy way.

"Now quiet I'm just preparing you for seventh grade."

Suddenly the bell rang. BRRRINGGGG!!! Then the doors slammed open. Kids running everywhere, screaming, shouting. They got on the bus and went home." So much for the pop quiz." Jacob said.

The next day shocked everyone in the subdivision. It started to snow. "Wow!" Jacob said. "Can I go outside can I, can I?"

"NO!" his grandma said. "All snow does is get your clothes dirty and I have enough laundry as it is!" Jacob couldn't believe what his grandma had said. His parents always let him go out in the snow. They even came out with him and built a snowman together.

"It's not fair!" Jacob said.

The next morning he had breakfast. He asked his grandma if he could go outside again but she still said no. Then... he got bored so he ate and ate and ate. He had tacos, suckers, candy, chocolate, chicken, fries, and a lot more. This is what happens when you get bored.

Then school started. You won't believe what happened. When he was in sixth grade he weighed eighty-five pounds. At the beginning of seventh grade he weighed a total of two hundred fifty-seven pounds. Pretty FAT!! All the kids thought he was a new kid until he told them who he was.

"What happened!" one kid said.

"What were you thinking?" said another in shock.

That day he sat all by himself in class. He felt left out. "I hate the way I look. Why did it have to be me?" Jacob said with a sob. He went to lunch and said to himself, "OK, I'm not going to stuff my face." Then he saw what was for lunch... PIZZA!!! He ate until he couldn't eat anymore. He blamed his grandmother. He never wanted to see the light of day again.

The next day his grandma yelled, "Time for school!"....there was no answer. She yelled even louder, "JACOB LEE GET DOWN HERE THIS INSTANT!!!"... still no answer. She went upstairs and came to know that he had locked himself in the bathroom. "If you don't come out I'm calling the police!" his grandma said with fury.

Jacob replied, "You can't do that."

His grandma replied, "How much do you want to bet twenty, forty?"

Jacob came out of the bathroom, got in the car, and went to school.

When Jacob got out of the car his grandma said, "Guess what Jacob... I lied."

Jacob yelled, "WHAT!!!" Then his grandma drove away.

"Guess what class?" the teacher said. "We have a new student. His name is Anthony. Say hello class."

The class replied, "Hello Anthony."

"Take your seat right next to Jacob," the teacher said with a smile.

Time passed fast that day and it was lunchtime. Like always Jacob got a lot of food. He sat at a big table in the corner with nobody else on it. Then came along Anthony.

"May I sit by you?" Anthony asked.

"Sure," Jacob said happily thinking he made a new friend.

"So," Anthony asked, "where do you live?"

"Small town down Merry Lane in the subdivision." Jacob replied.

"I live on Hampton Road." Anthony said.

Lunch ended and it was time for the "end-of-day" pop quiz. As usual nobody made a good grade.

Finally the day was over. Jacob, who was usually down in the dumps, walked home dejectedly, but he was happy he had made a new friend. He couldn't wait for school tomorrow.

The next day Jacob jumped out of bed, put on his clothes, got his book bag, got in the truck and yelled, "Grandma hurry, hurry I need to get to school!!!"

His grandma yelled, "Jacob, Jacob it's Saturday. There isn't any school today." Jacob's face turned redder than a brick wall.

That Saturday he begged and begged his grandma if Anthony could come over until his grandma, surprisingly, said "Yes." They played all weekend.

Many days had passed and it was the same routine over and over. Go to school, gossip, have boring day, go home, invite over, play 'til six, go to bed, and sometimes sleep over. Anthony didn't care if Jacob was fat, thin, short, or tall.

Then... the saddest day of Jacob's life started February 6 when he got a phone call from Anthony, "I don't know how to say this but my father has just got a new job in California... I'm moving." then he hung up. Jacob burst out in tears. His one and only true friend was gone.

Months had passed and still no sign of anybody who would be his friend. He was miserable. He had no friends.

Then it was Christmas. His grandma had an idea. Since he didn't have a human friend then maybe he could have friendship with an animal.

Christmas morning. Beautiful, bright, jolly. Then suddenly his present moved. He opened it. It was a dog! What a surprise.

School was the same. He couldn't wait to get home and play with none-other than his new dog. He always had fun. He knew of the hardships though. He had to clean it, feed it, and pick up after it. But he didn't care as long as he got to keep it and had a friend.

Then one night he woke up because of the wind. And right there next to him sat his dog. Then something amazing happened. "Hello." To Jacob's surprise the dog spoke.

"Ah, hi."

The dog spoke, "Run with me after school and on weekends and I assure you, you will be you in sixth grade."

So he ran with the dog over and over again until finally... he weighted only ninety pounds. Only five pounds more when he was in sixth grade. He was popular again. He felt confident in himself he could do it and he did it.

Just because people look different doesn't mean you can pick on them. But if you feel that way, you can always fix it.

Paul Jinkerson Jr.
Age: 11

THE BIRD WHO FOLLOWS GOD

There once was a bird named Mary who went to church every Sunday and Holy day. She always sat in the first pew. One Sunday she was flying to church and she heard a voice. She looked around, but couldn't see anyone. The voice called her again. If no one was around, who could be calling me? It must be God. She asked God, "Why are you calling me?

God answered, "I have a job for you. There are some orphaned chicks that need your care. They're down by the stream. I need you to take care of them like your own."

So Mary went down to the stream and picked the chicks up and took them to the church and taught them how to pray. From that moment on she fell in love with them. That night in bed she couldn't sleep. She thought she could make use of her time and think of names for the chicks. "How about Gabby, Maddy, and Jenny," she said. Mary thought they were cute names. After she prayed, she fell asleep. The next morning, she woke up and went into the living room. The chicks were gone! She tried to stay calm, but she just couldn't! Mary started to look for the chicks, but couldn't find them. Suddenly she heard a chirp. Her heart raced. She saw the curtains move. Then Mary saw three little yellow chicks.

The chicks said "Mommy, you look like you've seen a ghost!"

"I thought I had lost you all!" Mary said. She thought God had set her up. "I just don't understand" she said.

"Understand what, Mommy?" the chicks said.

Mary looked down at her kids and thought, I must be blessed to have such kids. The moral of this story is if you understood God, you'd be God.

Shayla Tanner
Age: 10

THE NORTH POLE

It was summertime in early August at Daytona Beach, Florida. The Polson sisters, Alexandra and Elisabeth, were in their bathing suits ready to go to the beach for a swim. Alexandra was nine and Elisabeth was six.

"Come on, Alex! I'm so excited!" cried Elisabeth. Alexandra and Elisabeth climbed into the car, towels in hand. Elisabeth also had her floaties.

The Polson's car drove up to the beach. Elisabeth couldn't sit still.

"Calm down, Elisabeth!" said Alexandra.

"I can't!" exclaimed Elisabeth, "Come on!"

Elisabeth ran into the water and then gasped, "Yuck! Ugh! Gross!" Elisabeth was spitting into the water.

"What are you doing?" asked Alexandra.

"Salt-water-in-my-mouth!" cried Elisabeth. Alexandra laughed, pulling her goggles over her eyes.

Suddenly, Elisabeth disappeared under the waves. "Elisabeth!" cried Alexandra. She dove after her, but couldn't find Elisabeth anywhere.

Alexandra felt herself being pulled under the sand. I'm going under the sand? That's impossible! thought Alexandra.

"Cold. COLD. FREEZING! COLD!" Alexandra saw Elisabeth lying in a heap next to her... IN THE SNOW! There was snow, IN AUGUST!

Then Alexandra saw a sign that read: THE NORTH POLE. There was a red and white striped pole in front of it.

"Look," gasped Elisabeth, "the North Pole. I never knew it was red and white before."

Alexandra giggled. "That's not the real North Pole. In fact, it isn't a pole at all! It's a snowy place around north Greenland. That's where we are."

"Oh," said Elisabeth. "Oh! You mean it's where Santa's workshop is?" she asked.

"There's no such thing as Santa's workshop," said Alexandra.

"Oh yeah," said Elisabeth, "then what's that?" She pointed to a huge building left of the girls. A sign on top read: Santa's Workshop.

Elisabeth had already started running to the workshop, stumbling in the snow with every step. "Come on, Alex!" she called.

"Unbelievable," whispered Alexandra. She started following Elisabeth anyway. "Wait up, Eliza," she called after her.

Elisabeth stood in front of "Santa's Workshop". "Wow!" she whispered. This can't be happening, thought Alexandra. Elisabeth thought exactly the opposite. "This is great!" she shouted. "Snow, when we're in our bathing suits! I'm not even cold!"

"Well, I'm sure you were before, in the snow. I sure was," said Alexandra.

"Maybe," answered Elisabeth, "but I'm not now, and that's all that matters!"

"Yeah, I guess that is kind of weird," agreed Alexandra.

"I want to go in! I want to go in!" screamed Elisabeth, jumping up and down in front of the door like it was going to open if she told it to.

Then something else caught Elisabeth's eye. "Look!" she exclaimed, "a real reindeer!" Elisabeth walked up to it. "Hello. I'm Elisabeth. Which one are you? Dasher, Dancer, Prancer, Vixen, Comet, Cupid, Donner, or Blitzen? You're obviously not Rudolph, because you don't have a red nose," she said. Alexandra rolled her eyes.

"Get back here!" a little voice yelled. Alexandra turned around and saw a little elf running out of the building. Get back here Comet!"

"Oh! So you're Comet?" asked Elisabeth turning to the reindeer.

"And who are you?" asked the little elf. Alexandra spoke up.

"I'm Alexandra, and this is my little sister, Elisabeth. We're the Polson sisters."

"Yeah, I'm Eliza. Call me Eliza. And call her Alex," said Elisabeth.

"Oh, whatever you say, Eliza and Alex. I need to get Comet back in here right now. Here, Comet. Comet. COMET!" yelled the little elf. Comet scurried along after the sharp tone of the elf.

"Wait!" said Alexandra, "Do you know how we can get back to our home in Daytona Beach, Florida?"

"Furyda? Never heard of it. Sorry," said the elf. "But, maybe Santa can help. Come inside."

Elisabeth suddenly started shouting, "Yeah! Yippee! Wahoo! I get to see Santa and all his elves and all the reindeer and the workshop and all the toys and..."

"Okay, we get the point, Elisabeth. Calm down and come on," said Alexandra.

The two girls walked into Santa's Workshop with the elf. "Wow!" exclaimed Elisabeth, her eyes growing wide.

There were elves everywhere, making all kinds of toys. There were even three floors, and the top two had an opening in the middle looking down on the first floor.

"I want to go to the top floor and look down!" demanded Elisabeth. "I thought you wanted to see Santa and the reindeer still," said Alexandra. "I had a longer list than that," said Elisabeth. "You already saw the elves, toys, and workshop," Alexandra reminded her.

"I'm going to look for Santa," said the elf. "You kids run outside and play so you don't mess anything up."

"I won't mess anything up!" mumbled Elisabeth.

"Come on, Eliza," scolded Alexandra. On the way out the door, the Polson sisters almost bumped right into someone. "Excuse us," said Alexandra.

"Are you Santa?" Elisabeth asked, suspiciously squinting her eyes.

"Why, yes, little girl," Santa answered. Alexandra's mouth dropped open. "Cool!" was all Elisabeth said. "Do you want to come outside and play with us?" she asked.

"I'm sorry, I have work to do. Oh, but this is for you. Have fun!" Santa called and walked away.

"Cool! I got to see Santa!" exclaimed Elisabeth. "I even got a little tin with candy canes." Alexandra said nothing.

The Polson sisters made their way outside. Quickly, Alexandra formed a snowball and threw is at Elisabeth. "Hey!" she called.

Now Elisabeth had a snowball in her hands. She snuck up on Alexandra and threw it as hard as she could. "You!" screamed Alexandra.

Alexandra frowned, but smiled at Elisabeth, and Elisabeth shrieked. Alexandra chased her all around through the snow until they exploded with laughter. "Let's take a walk," Alexandra suggested.

Alexandra and Elisabeth started walking down the street. At first it was a pleasant walk, until they reached Candycane Street in town. That's when the snow really kicked up.

"Snowstorm!!" someone called. The girls pulled their towels around them tightly. They were as warm as if they were in coats, hats, and mittens.

Suddenly the girls were blinded, not being able to see because of all the snow. Elisabeth clung to Alexandra's arm. They managed to walk though, but only a few steps at a time.

After a while, the snow cleared. The girls looked around. There was no snow anywhere! It was so hot, when Alexandra peeled off her towel; it was soaked with sweat, not snow. They were on the shore of the beach. THE BEACH!!

"Did that just really happen?" asked Alexandra. Elisabeth held up her tin. Alexandra smiled. They had really gone to the North Pole!

Ashley Lynn Kunze
Age: 10

ARIEL RUNS AWAY

My name is Ariel. I am four years old. I am not getting treated very fair. Last Sunday I wanted some ice cream 'cause I ate all my food. (Well I ate a few bites of pizza.) I asked for some ice cream and they said no I did not eat all of my food. Then I said please 'cause they said if I say please I could get anything I wanted. Maybe they said something different, I can't remember. But they still said no.

Tonight I wanted to cook dinner. But Mommy said I was too young to use the stove. So I said I'll just use the microwave. Mommy said no again and that was how come I had to throw a fit. Now I'm in my room 'cause of that. Then it hit me I'm gonna run away. So I packed my stuff, opened my window, and got out. I wanted to go to the park but I was not allowed to cross the street so I just went in the bushes behind my house. It was not the best place to be but it was better than that no-fair house I was living in. Then I got so sleepy I lay down in my sleeping bag and went to sleep.

The next day I woke up and peeked out of the bushes and I decided I was hungry. I do not want to be a crime person but I took my favorite box of cereal Cavity Krunch. I even know their theme song. It is "Cavity Krunch, Cavity Krunch, it's the best cereal for your lunch." I thought to myself this should last me about a week. But when I got back to the bushes I found out it only lasted two hours.

Then I got scared my mommy and daddy did not miss me. So I gathered my stuff and jumped in my window. When I got in, my mommy opened my door and asked me if I had a good night. I just looked at that lady like she was crazy. She had no clue I was gone. Good thing she didn't, or I would be stuck in my room forever.

Miranda Warner
Age: 10

"Bye Mom," said the fraternal triplets as they got on the bus to ride to school. Mom thought that they were going to have a great day of school. But little did she know that there was a big, bad teacher!

The teacher's name was Ms. Wacker. The teacher hated twins and triplets. Especially fraternal. As the triplets went into the classroom, Ms. Wacker gave them the look.

The look is the ugliest, meanest face you can imagine. As they turned their math homework in to Ms. Wacker, she said with a mean voice, "Ah gi-me that." The triplets try to be nice, they really do. But old Wacker the Quacker, (that's what the kids call her), just can't deal with them. So at recess, the triplets made a plan to sneak out.

"OK," said triplet number one. (The boss.)

"I hope it works," said triplet number two. (The paranoid one.)

"This is what we're going to do. I'm going to ask the teacher to go to the bathroom. Triplet number two, you're going to ask Ms. Wacker to get a drink. And triplet number three, (the helpful one that Ms. Wacker sort of liked,) ask Ms. Wacker if she has any papers for you to take to someone." Riiiiiing! The recess bell for recess to be over. Triplet number one said, "Let's do it."

As soon as they got into the classroom, triplet number one got out of his seat, walked to Ms. Wacker's desk and said, "Ms. Wacker, can I go to the bathroom?"

"Yeah, whatever," said Ms. Wacker. She started to pass out worksheets.

As soon as she got to triplet number two, he said, "C-c-can I g-g-get a d-d-drink?"

"Uh huh," said Ms. Wacker.

As soon as she sat back down in her seat, triplet number three went up to Ms. Wacker's desk and said, "Ms. Wacker, do you have any papers for me to take to someone?"

"Yeah, take em' to Mrs. Pen," Ms. Wacker said.

Triplet number three walked out into the hall, shut the door and said, "Boo-ya."

Now the hard part was to get past the teachers. But surprisingly, they did it without a sweat. They opened the door, stepped outside and they were free at last. Triplet number one did a dance. So then they started walking down the road.

They were about half a mile from school when they saw the worst possible thing they could see. A police car. They tried to hide behind a shrub of bushes, but they were too slow. The policeman saw the children. He stopped and got out of his car and said, "What in the world are you hooligans doing?! Why are you out of school?! Get in the car!!!" The hooligans did as they were told. "What school do you go to?" The policeman asked the triplets.

"Dooms Days Elementary," said triplet number three.

The policeman took them back to their school. "Which class are you in," he asked.

"Who do you think?" grumbled triplet number one.

"Oh," said the policeman. He took them to Ms. Wacker's class. Of course, they all got whacked by the automatic whacker. It ended up that the sneak out plan didn't work. But not for long!

To Be Continued...

Want to read the next book? Look for: The Three Little Kids and the Big Bad Teacher #2

Austin McWilliams
Age: 9

One day me, Cindy, and Emma were going to the water park. We went during the summer because it was warm. We went to the water park to mostly swim. Nothing really special happened we just had fun. Emma rode the water slide it was the blue one but I didn't. When I was there a wave came up and hit me in the face. We also went to the lazy river, that was fun. We had the best time at the water park.

Emily Hover
Age: 9

THE WITNESS

I have heard of this Stephen. It is said that no one can stand against his wisdom or the "Spirit" by whom he speaks. I patiently watched as Stephen was brought before the Sanhedrin. Witnesses were called forth and testified against him saying, "This fellow never stops speaking against this holy place and against the law. For we have heard him say that this Jesus of Nazareth will destroy this place and change the customs Moses handed down to us."

I could not believe what I was hearing. No man has the right to change the Laws of Moses, especially this Jesus of Nazareth, who had died some time ago.

"Are these charges true?" the high priest questioned. As Stephen answered, I began to notice how vigorously and fervently he spoke. There was a hidden power in his voice, something that took me by surprise. But when I tuned my ears from my thoughts and listened to his words, I became greatly angered. This preacher had the audacity to call us a stiff-necked people, and in the presence of the Sanhedrin as well!

Fortunately, I was not the only one to have felt such anger. Stephen's opposition, Jews from Cyrene, Alexandria, Cilicia, and Asia, snarled and gnashed their teeth in fury. However, Stephen gazed heavenward, his face bright and glowing like an angel, and declared, "Look, I see Heaven open and the Son of Man standing at the right hand of God."

With that said, the already furious crowd covered their ears and yelled at the top of their lungs. All of them rushed to him on one accord, grabbed him by his tunic, and began to drag him to the outskirts of the city. I followed closely in front, careful to see Stephen's reactions. He humbly allowed himself to be dragged away, knowing that his end was near. His face and gaze were filled with peace; I could tell that he was not afraid of his death, and that puzzled me. I have seen many executions where the convicted have renounced their faith so they would not die. But somehow I had a strange feeling that this execution would be different from the others.

However, all of my musings were forced to the back of my mind, as the execution was being prepared to commence. The executioners draped their cloaks over my arm, careful to keep their nice garments from being dirtied during the stoning. I hugged the garments close to me, as a reminder to myself that I was part of an important event, one that would be remembered as long as time existed.

Stephen's captors threw him onto the dusty ground, waiting for him to stand and oppose them. He rose slowly, ready to accept his coming pain. Finally, a man in front picked up a fairly large stone and hurled it with all his might. It smote Stephen on his cheekbone. The preacher was knocked backward, but quickly regained his ground, a slowly bleeding gash on his left cheek.

Another stone was released and smote him in the nose, drawing forth a trickle of crimson. One stone soon escalated to two, then three, four, and then five stones all at once. I watched in mixed emotions as Stephen continued to stand back up after being hit several times. His face was bruised and scraped, as were his arms and legs. He doubled over in pain as a very large stone belted him in the chest. He dropped to his scraped knees and gasped for air. More stones were released, causing Stephen an endless stream of pain, but he kept recovering.

Finally, when the last stone had been cast, Stephen was at the end of his strength and trembled in pain as he stood once more. His executioners were bending over and panting, out of breath from the rage they had unleashed on this Christian. They wiped several beads of sweat from their brow, but carefully watched Stephen, fearful that he would not die. Instead, Stephen tilted his head heavenward and prayed. "Lord Jesus," he called in a fading voice. "Receive... my spirit." It caused him great pain to speak. His legs became weak and he sank to his knees, his breath slowing. "Lord," he whispered. "Do not hold this sin against... " He sank lower to the ground, leaning on his bruised elbows for support. "... them." In that moment, Stephen breathed his last and collapsed on the dirt.

I stared at his bruised and battered body while the crowd retrieved their cloaks from me. One part of me felt sympathy for Stephen, even sadness. But the other part sought to congratulate his stoners for ridding this world of another one of those accursed Christians. That side triumphed. I became glad that Stephen was dead; his death would serve as a sufficient example to these Christians. And in that moment, I, Saul of Tarsus, resolved to get rid of them as well.

But what if... oh, never mind.

Erica Smith
Age: 14

DISNEY CARRY AWAY

Once upon a time there was an older woman and man. They lived in the woods in a small wood house. One day the woman was in her garden picking tomatoes and other things. Meanwhile, the man was picking apples and other fruits. When they were done they went inside to prepare supper. After they had eaten they went upstairs to their quiet, peaceful room and went to bed. While they were asleep there was something going on downstairs. It was Disney characters, like Cinderella, Snow White, Donald Duck, Goofy, and all the others. They were hosting a House of Mouse Episode.

Meanwhile, upstairs the woman and man were asleep. Ten minutes later the woman woke up and said to her husband, "Sam, do you hear something?"

"No. I don't," said Sam.

"Well, okay," she said. So, she went back to sleep.

At midnight she went downstairs to use the restroom. When she went downstairs there in her living room floor were the Disney characters. She hollered, "SAM GET DOWN HERE RIGHT NOW!" Because their grandchildren watched House of Mouse all the time at their house she kind of knew what was going on.

All of a sudden Mickey Mouse walked over to Linda and said, "Wanna dance?"

Linda said, "Sure." She looked at her husband who was darting toward her as fast as he could.

He got right up in between Mickey Mouse and his wife and said, "No. You will not! You will not dance with my wife!"

"Oh, please Mr. Walton," begged Mickey Mouse.

"Why don't you guys play the music and we will do the dancing," said Linda.

"Sure will," Mickey Mouse said.

"Well OK. I guess that will work," said Sam.

So, Mickey Mouse and his band started to play a song and the couple danced and danced song after song, move after move. Then everybody started to dance. Then afterward the wife treated everyone to lemonade and cookies, which were delicious.

Then the wife offered Mickey to sleep in the guest room. Mickey Mouse said, "OK, I will be delighted to."

"Well then hustle up. Come on now. Move it on upstairs." So, Mickey and his band went upstairs.

In the morning they were all treated to biscuits and gravy. "What a wonderful breakfast Mrs. Dutchman," said Mickey Mouse. "Well we must be on our way now," said Mickey Mouse.

"Well don't go without lunch," said Mrs. Dutchman.

"Well, I must say we do need something to eat," said Mickey Mouse.

Mrs. Dutchman said, "Well, I'll start lunch."

Before she turned away she said, "Mickey what would you and your band like for lunch?"

"Well, I don't care. Any special orders, band?" he asked.

"Nope," said the band.

"Okay then," said Mrs. Dutchman. "Well how do you like spaghetti?"

"Oh, we love spaghetti," he and his band said. "Well, then I will start getting lunch prepared," she said. Then she turned away. "Well," said Sam, "do you want to watch some television?"

"Sure," said Mickey. "What are we going to watch?"

"Whatever you want to. You're the company," said Sam.

While Mickey was flipping through the channels, Sam hollered, "Linda, when will lunch be ready?"

"In forty-five minutes," she answered.

Mickey came to a sudden stop and said to Sam, "Look, here's my show. Wanna watch it?"

"Sure," said Sam.

"Welcome to the House of Mouse," said the microphone. Then came the House of Mouse starter song and then the episode.

Mickey said, "Wow, I've never seen my show before! Can we watch it?"

"Sure," said Sam.

"LUNCH!" hollered Linda. They all ate lunch in the living room and watched Mickey's show.

After lunch they all cleaned up the mess. Mickey went upstairs and started packing up to leave. Then all of a sudden Linda heard a train noise but nobody else did. Linda wiped her hands on her apron and walked into the living room and said, "Did you hear something?"

"No," said Sam and so did Mickey.

Then Linda looked outside and saw a train. She told Mickey, "Come here." So he did. There was a train waiting outside that had a banner on it that said, Welcome home Mickey. Cinderella's coachman jumped out of the train and knocked on the door. Linda opened the door.

The coachman said, "I have come to save Mickey."

Mickey said, "I am fine here, but I must go home."

"Thanks for letting me stay," said Mickey.

"Well, stay while I make a phone call." She called her husband from work and told him.

He said, "Call the grandchildren and tell them I'm on my way. I want them to see Mickey Mouse."

Then they both said, "Good-bye," and then hung up. She called her grandchildren and said that Papa was on his way to come and get them she also said that she had a surprise for them.

Fifteen minutes later they arrived. They said, "Hi Mama." When they saw Mickey they opened their mouths and ran toward him and screamed.

"MICKEYYYYYYYYYY!"

Linda said, "Now kids, Mickey has to go I just wanted you to see him."

"Awwwww," said the kids.

They gave him one last hug each and then Sam took them home and went back to work. Then they all had cookies and milk and then Mickey said, "Thanks for everything."

Linda said, "Anytime you need to drop in, come to my house."
"We will miss you." Then he said he had to leave because he had a show to perform.
So he left and he thought about them all the way home. Linda said to Sam, "I miss Mickey."
"So do I." Sam said. "It's not the same but we will have to move on."
"I know," said Linda. They have done good ever since.

Lauren Zanette Dudley
Age: 9

"Come on we're going to be late!" Johnny said. Johnny was really excited. He and his friends Austin, Lauren, and I were all excited to go to Elvis' house on Elvis' birthday. Johnny and I were huge fans of Elvis so we couldn't wait to see his house. When we got there we went to our hotel. It was right next to Elvis' house! It was called Heart Break Hotel. First we unpacked. Then we went out for dinner at Ruby Tuesday. We were going to Elvis' tomorrow for his birthday. While we were there at night we tried to sneak upstairs but we never got too far because there were people guarding the staircase. When it was later we tried again and we got upstairs! First we went into the room on the right. "I think this is Lisa's room."

Austin said, "Lisa was Elvis' daughter."

"I think we should go back down with the group now." said Lauren. Lauren was a good girl. She never got in trouble at school.

"Let's go in the other rooms now," I said. When we got there we couldn't believe our eyes. It was Elvis' ghost! I started to gasp.

He said to us "Hey baby." Lauren almost ran downstairs but she didn't because the guards were back! They had gone out for dinner they're back! Elvis said, "looks like you're stuck up here for the night." In the morning we all got up at the same time. Elvis wasn't there anymore. We avoided the guards and ran to the hotel. When we got there we went to our room and packed. We went home after that.

On the way back I said, "Well that was scary I've never seen a ghost before."

Siobhan Campbell
Age: 9

THE LION AND THE RAT

It is Baby Rat's birthday and he invited his friend, Baby Lion, and they played tag outside. When they were done playing tag they ate dinner and cake. Then Baby Rat got to open his presents and he was so excited. Baby Rat got a bike, Play Station, and a Nintendo 64. Finally he opened the present from Baby Lion, it was a Tonka set. He loved Tonka sets. Baby Rat ripped open the box and it was a boat. He put everything together right until the trailer and Baby Rat gave up. Baby Rat had a hard time putting the trailer together. Baby Lion loves Tonka sets too and Baby Lion helped Baby Rat put the trailer together.

Moral of the story is never give up.

Hunter Bajkowski
Age: 9

THE BUNNY PRINCESS AND THE KNIGHT

Once upon a time, there was a beautiful princess. She was a friend to all creatures. One day she went into the forest with her friend, the rabbit. They stopped by the pond to see Frog. Frog said, "Hello." Then Frog saw a monkey knight. So the monkey knight grabbed the princess and ran away with her.

The monkey didn't know that the princess had mud on her shoe. Rabbit found the king and queen and they followed the foot tracks. They found the Bunny Princess.

Now the princess knows to stay with somebody that she knows so that she will not be taken away again.

The moral of the story is to always stay with somebody you know.

Kennedy McGuire Jones
Age: 9

THE NIGHT OF THE MYSTERIOUS PSYCHIC

Boom! A car lost control on a sharp turn and smashed into a large oak tree on the side of the road. A tall, slim figure stepped out of the damaged vehicle and into the moonlit night. The figure was slightly injured from the impact of the sudden incident, but had managed to get up and walk around.

This particular figure's name was Ronald Caneshape. The man looked around the area. Then his eye caught a path into the forest. Ronald Caneshape followed the winding path, and suddenly there was an object showing through the fog. The lost figure walked toward it. The object was a house! A small house. Ronald kept on walking toward the house until he found himself rapping upon the door.

The door opened and an old, short woman appeared in the doorway. This particular woman looked strange to Ronald, for she wore a turban upon her head and so many rings on her fingers that her hands look like diamonds themselves. "Yes, what do you want, my dear?" asked the strange looking woman in a calm voice.

"Well, I..."

"Oh, come in dear. You must be all shaken up from that dreadful car accident," said the old woman, pulling the man on her doorstep into her home.

Ronald's lips were glued together. How did the woman know what he was about to say? He was amazed.

Minutes passed, and Ronald Caneshape found himself drinking a red disgusting medicine to kill his pain. "Ugh!!" exclaimed Ronald as he choked on the medicine. "What is this?"

"Turtshwaite", answered the old woman. "It's made of turtle shells and beetle guts."

Ronald's face shriveled.

"I know what you are thinking Ronald Caneshape. You want to know who in the world I am," said the woman.

Ronald almost bit his tongue. How did the woman know his name? And how did she know what he was thinking? "Who are you?" Was all he could say.

"Well, my dear, I don't think you need to know this personal information."

"Then what are you?" asked Ronald, still shocked.

"I am a psychic, one who interacts with the spirits beyond this world", the psychic said.

Well, that answered all of Ronald's questions even though he thought there were no such things as real psychics. "Then what are you doing, living in this dark forest all alone I mean?" asked the curious man.

The psychic grinned, drumming her long fingernails upon the table of which they sat across. "Waiting for you my dear," answered the mysterious woman.

Ronald didn't know what she was talking about, and the only thing he could say was: "What?"

"I've been waiting for you. I knew that you would end up here one day, so I stayed in this forest 'til the day you'd come -- and you did!"

Ronald was puzzled. "So why am I so special? And why did you wait for me?"

"Well, you see, long ago, when I was young, I lived in a great land called Janemia. And every thousand years there would be a new King of Janemia. Well, about seven hundred years ago, a King was about to step down from his throne -- but first, he had to choose between his two sons for the title of King of Janemia. So he picked the younger one, who stood by his side every minute. The older one who disobeyed his father's rules and never stayed by his side, was very jealous, so he killed his father and brother and declared himself King of Janemia. And so, after he declared himself king, he made all of the residents slaves, and made all of the slaves work from sun up to sun down. Trust me -- I was there. But anyway, one morning, while some slaves and myself were chopping wood, I had a vision," said the woman.

"What kind of vision?" asked Ronald curiously.

"A wonderful vision, my dear, a wonderful vision. A vision so wonderful and so great that I told all of the slaves and they called me a prophet! But, nowadays I call myself a psychic -- I'm not worthy enough to be called a prophet."

"What was your vision about?" Ronald became lost in his curiosity.

"Well, of course, it was about you. My vision was that there would be a hero in the future. The only sorcerer who could defeat the king and be worthy to become king himself. And now the vision is fulfilled. You are here! You are in my very home at this moment! You are the hero!"

Ronald was shocked. A normal, middle-aged person couldn't possibly become a king of a magical land! Ronald didn't have any words in his mind. And all he could think of the final words of the psychic was that it was a joke.

Suddenly, the psychic pushed her chair away from the table and stood up. "Come, follow me." And as soon as Ronald got up and followed the old woman, he realized that she knew that he had doubted her.

The psychic led Ronald through a doorway of beads and into a very strange room. The room was very long, and on each side there was a row of candles, and at the far end of the room was a long, thin case sitting upon a bunch of pillows.

The two figures walked to the far end of the room until the psychic bent down and picked up the case. The woman put the case in Ronald's arms, which was very heavy to his surprise.

"Open it, my dear," urged the psychic.

Ronald carefully opened the case, and inside of it was a big bundle of paper, which obviously caused most of the heaviness of the case. He unwrapped it nimbly and found a stick made of silver, and the bottom made of gold.

"What is this?" he asked the wise woman.

"A wand," she answered.

"A wand?" Ronald spluttered with disbelief.

"Yes, a wand."

"What is it for?"

"What is it for? You can't just step into a magical land without a wand! It's dangerous! And besides, it will help you in desperate times. It will help you even more to defeat the king and his evil powers. You see, when I escaped from Janemia, it was up to me to find you. And since now that you're here, it's up to you to save Janemia."

Ronald was afraid. It was up to him to save that great land. "So does that mean you're not coming with me?" Ronald asked.

"Yes, my dear, it does. My bones are brittle, so I cannot travel anymore," explained the psychic. "But I do have someone who will go with you." The old woman beckoned him to follow her and they stepped outside into a small, stable-like shelter. And inside was something so unbelievable to Ronald that he rubbed his eyes to make sure that what he was seeing was real. There, in the middle of the room, tied to a pole, was a large dragon.

"This is Duglo," said the psychic. "The very dragon who helped me escape from that horrible land many years ago -- and he will be as faithful to you." Ronald was amazed at the creature standing before him.

"Come with me, my dear -- we need to gather supplies for the journey," the psychic said. So Ronald followed her back into the house.

About one hour passed, and Ronald came out with a knapsack filled with supplies, while the woman followed. Ronald stopped at the doorway of the shelter and pulled the straps of the knapsack over his shoulders as the psychic stepped into the shelter and put a saddle upon the dragon's back. "All right, you are ready to go. Get on." The woman patted the saddle on the dragon's back.

Suddenly Ronald became hesitant. He wanted to know more. "But why am I supposed to save this land? I know nothing of magic, or sorcerers and such."

"You were chosen, my dear. It is a mystery why you were chosen -- even I don't know why. But the spirits told me and I believe them with all my heart," explained the woman.

"But you never told me how to get to Jamenia."

"Don't worry. Duglo will know the way."

"But why am I doing this?"

"You want to be a king, don't you?"

"Yes." That made Ronald feel better, so he climbed onto the dragon, and the woman handed him his wand, which he then put in his coat pocket.

"Are you ready?" the psychic asked. Ronald nodded his head.

"Good luck," said the woman with a smile. She freed the dragon from the pole and watched it swiftly fly out of the shelter opening.

"Behold, the future King of Janemia," muttered the psychic.

Alex Richard Fisher
Age: 12

THE MONSTERS ATTACKED MY HOUSE

Three days ago one hundred great big monsters attacked my house. My gecko chased the monster into the toilet. Then more monsters came. And then every animal in my house came. And then a freak of nature came, a polar bear came and a dog came. My dog was on TV. Then he jumped out.

Robbie Bluett
Age: 7

DEATH MOUNTAIN

Death Mountain that's what most people call it because over one hundred people have tried to get to the top. But what many people say the theory is, is that this old man who lives in a cave at the top of the mountain has set traps all around the mountain. His best trick is a hole covered over with leaves and sticks. But people don't know where the hole is because he puts leaves and sticks down the whole trail. The other person that is with them always tries to get the person out, but they never can, so they go back down the mountain to the town to get help. The name of the town is Hill Valley. But by the time the person gets back with a search party, the person is always gone and is never seen again.

Myths are told about the man, they say that he eats the people that he captures. People say they have seen him, they say that his face is so scary that if you saw it, it would make you pass out! But there was one mysterious thing that he did, but most people think that he only did it once, but there were some people who think he did it more than once. Anyway what he did, he would torture the person for days and days, then he would cook them over a fire and eat them. There was only one person that ever made it up the mountain and back down to Hill Valley.

Ray Smith was the man's name, although he didn't live in Hill Valley. About three years later, Ray Smith came back. He made it up the mountain and then he found the old man murdered, lying on the ground. Ray went back down to Hill Valley and got a search party together. He and the search party went back up the mountain and got the old man's body and went into the cave where the old man had lived. There they found enough guns and bombs to fight a war. People who go up the mountain now go into the cave and they say they hear spooky noises, they also say when they leave and they turn around and look back inside they can see blood on the walls and when they leave they say that they can see the old man's ghost.

Jordan Dunlap

THE TRAP DOOR

On a rainy, dark Saturday morning Mary had to clean her closet because it was a pigpen. She had all her stuff out so she could organize it a little better. She took her shelf out of the closet and saw a door. It was made out of wood and it was dusty. She had never seen it before. It's like it just appeared. So she went in the door and it shut behind her. She was locked in.

So Mary started to explore. She found a trunk. It was black, dusty and it had spiders on it, so she wiped them off. It was as weighty as a grand piano. She couldn't pick it up, so she dragged it across the floor. She thought that she could bang it against the door to get back into the closet. Bangggg. It didn't work. The door was too strong. Mary was worried that she would be stuck because she was on the third floor and her mom was in the basement. She couldn't yell that loud.

She was just about to yell for help when she heard footsteps. She was fooled by the sound of the footsteps. She was not the only one in the attic. She found an old man. He looked like a rag with all his long hair. It was gray, very gray. His clothes were raggedy too. She started to talk to him. She asked him if there was a way out. He said he was trapped in there for thirty years. Mary asked him how he stayed alive. He said that he found scraps of food in corners and in cracks. Mary thought that it was weird that he found food. She asked him how he got in there. He said that he got stuck in there when he was a kid. His parents were moving. They thought he died because he got stuck in the trap door. So they moved without him. Mary didn't want to get stuck in there, so she asked him if she could get out. He said yes. He found a key in the crack in the wall but his arm was too big to fit all the way down. Mary had a small, long arm. So they walked to the crack in the wall. It was a long walk back to where she found the trunk. Mary reached down and got the key. She was so relieved. They dashed as fast as a pack of wolves catching their prey to the door. The lock on the door was hidden. She had to find it. She tried several different places and in about ten minutes she found it in the middle of the door. She quickly unlocked the door and got out. She felt better. Now she didn't have to think of being stuck in there with the old man.

Mary got out with the trunk and the old man. She called her mom. Her mom raced up the stairs because she thought Mary finished cleaning her closet out, but she didn't really even begin. Her mom had a better surprise than she thought. She came up and saw an old man standing next to Mary. Mary had to explain to her mom about the trap door and the old man that he was not going to hurt her. Then they opened the trunk and they found GOLD, diamonds, and other treasures. The old man went and found his parents and he got half the gold. Mary and her family were rich. They used the money for a house cleaner so they didn't have to clean the closets again.

Ali Goeckner
Age: 11

LIFE LIKE NONE OTHER

The sun was shining brilliantly over the Hawaiian waters. I felt the warm sun on my skin as my dad and I pushed the red kayak slightly into the cold water. My little brother, Jacob, followed close behind carrying two long black paddles. We all waded into the water and got into the kayak ready for a very exhilarating experience.

As my dad taught me how to paddle the front of the kayak, I listened very carefully. I was in no mind to tip the boat over! We finally got the hang of it and pushed off of the sandy shores where the kayak began its journey through the lagoon.

We paddled parallel to the shore where children made little sand castles near the water's edge and attempted to catch the elusive little minnows. Jacob waved to my mom who was tanning leisurely on a chair. Many other beach-goers were doing exactly the same thing. We saw people snorkeling and water-biking, too. Laugher and talking rang loudly through our ears as we moved on.

I looked down into the crystal clear water and saw much life beneath me. A small school of black and light yellow striped angelfish darted beneath us in a flurry of color. Hiding behind seaweed and lava rocks they played hide-and-seek with each other. Jacob exclaimed in a series of oohs and ahhs at the little puffer fish that swam next to my paddle. It reminded me of a little train. Just chugging slowly along, not really afraid of the humans around it.

After a few minutes we switched our seats. I sat down in the middle, for my brother wanted to try and paddle. That didn't last too long. I moved to the back so that I could steer. Our little kayak picked up the pace. I tasted salty air blowing into my face. The smells of suntan lotion teased my nose. I heard a splash behind me and saw a fish leap out of the water. This was no angelfish, it was a huge flying fish at least a foot and a half long! Then a few yards away little silver fish jumped like a fountain. Their little scales shimmered in the golden sunshine. When they submerged back under the water it made a sound like a marble being dropped into a pool. It was miraculous.

We paddled out towards the waterfall. My dad wanted to push me under it. I steered away quickly. When we were clear of the foaming white waterfall, suddenly I heard a bubble pop. I snapped my head towards the water and saw a mother and baby sea turtle. It was a beautiful sight. I reached out and stroked the mother's shell. She turned around and swam under in one graceful motion. The baby blew and popped another bubble and then followed close behind.

I will never forget that day. It was an amazing experience in my life. I hope many more people get to experience the wonders of nature like I did.

Samantha Otto
Age: 11

BYE

Chapter One: Scary Night

One night I was lying in my bed and just looking out the window. I saw something scary. I got out of my bed and I saw some glass on my bedroom floor. I was scared because there was a hole in my window. I got on top of my desk and I saw some eyes.

I got a long quilt and put lots and lots of knots in it. I tied it to my bed posts and threw it out of my window. I climbed down the quilt and something grabbed my foot. I screamed! I heard my mom calling, "Jenny! Jenny!" I tried to yell but a person had his hand over my mouth. When my mom went to go get the car, we left. The man took me to a dump. There was a big building that said "People". He took me in the building. There were all these children in there, tied up in chains. He threw me in a ditch and tied me up in chains too. There was another kid in the ditch. His name was Alex. Alex told me all about this place. Then they got to work. Then it turned out that Alex was bad. He was talking to the people who own the building who are keeping the kids. He uses a walkie-talkie to talk to them.

Chapter Two: I Got Stolen Again.

Alex's walkie-talkie started beeping and we both heard it. The walkie-talkie started floating. We tried to get it but the hole was too deep. We were stuck.

I said, "Give me a boost." I got out and pulled Alex out. "Let's split up, you go left, I'll go right," I said. So I went right and I saw something. It was a person. I asked if he knew the way out. But I got too close and he grabbed me and threw me into a car. I grabbed the keys and threw them out the window. He got mad and threw me in the backseat. He had a trunk. I lifted the trunk and I tried to jump but his friend grabbed me. He threw me out and I ran away. I saw my dad on his motorcycle. I yelled, "Dad!" He stopped.

I said, "Why are you crying?"

He said, "They are happy tears, I missed you."

"I missed you too!" I said.

Jessica Ritchie
Age: 9

WILLIAM'S STORY

My real mother always said, "There is always a way out." I remember her cradling me in her arms when I was a baby. I remember.

I remember our trips to the beach, he loved the beach. I remember our fun times together on the coast. His tan slim body his rosy cheeks. I just don't remember if he told me he loved me.

The nurse handed me a paper cup full of water. I was fifteen, so I was pretty smart. I could see her comforting face was full of worry. "He's - gonna die isn't he." I said slowly. I looked up at the nurse. She had her hands on her hips, and was pouting. Then lowered her hands and sighed. I was told to go to the waiting room.

I walked out in the hospital hall and almost cried. "I have been living in a foster home for six years and now- I - I was..." The nurse stopped me.

"Come back in here!!! she interrupted. I ran back in. "Are you in love?"

It was early in the morning on Wednesday I slept in. My foster mom had to drive me. I didn't realize that God had given me a second chance. I should have been on the bus with Willam. I should be dying too. It was my fault. I should be in that room next to him. I loved him.

The doctor came in at 3:00 p.m. I didn't leave that night, but had to sleep in the waiting room. His name was Dr. Beck, he went to Willam's mother, talked for ten minutes, and then left. My surroundings looked strange to me. Everyone was carrying candy, and get well balloons. Everyone seemed to be here to see Willam, but none of the girls were allowed in, not even Willam's mom.

Dr. Beck came back in and the chatter stopped again. He started whispering in Willam's mom's ear again. She looked very pale. When the doctor stopped talking she looked like she was half crying. And yet, she also looked half amazed.

I remember. Willam's mom came close to my side I could smell her fear. I could see how sad she was, like someone had thrown ice water on her warm heart. The room seemed as dark as night. Everything was dull, even the sunflowers on the table seemed to wilt. Everyone knew death was upon us.

I walked into Willam's hospital room I felt his cold clammy hands. He looked so peaceful. He had blood on his forehead. He was awake but barely moving.

"I need to tell you something." I came close and listened hard because this may be the last time I heard him speak again. "Since the day I met you, I loved you." His pale face turned red. "And if I die today I still will."

I felt tears come down my cheeks. I tried to stop but they kept coming. Willam took a ring off his finger and placed it on mine. "I'll always be here for you." he said.

I have never told anyone what happened to William, and I have never taken the ring off until now.

Margaret Mary Baine
Age: 10

LIFE

Life is so beautiful simple and sweet. I love my family more than any kind of a treat. The grass is green. It grows really fast. Sixty minutes in an hour the days don't last. The trees' leaves are all different colors. Girls, boys, men, women, and many more others. Some days I'm happy, some days I'm sad. Some days I feel like crying and feel so bad. Some days people make fun of me sometimes they don't. Some days I want to move, but I won't. I hate these blues. The days I hate the most are the days where everything is black and white and not one color is in sight. I love being happy and so bright. There are a lot of people in this world men, women, boys, and girls. We're all different in our own kind of way. I try to listen and forget what people say. We all have one, two, or maybe even three things in common. I like to watch the Lord of the Rings especcially that crazy little hobbit. Our world is made up of all different skin colors, that's why we're called the United States. There is no other. Friends help you when you're down, sad, or even don't feel right. Your friends would give you advice or when your clothes are a little bit too tight your real friends would never make fun of you or leave you crying. They go help you. I'm not lying. When with your friends you can't ever lose. But remember you don't want the blues. I guess I'm just a shadow. You never smile at me you just look at me weird. I bet you if I walk down the hallway I'll bet you never say hi. I bet ten dollars that this is not a lie. You never look at me or even say good-bye. You might as well call me a shadow but I forgot I already am. I'm wrapping this up because it's getting too long. When I get older I hope to be famous for a lot of things, one is writing songs.

Theresa Ford

THE ANIMALS' PARTY

Once there were animals in the woods. They were having a party and were having a "BLAST!!!" There was a bear, deer, raccoon, owl, snakes, fish in the creek, Mr. Frog, and bunnies. The raccoon was old. He could barely walk he was so old. The deer was so young. She would run around and around teasing the raccoon. The bear was BIG, too!!! The owl was hooting, "Hoot, hoot." The snakes sssslithered along. The fish jumped into the air. They all had punch, cake, and ice cream. They all had a good time. But the house near the woods had singing coming from it. They went out to see what they were doing out there. The dad had a gun just in case he needs it for safety. As they were walking closer and closer, "Boom!" He shot it in the air. The animals heard the gun. So they ran off to hide. They said, "Go, go, someone is coming!" They ran off to another place.

Kayla Green
Age: 8

THE WONDERLAND

One Saturday morning Mary was cleaning a closet in the attic when she found a little door. She opened the doorway and went in. There was a sign that said, "You are in Wonderland." Mary found a gold key on the ground. She put it in the little key hole and she went inside. She locked the door behind her. She did not want her mom to know. How would she get back to the real world?

After she locked the door she looked around and saw a crimson rose bush nearby start to wiggle. She started to shake because she was so scared. Then something came out of the bush! Mary shut her eyes. The next moment she was in a little carriage pulled by four beautiful white horses. All around her were elves. They were very little and looked kind of funny. They took her into a tunnel. The tunnel was so dark you couldn't see the end of it. It smelled like dried fish. When they got to the end the elves locked her up in a cage.

Mary was confused. First, she tried to use the key that she used to lock the door to scrape the metal bars of the cage. It didn't work. The keys only made marks on the metal bars. Then, she tried using the key to unlock the lock on the cage. That didn't work either. The key was too big to fit into the tiny hole. Finally, she tried to talk the elves into giving her the key because she needed to go back to her room to finish cleaning her closet. That still didn't work. The elves didn't believe her.

While everyone was sleeping a dainty fairy came. She was very elegant. Her dress was as beautiful as a flower garden. Then the fairy used her wand to unlock the lock. Pow! The lock was unlocked. After that she gave Mary magical wings to fly away and a wand to defeat the elves. Mary flew home and started to clean her closet again but this time she used her antique bookshelf to block the secret door.

The next time Mary went through the door she made sure to bring her magical wings and her new wand. Before she started her next adventure in Wonderland, she wanted to make sure she had the help of magic. She planned to bring a friend or two along with her also. Every day she went to Wonderland and had a new adventure.

Amy Chen
Age: 11

ONE MONTH CAN MAKE A DIFFERENCE

It all started when a neighbor heard a loud sound outside his window. He was wondering what it was so he walked outside and saw a guy slapping his own horse. The neighbor called the animal shelter. The animal shelter and the police came out to the farm where the horse lived. They found out that the horse's name was Buttercup, and they also knew that Buttercup had been abused by the owner Boltum Walter. The animal shelter took Buttercup and the police gave Boltum his rights.

After the animal shelter ran some tests they nurtured Buttercup back to the way she was before Boltum got his hands on her. Soon she was back to normal. Soon she was also sent off to be sold.

Buttercup was sold to a nice old man who lived in the country. Then one night the old man who bought Buttercup gave a call to the police, and he told the police that someone had tried to take Buttercup away from him. That person had gotten away with it too. Then to their surprise they found Buttercup in a different state and being used for a petting zoo. When the police got their hands on the owner, they weren't surprised that it was Boltum Walter. He would take Buttercup to the petting zoo and Buttercup would stay there all day, then Boltum would take her home and the abuse would start all over again.

They took Buttercup back to the animal shelter and took Boltum to jail. The animal shelter made Buttercup better once again. Buttercup was then taken back to be sold again. Buttercup was sold to a very nice family. They lived in Paola, Kansas. Buttercup was one of the Barkson's family now. Days went by very fast.

One month after the Barksons had gotten Buttercup and had been told her story, Buttercup passed away from old age. At least Buttercup had one good month. Now the Barksons started a foundation for abused animals. Buttercup has never been forgotten.

Katlyn Kitchen
Age: 10